DEEP BLUE

MARK MORRIS

BBC

Published by BBC Worldwide Ltd,
Woodlands, 80 Wood Lane
London W12 0TT

First published 1999
Copyright © Mark Morris 1999
The moral right of the author has been asserted

Original series broadcast on the BBC
Format © BBC 1963
Doctor Who and TARDIS are trademarks of the BBC

ISBN 0 563 55571 8
Imaging by Black Sheep, copyright © BBC 1999

Printed and bound in Great Britain by Mackays of Chatham
Cover printed by Belmont Press Ltd, Northampton

Many thanks to Paul Tye for information about boats and David Howe for information about families.

This is for Kevin Mullins, a great friend who was there at the beginning and who has shared so much of the magic.

Part One
Seeing Stars

With a grinding of machinery and a clanking of chains the trawl was winched aboard. As the huge net broke the grey surface of the sea and rose into the air, it looked like a living thing itself. Beneath its thick mesh thousands of fish thrashed and writhed, their silver bodies flashing beneath the blazing summer sun. When the trawl was clear of the sea, Terry Robson operated the gantry arm and the net swung out over the deck, drooling water which splashed around the boots of the six-man crew.

The *Papillon* had been built in the thirties, a decade or so before Terry was born. It was rusted and patched up, its engine in need of constant attention, but Terry's old grandad still referred to it as 'the new boat'. The Robsons had been fishermen for generations, perhaps even centuries, but in recent years Terry's dad, Malcolm, skipper of the *Papillon*, had been muttering with no real humour about there being 'a sea change' on the way.

The big factory trawlers, with crews of up to a hundred and no reason to come ashore except for the occasional repair, were putting sole traders like the Robsons out of business. For the moment they were still making ends meet – just – but Terry was realistic enough to realise that it wouldn't be too long before they would have to diversify. Already many of their friends and neighbours were supplementing their income by taking groups of overfed businessmen for a day's sea fishing. If it hadn't been so depressing it would have been funny, making executive types pay for the privilege of freezing their nuts off and chucking their guts up all day.

As Joe Tye, Terry's cousin by marriage, released the cod end, sending fish cascading in a slithering heap across the deck, the gulls circling above the wheel house began to shriek with frantic hunger. Terry moved forward to help sort through the catch. A lot of the stuff that the trawl ensnared would have to be thrown back – crabs, eels, pregnant females, fish smaller than regulation size – but there looked to be enough viable fish here, cod and haddock, herring, whiting and plaice, to make this a good haul.

Joe's son, Barry, who at twenty was the youngest of the crew, and who wore his blond hair long like his pop-star heroes The Sweet, was bending towards the mass of fish slithering around his boots when suddenly he recoiled. Terry's Uncle Pete, his dad's younger brother, glanced up. Uncle Pete was a fearsome character, six-and-a-half feet tall, with a bushy black beard, piercing blue eyes, and hands like shovels. Barry was often the – mostly undeserving – butt of Pete's abrasive manner, which did little to sweeten the already volatile relationship between Pete and Joe. Terry didn't know why his dad's brother and his sister's husband disliked each other so much. Maybe it was just one of those things, or maybe there was some history between them. The fishing community at Tayborough Sands was tight-knit, contained within such a small, neat block of the tourist town that it could almost be termed an enclave. In such communities favours were always returned in kind, and often with interest, but by the same token no grievance was ever forgotten. Grudges were worn like insignia and even passed down through subsequent generations.

'Something frighten you, lad?' Pete growled. He had a knack of making every sentence he uttered sound as if he was accusing someone of spilling his pint in the pub.

Barry's face creased in revulsion. 'There's another one of them bloody fish,' he said.

John Baycock, Terry's best mate and the only non-family

member of the crew, piped up with his usual good humour, 'Aye, you tend to get a lot of 'em around here.'

Barry looked at him as if he didn't realise John was joking. Barry was a good lad and a willing worker, but he was not over-endowed in the brains department.

'No, I mean… one of *them* fish. Horrible it is. Ugliest one so far, I reckon.'

'You sure you've not just come across a bit of broken mirror caught in the net?' John said, making Terry and his dad laugh.

Barry shook his head and shuffled backwards. 'Horrible it is,' he said again. '*I'm* not touching it.'

'Oh, for Christ's sake, you big pansy,' growled Uncle Pete and strode forward through the slimy carpet, beetle-brows knit together in a scowl.

Terry moved forward too. He wanted to get a closer look at the deformity. There had been a lot of them these past couple of weeks. Some said it was to do with the strange light that Bob Elkins had seen land in the sea, but Terry thought it was all down to pollution. These big chemical companies and what-have-you dumped God knows what into the water these days.

Barry was right about one thing: this particular specimen *was* the ugliest one so far. Terry saw it immediately amongst its suffocating brethren, and recognised it as a cod despite its hideous abnormalities. Oddly it was not flapping frantically as the other fish were, but was lying still on its stomach, its sides moving slowly in and out, almost as if it had adapted to breathe the air. Its flesh was discoloured and bulging with lumps that seemed to shift sluggishly beneath the skin, its mouth hung open, revealing small but razor-sharp teeth, and its eyes bulged as if it was glaring at its captors. Most grotesque of all, though, were the black, porcupine-like quills which had sprouted all over its body. Looking at it, Terry felt not just repulsed but uneasy. Perhaps it was the creature's huge eyes, but it felt as though the thing was watching them broodily, as if there was a nasty little intelligence working away in there somewhere.

Although he had never been deep-sea diving, Terry knew a couple of lads who had. They came into the Mutton for a pint or two most Friday nights. The words of one of the drunken conversations he had had with them came back to him now. He remembered them telling him that divers were more worried about cod than they were about sharks, because whereas sharks would ignore you most of the time, cod were vicious little buggers. They would latch on to your face with their teeth if they could, then spin themselves round and round until they'd torn off a circular chunk of flesh. Terry remembered making a joke about it, telling the lads that the cod were only getting their own back for all the fish and chip suppers eaten over the years. Now, though, the recollection filled him not with amusement but alarm, and as Pete bent forward, extending a hand towards the fish, he couldn't help blurting, 'Don't touch it!'

Pete paused and half-turned, his blue eyes drilling into Terry's own. 'What's up wi' you? Don't tell me you're as much of a lass as Shirley Temple here.'

'No, it's just that… you might catch summat, that's all. We don't know what's wrong with it.'

'Terry's right,' said Joe. 'At least get yourself some gloves. I don't like the way that bloody thing's looking at you.'

Pete shook his head, an incredulous look on his face. 'I don't believe you lot. You're like a bunch of frightened kids. It's only a –'

'Look out!' Barry screeched.

Moving so swiftly that it was almost a blur, the fish launched itself at Pete. He span in surprise, hand raising instinctively to protect his face. The cod opened its mouth wide and clamped its teeth around his upraised fingers. Pete yelled in pain and fury and swung round in an arc, the fish clinging to him like some grotesque silvery glove that he was unable to shake off. It would have been funny if it hadn't been so alarming, if the fish hadn't then dropped some ten yards away to the deck with a squishy thud, and if Terry had not looked at Pete's hand and seen only ragged stumps gushing blood where three of his fingers should have been. Pete held his hand up in front of his face, his mouth wide open, and the furious roar died in his throat like a wave spending its strength on the shore. For a moment the sea was reflected, a dense grey, in his wide, astonished eyes before they glazed over, his eyelids flickering.

'Catch him, lads, he's going down,' Malcolm shouted, breaking the stunned silence.

Perhaps it was his skipper's words that revived Pete, perhaps just sheer bloody-mindedness. For even as his fellow crew members moved forward, stretching out their arms to keep him upright, giving the spiny, malformed cod a wide berth as they did so, Pete roared like a battle-charged warrior and thundered towards the fish still some ten yards away.

Terry wasn't sure what his uncle planned to do – perhaps mash the fish to pulp beneath his boots and retrieve his bitten-off fingers from its gullet. But whatever his intentions, Pete never got the chance to realise them.

The lumps that had been moving sluggishly beneath the cod's scaly skin suddenly seemed to coalesce into a single bulbous mass at the apex of its spine. The cod opened its blood-smeared mouth and let loose a shrill and raucous cry, almost like the caw of a crow, which made Terry's skin crawl. Almost simultaneously the fishy lump swelled and the skin ripped open from the pressure like cheap cloth. Barry let out a squeal of horror and Terry felt a surge of fear as several long, spiny, crab-like legs quickly unfurled from the rent in the creature's back.

Pete might still have caught and crushed the thing beneath

his size twelve boots if he had not stumbled to a faltering halt at the sight. The newly hatched legs stretched out, four on each side, clicking like knitting needles as they found the deck. Gaining strength, they flexed, grotesquely lifting the body a few inches upwards. They quivered for a moment, then, moving with astonishing speed, scuttled the creature away towards the prow of the boat.

'Hey!' Pete yelled, as if to a purse-snatcher, and gave chase once more. It was too late. The mutant halted a few feet from the prow, bent its spiny legs in a crouch, and sprang over the side. It hit the grey water with a splash and was gone.

For a few moments nobody moved. They stared at the patch of churning, foamy water that briefly marked the creature's passing, transfixed with mouths agape and eyes wide, until the sea smoothed itself over as if to deny the existence of such a monstrosity. His voice clotted with awe and dread, Malcolm said slowly, 'Twenty-eight years on the sea, and I've never seen anything –'

Pete interrupted him with a rattling groan. Then he keeled over face-first, crashing to the drenched, slippery deck like a felled oak.

Terry realised with a guilty start that for the past moments he had forgotten about the terrible damage to his uncle's hand. For the first time he saw the blood pooled and spattered around Pete's prone body. There was an alarming amount of it, and the wound was still pouring with blood. Terry rushed forward, skidding to his knees beside his uncle at the same time as John Baycock and Joe Tye. A few moments later they were joined by Malcolm, who thrust the first aid box from the wheel house into his son's hands. Only Barry hung back, his face ashen.

Terry had to will his hands to stop trembling in order to open the box. He took out a bottle of antiseptic, oily with fingerprints from previous mishaps, and a roll of bandage in a cellophane sheath. He tore the sheath open with his teeth and began to tug at the bandage inside, dismayed to see his own grubby fingerprints instantly soiling the pristine white gauze. He was about to pour some of the antiseptic on to the bandage when Joe Tye muttered, 'What's that stuff on his hand?'

For a guilty moment Terry thought Joe was accusing him of being unclean, but then realised he meant Pete. The big, bearded man's breath was a rattle in his throat, his eyelids flickered, his body shook as though with fever. Perhaps it was shock or loss of blood. In a daze, Terry looked down at his uncle's mutilated hand.

It was the blood that had swamped his attention before, but Terry now saw the 'stuff' that Joe had pointed out. Through the blood he saw that Pete's wound was coated with a glutinous, jelly-like ooze. Terry swallowed and shuddered. He imagined the creature disgorging the gluey substance like poison from its diseased body on to his uncle's. Frantic to prevent the stuff from penetrating the wound, Terry yanked at a length of bandage, but it refused to tear, merely stretching instead.

John Baycock delved into the first aid box, grabbed a swab and began to wipe the gel away from the wound. Terry flashed him a glance of gratitude, unscrewed the lid of the bottle and poured antiseptic directly on to Pete's hand. Semi-conscious, the bearded man hissed and muttered, his body tensing momentarily.

'Easy there, big man,' Joe Tye soothed with a tenderness that surprised Terry despite the circumstances.

When he was satisfied that the wound was entirely clean, John Baycock applied a lint dressing, holding it in place as Terry wound the bandage tightly around his uncle's hand. He worked swiftly and carefully, trying to outpace the blood that continued to soak through the lint and the gauze and

7

threatened to reduce his good work to a sodden red mess. As more and more bandage was applied, an almost palpable relief coursed through the men, as if hiding the terrible injury from view could somehow quell the horror of the incident that had caused it. When Terry was finished it looked as though his uncle was wearing a single white boxing glove.

'Will he be all right?' Barry murmured, stepping hesitantly forward now.

Terry shrugged and felt his dad's hand pat him twice on the shoulder.

'Good work, son,' Malcolm said in a low voice as if his words were meant for Terry alone. Then raising his voice, the skipper added, 'All right, lads, keep him as comfortable as you can. I'm taking us home.'

In the two weeks since he had been given his new job title, Jack Perry had been practising the term in his head and in front of the mirror in his bedroom. 'I'm an environment co-ordinator,' he would say, qualifying the statement with a slight raising of the left eyebrow and a smug little smile. In his mind he would be at a party, sipping Pina Colada and speaking to a woman who looked like a cross between Sally Thomsett from *Man About the House* and that girl from the *Hai Karate* ads. The woman would gasp in admiration and her eyes would brighten with interest. Perhaps she might even lick her glossy red lips in lascivious anticipation.

It was at this point that the fantasy would begin to dissolve. If the woman enquired further, Jack would have to admit that he drove a truck for the council and that the only authority he wielded was over a bunch of moaning, long-haired students who were simply out for a bit of holiday money. Not only that but every morning at 5 a.m. he and the students – most of them hungover, or soporific from the pot they had been smoking the night before – pulled up on to the promenade, got out clad in overalls, boots and thick rubber gloves, and tramped down to the beach, laden with shovels and industrial-sized refuse sacks.

Environment co-ordinator. In his more bitter, disillusioned moments, Jack would see the job title for the joke it really was. Nothing more than a fancy name for a rubbish-collector, a street-sweeper, someone who trailed behind the rest of mankind, picking up the filth that they left strewn in their wake.

Sometimes, lying in his bed at night and hearing his widowed mother in the bedroom next door tossing restlessly in hers, Jack would wonder where it had all gone wrong. There were no parties in his life, no Pina Coladas, no Sally Thomsett lookalikes. There were not even any friends to speak of – not real ones at any rate. Just casual acquaintances, people he knew on a superficial level: people at work; people he bumped in to now and then who had been to school with him, and who, like him, had never moved away; fellow enthusiasts at the steam railway where he did voluntary work every Sunday.

If it wasn't for his trains – his weekly pilgrimage to the railway itself, the books he spent hours poring over, the beautifully complex model rail network he had set up in the attic and which he added to constantly – he didn't know what he'd do. Oh, he had dreams of going to parties and meeting beautiful women, of being the pivot of an uproarious circle of friends, but when it came down to it he was only ever happy in the company of his trains. His trains were a constant, his trains never let him down. The only thing that ever blighted the time he spent with them was the knowledge that sooner or later reality would impinge again, highlighting his inadequacies, crushing his spirit with its casual cruelty.

Hell is other people, he thought on this particular morning as he crunched the truck down through the gears and brought it to a shuddering halt on the seafront. Even if by some miracle he did one day meet Sally Thomsett or the *Hai Karate* girl and she did, by some far greater miracle, turn out to fancy him, he honestly doubted whether he would be able to cope. Part of him desperately wanted to be loved and accepted, but the more dominant part balked at the prospect of what that would really involve. People – *real* people – were different to fantasies. They were too unpredictable, they wanted to enter into relationships that needed to be worked at, partnerships in which compromises had to be reached, sacrifices made.

'What's this? Offering a silent prayer to Neptune?' said a voice from the back of the truck, and Jack realised he had been daydreaming again. It had been happening with increasing regularity this past week or so, an inability to concentrate on what was happening around him, a tendency for his thoughts to drift inward. By now he was finding it difficult to keep track of conversations without his mind slipping away. It was almost impossible to settle down to read or watch TV for any length of time. Perhaps it was all to do with the fact that he'd been sleeping badly of late. His dreams had been full of dark, unsettling images that caused him to wake several times a night, sweating and gasping for breath. The frustrating thing was, he could not recall the specifics of any of these nightmares. If something beyond his usual anxieties was bothering him, he had no idea what it was.

'Sorry, just… erm… just collecting my thoughts,' he mumbled in reply and, twisting round, attempted a grin that he couldn't help but feel sat awkwardly on his face.

The group in the back, his eight-strong workforce, four lining each interior wall of the truck, stared back at him sullenly. Jack felt sweat trickle down his forehead, moisten his armpits. At forty-four he was a good quarter-century older than every one of these boys. They made him feel dull, fat, ugly and unaccountably nervous. They made him feel like a teacher in dubious control of a class of students who felt nothing for him but contempt, or perhaps, even worse, pity.

'Right,' he said with hollow bonhomie, 'let's get to it then,' and he rubbed absently at the rash that had sprung up on his arms in the past week, and which in the muggy, sweaty heat was itching more than ever.

They climbed out of the truck, carrying the paraphernalia they would need to clear the beach of rubbish left by both holidaymakers and the outgoing tide. Jack had been doing this job for a long time and had seen enough stuff washed up on the beach to put him off swimming for life. As well as the usual rubbish – bits of old fishermen's netting, plastic bottles, rusty tins – there had been dead animals (dogs and cats mainly, and once half a horse, trailing bluish-white guts bleached of blood), syringes, surgical dressings, raw sewage and chemical drums rusted and punctured. He had never found a person, or bits of a person, but he knew one or two workers who had. Mike Salters and Craig Branch had once found the body of an old woman floating in on the tide, her face black and eyeless, shrimps and baby crabs spilling from her mouth as the waves dragged her up on to the beach. And there was talk that Tony Carver had once found a man's decomposed head in a Sainsbury's bag, the victim of a gangland killing whose dismembered body – minus the hands – had apparently been recovered later from a skip behind one of Tayborough Sands's plusher hotels.

Jack adjusted his spectacles and looked out over the clay-coloured expanse of beach. Although it was already muggy, the day was still struggling to open its eyes. Dark clouds smeared the sky like old mascara. On the horizon, the rising sun was a blur of lipstick-red. As they trudged down the uneven stone steps on to the beach, a sea-breeze ruffled over them, which, while bringing welcome relief from the humidity, carried with it a stench of rotting seaweed and dead fish.

Vaguely Jack waved his troops off to cover different sections of the beach, noting that their grunts of acknowledgement were becoming surlier by the day. He ought to do something about it, he supposed, assert his authority, but he felt both too intimidated and too lethargic. As he moved down the beach armed with his shovel and his roll of refuse sacks he noticed that one of his workers, Simon, a thin seventeen-year-old with straight blond hair cut in a pageboy style, was scratching feverishly at the crook of his elbow through his overalls, his teeth clenched in a grimace.

If it had been anyone else, Jack might not have said anything, but Simon was quiet, softly-spoken, generally polite.

'You all right?' Jack asked.

Simon looked momentarily dazed, as though Jack had sprung up from nowhere, then he blinked and nodded.

'I've got this rash. On my arms and across my chest. Itches like mad.'

'Me too,' said Jack, and felt compelled to rub at his own arms. 'Must be the heat. These overalls. Make you sweat a bit, don't they?'

He offered an uncertain smile, which wavered when Simon shook his head. 'I don't think it's the overalls.'

'Don't you?'

'No. I think it's *this* stuff.'

Simon jabbed at the sand with the toe of one booted foot. Jack looked down and saw a few stringy clots of the strange deposit that the tide had been leaving behind for the past week or two. It was like half-set jelly, though colourless and transparent. It had been everywhere recently, each rolling wave bringing more of it up on to the sand. Jack and his team did their best to clear it from the beach, but they were fighting a losing battle. Jack held up his gloved hands and announced,

'It can't be that. If we're careful it shouldn't get on our skin, whatever it is.'

'I know that,' continued Simon, his brows crinkling in a frown, 'but what if it's giving out fumes or something and we're breathing it in? I mean, what is this stuff? It might be some killer chemical; it could be nuclear waste for all we know. I mean, there was that thing in the paper a couple of weeks ago, wasn't there, about that lighthouse keeper who saw some weird light come down in the sea? Why hasn't anyone come out to investigate that? Why isn't the government doing anything? I mean, it might have been some Russian secret weapon, mightn't it? Maybe they're planning to poison us all by contaminating our water. I've read all about that sort of stuff, chemical warfare and that.' He came to a sudden breathless stop, his cheeks red, eyes wildly searching Jack's face. Then, as though embarrassed, his gaze flickered away, he turned his head and re-focused on the sea.

They stood in silence for a moment, then Jack murmured, 'Maybe I ought to report it. Just to be on the safe side. I could even save some in a jar and take it to a laboratory or something.'

For a moment Simon didn't respond, then he nodded. Dreamily he said, 'The sea's such a big place, isn't it? I bet there's stuff out there that no one's ever seen.'

Jack followed his gaze. His arms were itching. He shivered.

The sun was tearing itself from the water now, leaving blood on the ocean.

As he walked up the steps to the front door of Ambrosia Villa, Captain Mike Yates couldn't help feeling guilty. Although his little trip to Tayborough Sands wasn't exactly a holiday, it felt as though it was, as though he was having a jolly at the taxpayer's expense.

'Light duties,' the Brigadier had called it, and then later, registering Mike's dismay, he'd amended that to, 'Vital intelligence work.' 'I need someone I can trust, Yates,' he'd said, 'someone with integrity. Someone with a clear head, who can sort out the wheat from the chaff.'

A clear head. That was a joke for a start. It was precisely because of his inadequacy in that department that Mike had been given this assignment. He couldn't believe that almost six months had passed since it had all begun. It seemed like no time at all since he had been sitting behind the desk at Global Chemicals in Llanfairfach, purporting to be the 'Man from the Ministry'. As usual things had gone a bit haywire before the Doctor had managed to sort it all out. Turned out the company, which had been pumping lethal industrial sludge into the village's abandoned mine workings, was being run by some sort of super computer which called itself BOSS and which could scramble its employees' brains, turn them into mindless zombies.

For a while Mike himself had fallen under its influence. BOSS had dismantled his thoughts and put them back together in a different order, had made him believe his friends were his enemies. He'd nearly shot dead the two people he trusted most in the world: it had seemed perfect sense at the time, before the Doctor had shown him the error of his ways with the aid of a blue crystal he'd picked up on some far-flung planet or other.

After that, Mike had been fine for a while, had felt better than he'd felt for a long time in fact. But then weird thoughts and feelings had started to spring up, like weeds in a well-ordered garden. He had begun to suffer odd bouts of depression, feelings of futility. Despite the vital part he'd played in repelling the many and various threats to Earth over the years, he had started to convince himself that his life was meaningless.

Eventually, inevitably, this emotional instability had affected his work, and the Brigadier had ordered him to undergo a course of pathological assessment and then to take some compassionate leave. Perhaps if the Doctor and his blue crystal had been around all of that might have been avoided, but he had been distracted and irritable ever since his assistant, Jo Grant, had quit UNIT after announcing her intention to marry Llanfairfach's resident eccentric, Professor Clifford Jones. The Doctor had spent most of the past six months going off for solitary jaunts in his TARDIS, sometimes for several weeks at a stretch.

He had been absent when Mike's problems had come to a head three months ago, and was absent again now, having slipped away in the night two weeks ago, much to the Brigadier's chagrin.

It had taken Mike a month or two to sort himself out, but now he was back for good and itching to get down to some proper soldiering. However, his return, and the Doctor's increasing absences, had coincided with a lull in the type of incident UNIT usually dealt with. Perhaps that was a good thing, Mike thought. Perhaps it was better to ease himself back in gently rather than throwing himself head-first into the fray.

It didn't *feel* better, though; that was the thing. It felt to Mike as if he was cheating. He set his jaw, gripped the handle of his small suitcase more tightly and rapped sharply on the lemon-yellow front door of the guest-house. 'I *am* making a difference,' he whispered to himself as he waited for an answer, and instantly felt a little better, as his psychologist, Dr Cutler, had assured him he would.

As the door opened a pair of seagulls began squabbling directly overhead, as if some flapping, screeching entity had been released from the house. He quickly recovered his composure and smiled at the woman who stood on the threshold. Her bird-like face was austere, her lips pressed so tightly together that they seemed bloodless. She looked disapprovingly at Mike's burgundy cords and brown suede jacket.

'Mrs Macau?' he enquired, pronouncing it 'Macow'.

'Macau,' she corrected, so sharply that he bit back the response that sprang to mind: 'Ah, like the exotic bird.'

He covered his near *faux pas* with a smile and said smoothly, 'Of course. My name is Mike Yates. I understand you're expecting me?'

'I expect we are, Mr Yates,' replied Mrs Macau coldly, and turned into the house. 'Please follow me.'

After the brightness of the sun, the hallway seemed dingy, the walls cluttered with clocks whose sombre, somehow ominous symphony of clunks and ticks made him think of little knives chopping away the seconds. Mrs Macau asked him to sign the register, then gave him a perfunctory tour of the guest-house: the lounge where two old ladies sat knitting, their faces rouged by the effect of the red flock wallpaper; the dining room where breakfast was served between 7.30 a.m. and 10 a.m. *precisely* (she scowled as if he had already contravened this rule); the bathroom on the second floor, with black pin-mould collecting in the corners and ever-present condensation fragmenting the sunlight through the stippled glass of the window; finally, his own room on the top floor, which instantly became his favourite part of the house. It was an attic room with a sloping ceiling, a brass-framed bed and a small window in an alcove offering a seagull's-eye view of the fishing harbour.

'Thank you, Mrs Macau,' he said, putting his suitcase on the bed. 'I'm sure I'll be very comfortable here.'

She started to list the rules of the house. No alcohol. No pets. No visitors after 10 p.m. Mike listened patiently till the end and replied, 'That all sounds perfectly fine, Mrs Macau.'

With a final suspicious glance she left him alone. Mike pursed his lips and expelled a heartfelt sigh of relief, then snapped open the catches of his small suitcase and lifted the lid. Although he had been booked into the guest-house for two nights with an option to stay longer if required, he was hoping to be back on a train to London by tomorrow afternoon, his business concluded.

Not that he would only do half a job, of course. No, Mike was too thorough, too conscientious, for that. It was simply that he expected nothing to come of this little investigation. From his suitcase he took an army-issue toiletry bag, the latest in a series of psychology textbooks he had been reading recently (his immediate subordinate and good friend, Sergeant John Benton, had picked this one up from his desk a couple of days previously, flicked through a few pages and then replaced it with a baffled, slightly troubled expression), and a small selection of clothes, which had been meticulously ironed and folded by his own fair hands.

He put the clothes and the toiletry bag away in the chest of drawers that stood against the wall beside the door and placed the book on his bedside cabinet. The suitcase now contained only three further items – a file pertaining to his assignment in an anonymous, buff-coloured document wallet, a chunky two-way radio and a Colt .45 semi-automatic handgun in a body holster.

He felt rather foolish bringing along a gun when all he was required to do was chat to a local lighthouse keeper about a strange light he had seen come down in the sea twelve days ago, but the Brigadier had insisted. 'Always be prepared, Yates,' he had said in that brash, rather pompous way of his. 'First rule of soldiering.'

'I thought that was the boy scouts, sir,' Mike had replied with gentle good humour.

The Brigadier's moustache had twitched. 'Same principle, Yates. You've worked for UNIT long enough to know that you should always expect the unexpected.'

Mike put the radio in the drawer beneath his underwear, placed the gun on the bedside table next to the book, tossed the document wallet on to the armchair beside the alcoved window, then closed his suitcase and slid it under the bed. He spent the next twenty minutes reading the documentation, which didn't amount to much: a local police report comprising a short statement from the witness and a photocopy of the story as portrayed by the local newspaper, which treated the whole thing as a bit of a joke.

Mike sighed. Ninety-nine per cent of such incidents proved to have no basis in fact, but UNIT were obliged to follow up each and every one of them as a matter of course. Often it was the Doctor (and, before her departure, Jo Grant) who undertook such assignments; indeed, this was one of the tasks which the Doctor performed only too willingly – largely, Mike suspected, because it gave him the chance to distance himself from the military activity at UNIT HQ and to whiz about the countryside in Bessie, his little yellow car.

This particular arrangement worked out well for all concerned, not least because the Doctor had an uncanny knack of distinguishing between the genuine and the bogus, a sixth sense when it came to detecting alien involvement or even a serious home-grown threat to planetary stability. Mike, however, suspected he would speak to Mr Elkins and come away with nothing further to add to what he had just read. Although his mother had always described him as 'the sensitive one' of her four boys, he was not adept at picking up on the subtle, hidden clues that the Doctor seemed to pluck from the air with ease. Indeed, watching the Doctor at work, Mike often felt like a dull and plodding beat constable confronted with the dazzling and enigmatic presence of Sherlock Holmes.

It was raised voices from outside that plucked Mike from his reverie. Putting the folder aside, he stood up and crossed to the window. There seemed to be some commotion down by the harbour, several uniformed policemen holding back a crowd of curious onlookers. From his vantage point, Mike could see that the object of their attention was a small, battered-looking fishing trawler. Already other policemen were in the process of erecting an exclusion barrier of sawhorses and yellow tape around the trawler, effectively closing off the jetty. From here Mike could see what he suspected the crowd couldn't. Scattered on the deck were a number of red blankets, clearly covering some irregularly shaped objects.

That could mean only one thing. Hastily he picked up his holstered gun and strapped it to his body. Then, patting the back pocket of his cords to ensure that he had his UNIT pass, he hurried from the room.

'You mean we've actually arrived where you said we were going to?' Tegan muttered scathingly.

The Doctor looked pained. 'Well, of course.' Then his voice dropped as he hunched over a panel on the TARDIS's hexagonal control console. 'Give or take a year or two.'

Tegan shut her eyes briefly. 'Don't tell me. We've landed in the Bronze Age.'

Turlough, standing beside the Doctor like an attentive pupil, the fingertips of his hands pressed together as if he was about to lead them in prayer, tilted his head and gave her a look of condescending disapproval. 'Come on, Tegan, be fair,' he said mildly. 'The Doctor's doing his best.'

Tegan grunted, meeting his pale blue gaze for only a moment before looking away. Despite being thrown into a series of life-threatening situations with the sallow-faced, red-haired public schoolboy, the bond between them was not particularly strong. Tegan was all too aware of her own failings – her brashness, her quick temper – but at least she was honest, at least people always knew where they stood with her. Turlough, on the other hand, was devious, underhand, duplicitous, and not only that but he was smarmy with it. And a coward, too. Tegan suspected he'd sell his grandmother if it meant saving his own skin (if he *had* a grandmother, that was; he had always been as evasive about his origins as he was about virtually everything else).

When he had first wriggled like a maggot into the core of the TARDIS crew, he had been working for an entity called the Black Guardian who wanted the Doctor destroyed. Turlough had apparently seen the error of his ways at the last minute but Tegan still didn't trust him. The boy always seemed to be working to his own, hidden agenda; always seemed to be striving to divide and conquer, playing her and the Doctor off against each other. And the thing was, he did it so slyly, so subtly, that all too often Tegan didn't see the trap until she had fallen right into it.

It was maddening, even more so because the Doctor seemed oblivious to his male companion's mind games. Indeed, the Doctor infuriated Tegan as much as Turlough did, albeit for different reasons. In his fifth incarnation he was a baffling mix of contrasting characteristics. He was brilliant and feckless, knowledgeable and naive, resourceful and disorganised, thoughtful and compulsive.

'How many years out are we?' she asked, addressing the Doctor and making an effort not to sound exasperated.

He glanced up at her, narrowing his eyes as if to judge her mood. 'Oh, only a few. Ten or so. Twelve at the most.'

'Forwards or backwards?'

'Backwards.'

'Well, that's OK then.' She spread her arms to better display the bright print dress she was wearing. 'I'll be a trend setter.'

'Hmm,' said the Doctor non-committally and, straightening up from the console, took a rolled-up object from the pocket of his knee-length, cream-coloured coat. He gave a practised flick of the wrist and was suddenly holding a white panama hat in his hand which he placed on his head with a casually stylish movement. 'Everyone ready?' he asked, all at once full of child-like eagerness.

Tegan couldn't help but respond to his mood with a smile, but Turlough merely raised his eyebrows and said with the trace of an indulgent sigh, 'Ready, Doctor.'

The Doctor operated a lever and with a hum of power the TARDIS's double doors smoothly opened. Tegan turned to face them, feeling a little quiver of excitement and apprehension. She wondered what the Doctor's surprise would entail. He'd said they all needed cheering up after the terrible events they had witnessed on Sea Base Four in the Earth's future. The Doctor had told his companions nothing else except that the surprise would take place on Tegan's present-day Earth.

'Shall we?' the Doctor said cheerfully and swept out of the TARDIS, the tails of his coat flapping behind him. Tegan glanced at Turlough, saw the expression of complicity he was offering her, and strode determinedly after the Doctor.

She emerged blinking into the sunlight that streamed into her eyes. Sounds filled her ears – gaudy music, excited chatter, delighted screams – and deliciously familiar smells kicked her taste buds into instant life: candyfloss, frying onions, fish and chips.

'It's a fun-fair,' she exclaimed delightedly as the glare of the sun faded and was replaced by the bright, shifting primary colours of revolving carousel horses and lurching dodgem cars, stalls offering pink teddy bears as prizes, the House of Fun with its unseen perils and pitfalls.

They had materialised between two quiet stalls, apparently unseen, as if the TARDIS had deliberately picked its moment. Even the grinding cacophony of the time machine's ancient engines appeared to have gone unheard, drowned out by the sound of Slade blaring from a swooping, spinning ride in the shape of a gigantic spider some twenty yards away.

The Doctor was standing with his hands stuffed into the pockets of his striped trousers, beaming round at the scene like a satisfied proprietor from beneath the brim of his panama hat.

'It's the seventies, all right,' Tegan shouted, walking up to him and gesturing at the long-haired men with their wide-collared shirts and outrageously flared jeans, the girls with their denim caps and platform shoes.

Unseen by Tegan, Turlough had sidled up behind her. 'What is this place, Doctor?' he shouted, making Tegan jump.

'Tayborough Sands pleasure beach,' the Doctor replied. 'As I recall, there's a particularly fine toffee-apple stall beside the Waltzer.'

'Pleasure beach?' echoed Turlough incredulously. 'You mean people come here to have fun?'

'Of course they do!' exclaimed Tegan. 'And that's exactly what we're going to do. Right, Doctor?'

The Doctor grinned in reply.

'But it's so vulgar...' complained Turlough.

'Just go with it,' replied Tegan and grabbed his arm. 'Come on, I've got some money. I'll stand you a ride on the roller coaster.'

'Roller coaster?' said Turlough doubtfully. 'What's that?'

'You mean you don't know?' She glanced at the Doctor, a wicked glint in her eye. 'Boy, are you in for a treat. Come on.'

She dragged him, protesting, away. The Doctor turned back to lock the TARDIS door, then headed after them. However, he had taken no more than a couple of steps when his senses were overwhelmed by a slew of images. It was as though a black cloud had crossed the sun of his thoughts, nightmare shapes twisting within the dense formations. He had an impression of something alive yet in constant flux, of oozing, jelly-like flesh from which claws sprang and eyes blinked and mouths opened before dissolving back into the main mass just as quickly.

Then the cloud passed and he was back in the fairground again. Released, he staggered slightly, steadied himself with a hand on the TARDIS door. He looked around, half-expecting his senses to be snagged by something untoward, something not quite right. Sensing nothing, he took a deep breath, and hurried to catch up with his companions.

'This looks nice,' said Charlotte Maybury brightly, momentarily resting her suitcase on the pavement. Her father, Tony, glanced up at the yellow door and hanging baskets of Ambrosia Villa without enthusiasm.

'It'd better be, the amount of money we've wasted on it.'

Charlotte's mother, Imogen, who had stoically maintained a brittle good humour throughout the hot and tedious train journey from Wolverhampton, suddenly snapped, 'Wasted? Don't you think we deserve this holiday? Don't you think we *need* it?'

'It's not a case of needing it, it's a case of bloody affording it,' said Tony, aggressive with the alcohol he had consumed on the train. 'We'd have been better off buying a car.'

'One of those old boneshakers you always throw our money away on that fall to bits after three months, I suppose?'

'If I had a car I could get a job,' retorted Tony.

'No, if you had some self-respect you could get a job. Look at the state of you. It's not even lunchtime yet and you're plastered.'

'I'm on holiday, woman. Or hadn't you noticed?'

Before the argument could escalate into a full-scale slanging match on the pavement, Charlotte said placatingly, 'Come on, Dad, don't let's row. Not on the first day of our holiday.'

'It's not me who wants a row,' Tony muttered. 'I just want to have a good time.'

'Yes, at everyone else's expense,' Imogen said sourly.

'Mum,' pleaded Charlotte.

'Sorry, love, it's just your father.'

Charlotte sighed. Her parents' arguments had been getting more frequent and increasingly vituperative recently. With each passing day she saw further cracks appearing in their relationship. As far as she could recall it had started two years ago when Dad had lost his job at the ironworks, though their problems may well have been more deep-rooted than that. Indeed, as she grew older Charlotte was not only beginning to realise that her parents had been growing apart for years but was also more willing to admit it to herself.

In many ways she was viewing this holiday as a make-or-break period for all of them. Whatever happened between her parents, it would certainly be a watershed of sorts. This time next year she would be eighteen, and, if her suspicions were borne out, the mother of a child. She wasn't *certain* that she was pregnant, but she intended to pluck up the courage to take a test some time within the next few days. Here, away from the stifling familiarity of everyday life, she had assured herself that it would be easier to bear somehow. And if the test proved positive, she would tell Mum and Dad and take it from there.

She glanced at her brother, Chris, in the vain hope of a little moral support, but he was being his usual moody self. He had hardly strung two words together since they had started out early this morning, and not for the first time Charlotte found herself wondering whether it was their parents' problems that were causing him to withdraw into himself or whether his behaviour was simply that of a typical acne-ridden, rebellious fourteen-year-old. Not so very long ago she and Chris had been quite close, but these days he was behaving as if she and their parents were the three people on the planet he'd least like to be with.

'Come on,' Charlotte said with mock cheerfulness, hefting her suitcase, 'let's see what our rooms are like.' She climbed to the top of the steps and stretched out her hand to the doorbell. Before she could press it, the door was yanked open.

The tall, thin-faced man in his late twenties looked almost as surprised as she must have done. He was hurrying out of the house and had to stop dead to avoid barging straight into her. They both apologised in unison, then laughed. 'Are you staying here too?' Charlotte asked, immediately blushing and hoping she hadn't made it sound as if she wished that he was.

'Just for a night or two. Here on holiday?'

She nodded. 'What's it like?'

The man grinned. He had a pleasant smile, easy and unself-conscious. Glancing behind him, then leaning a little closer, he murmured, 'Oh, it's fine, just as long as you watch out for the dragon.'

The sun had climbed to its zenith, and even though sweat rolled down Mike's back as he hurried along, he couldn't afford to take off his suede jacket because of the gun he wore strapped to his torso. The distance to the mouth of the fishing harbour was further than it had appeared. By the time he arrived at the edge of the police cordon, the crowd had grown. The majority were rubber-necking tourists, but there were also a number of locals, frustrated because they couldn't get to their boats.

He excused his way quietly and politely through the throng, offering a conciliatory smile and an apology when people scowled at him, not wishing to draw attention to himself. It was ironic really; the United Nations Intelligence Taskforce was a top-secret organisation, and yet the Doctor, who usually undertook such investigations for them, did nothing *but* draw attention to himself. Mike imagined how different the scene would be if the Doctor and Jo Grant had been here. The Doctor would no doubt have been elbowing his way through the crowd, Jo in tow (and she alone was enough to draw the attention of most men), proclaiming, 'Do excuse me, old chap,' in that loud, theatrical manner of his. Then, flouting authority, he would no doubt have ducked under the police barrier without explanation, leaving Jo to root out their UNIT passes to avoid arrest.

Mike smiled to himself. The Doctor's showmanship and his blatant disregard for protocol used to drive the Brigadier to distraction, and sometimes still did. Still, at the end of the day, the Brig was first to admit that if the Doctor came up with the right result then a little unwanted attention was a small price to pay. In some ways, Mike thought the Doctor's flamboyance worked to UNIT's advantage. It caught people off-guard, made them take the Doctor less than seriously, which often proved to be their undoing.

He reached the barrier and leaned towards the uniformed constable standing a few feet away. 'Excuse me.'

The constable ignored him, just as he was ignoring all the other comments and questions being hurled in his direction. Mike sighed, reached into his back pocket and produced his UNIT pass. He held it out for the policeman's inspection and said with a little more urgency, 'Excuse me, but would you mind having a look at this, please?'

The policeman's eyes flickered in his direction, focusing on the pass. Mike gave him time to read it, then asked, 'Would it be possible to come through, do you think?'

The constable reached for the pass. 'May I take this, sir? I shall have to make an enquiry.'

'Of course.'

A couple of minutes later, the policeman was back. He returned the pass to him, and lifted the tape barrier for him to duck beneath. 'If you'd care to follow me, sir?'

Mike heard a few comments behind him as he followed the policeman along the jetty. Someone muttered something about MI5 and several people laughed. A plain-clothes detective was waiting for Mike on the jetty beside the trawler. He had a square, pock-marked face and a C-shaped scar on his chin. His green suit sagged on him as if he had been wearing it for a long time without a break, and the top button of his shirt was undone beneath the fat knot of his tie.

'Mr Yates,' he said, offering Mike a strong but sweaty handshake, 'Detective Inspector Pickard.'

'Inspector,' said Mike. 'Good of you to see me.'

'Not at all. I'm a bit intrigued to be honest. I'd have thought something like this would be well outside UNIT's area of interest.'

Mike shrugged. 'Perhaps it is. To tell you the truth, I'm only here on a hunch. I saw some of what was going on from the window of my boarding house.'

'I see. So what really brings you to Tayborough Sands? Oh no, don't tell me. The so-called UFO that came down in the sea?'

Mike smiled, a little embarrassed. 'I don't expect anything to come of it, believe me, but UNIT is obliged to look into such matters.'

'Of course it is,' said Pickard, struggling to conceal his smirk. 'But if you're thinking what happened here is related to your flying saucer, then I'm afraid you're going to be disappointed.'

'And what *did* happen here?' asked Mike, hiding his irritation behind a mask of breeziness.

'Murder,' said Pickard bluntly. 'Multiple murder to be precise. Six-strong crew and not a single one left alive. Very nasty. Bloke who did it must be a madman.'

'Do you mind if I take a look?'

'Help yourself. Hope you've got a strong stomach, though,

Mr Yates.'

'Cast iron,' said Mike evenly.

Pickard raised his eyebrows and Mike followed him on to the trawler. The deck was wet, oily. The stench of rotting fish was almost overwhelming. Pickard said, 'The stink was even worse when we found the boat this morning. It was reported missing last night by the skipper's wife and we spotted it at first light, drifting on the sea. The murders must have happened right after the catch was winched aboard. There were dead fish all over the deck. We reckon there must have been some sort of argument. It's a bit early to say, but what we think is that the killer may have been mortally wounded by the last man left alive, who then died of his injuries.'

'How did the men die?' asked Mike.

Pickard fixed him with a deadpan gaze. 'Why don't you take a look for yourself.'

Mike held his gaze for a moment, then smiled and nodded. 'Thanks.' He moved to the nearest red blanket, noting the thick runnels of now-dried blood that meandered from beneath it and ran into the drainage gutters on both sides of the deck. He had seen death before in many forms and lifted the edge of the blanket without hesitation. He saw an arm that looked like it had been torn from its socket, lying in a pool of blood that had congealed to the consistency of black glue. The arm was mottled blue, purple and black in the places where the blood that was left inside had settled. On the bicep were four small circular bruises that could have been caused by the tight grip of a human hand.

Mike replaced the blanket and straightened up.

'What do you think?' said Pickard, in a challenging tone.

Mike had not been wholly unaffected by what he had seen – he was aware of the quick pumping of his heart – but he was calm enough for his response to sound clinical, considered.

'The arm wasn't severed by a blade. It was torn off. Which

means that, unless I'm missing something, your killer had incredible strength.'

Pickard nodded as if in satisfaction and moved to the second blanket. 'What's under here is even stranger,' he said, and lifted a corner of the blanket up for Mike to peer beneath.

It took Mike a few moments to work out what he was looking at. Finally he said, 'My God, that's part of a ribcage, isn't it? And that... that must be a heart.'

Pickard let the blanket fall back. 'Ribcage, heart, lungs and some surrounding tissue. They're quite badly crushed, but it's as though –'

'– someone or something reached in and ripped them out of the body with their bare hands?'

Pickard nodded. 'Exactly.'

'And you don't think that's at all unusual, Inspector?'

Pickard shifted uncomfortably. 'Well, of course it's unusual. To tell the truth I've never seen anything like it. But crazy people are capable of performing incredible feats of strength you know, Mr Yates.'

'Captain,' said Mike quietly.

'Pardon?'

'I hold the rank of Captain.' Then he smiled. 'Not that it matters. I'm just a bit of a stickler for detail, that's all.'

Pickard looked a little baffled.

'So is this all you have to show?' Mike continued briskly. 'Butcher's leftovers? No complete bodies?'

'There's one,' said Pickard. 'We haven't had a formal ID yet, but we think it's the skipper's son, Terry Robson.'

'But the entire crew have been accounted for?' said Mike. 'I mean, among all these bits and pieces?'

Pickard shook his head. 'It's still too early for that. We won't know for sure what we've got here until later this afternoon. Unofficially we reckon we've got the bits of at least five bodies here.'

'And the sixth crewmember?'

'Dead too, I'd guess.'

'What makes you so sure?'

Pickard led the way across to a blanket beside the wheelhouse. The bulge beneath this blanket was more substantial than the others. Glancing back at the police line at the end of the jetty – Mike guessed to ensure that the public couldn't see what he was about to reveal – Pickard pulled the blanket back.

The man was lying on his back, eyes partially open and glazed with death, head lolled on to his left shoulder. The exposed side of his neck and throat was ripped and gouged as if he had been attacked by a wild animal. His clothes and the wooden deck of the boat beneath him were soaked with blood. By his side, inches from his hand, was a stubby handgun with a wide muzzle.

'Flare gun?' said Mike.

Pickard nodded. 'I think Terry here fired it point-blank at his attacker, who then either fell or was blown overboard.'

'And Terry died later from loss of blood,' murmured Mike.

Pickard let the blanket fall back over the corpse. Mike straightened up.

'Well, thanks again for your help, Inspector. You will keep me informed if there are any developments, won't you?'

Pickard smiled thinly. 'If that's what you want. Though I don't think we'll be arresting any little green men from Mars for this.'

Mike matched Pickard's smile with a disarming one of his own. 'You never know, Inspector,' he said. 'You never know.'

Guy Elkins woke up thinking about who in the world he would most like to kill. Just lately his mind was refusing to turn itself to any other subject. If his mates started talking about football or motorbikes or girls they'd like to sleep with, his thoughts would begin to slip and a strange buzzing would start up in his brain, drowning out their words. The last time he had been in the pub, four days ago, all he had been able to think about was smashing his beer glass on the counter and ramming the jagged edge into Carl Collier's throat.

Carl was his best mate, they had known each other since they were babies, but the thought of Carl's blood spurting out filled him with a shudder of excitement he could barely control. He had felt sweat spring up on his brow, had clenched his teeth and gripped his beer glass so hard it was a wonder it hadn't exploded in his fist. Carl had noticed the state he was in, had frowned and asked Guy if he was feeling all right. Guy had known what Carl was saying despite his words being drowned out by a buzzing so loud it was like having an electricity pylon in his head.

The only reason he hadn't slashed his best friend's throat on that occasion was that he had forced himself, with a mighty effort of will, to let go of the glass, shove Carl out of the way and stagger out of the pub. He had set off for home at a stumbling run and hadn't stopped until he got there. He had no idea whether Carl had come after him to find out what was wrong. Certainly Guy hadn't seen him since he'd left him sitting bemusedly in a pool of beer on the pub floor.

Guy and Carl, both eighteen now, had been getting into trouble together almost since they could walk. They'd been done for affray, burglary, vandalism, shoplifting, stealing cars. They knew each other's strengths and limitations, knew they could rely on one another in a crisis. At least, they did until about ten days ago. It was then that Guy's mind had started to... change.

Guy, like Carl, had always enjoyed a good scrap. He believed there was nothing better than hearing the crunch of somebody's nose breaking beneath his fist, of knocking somebody to the ground, spilling somebody's blood. Just recently, though, the desire to inflict violence on other people had grown into an obsession, an addiction. It was as if something had taken him over, latched on to that desire within him, and had begun to feed it. In turn, the desire had responded, growing and flourishing like some rampant weed in his brain, and in the process strangling all other thoughts and needs. Today Guy didn't just want to hurt people, he wanted to kill them, wanted to rip them apart, bathe in their blood. The sheer ferocity of his thoughts was terrifying and exhilarating. Yet although his bloodlust had engulfed him to the point where he could barely function on any social level, he had never felt more alive.

All week he had been roaming the streets for stray animals or raiding people's gardens for their pets, bringing them back to the house, torturing and killing them in his room. It assuaged his desires a little, but it was not enough. Sooner or later he knew he would have to move on to people. The only thing that had held him back was the extra attention it would bring, the fear of getting caught.

It was not prison that scared him, though; far from it. He was simply terrified of being deprived of what he needed to feed his addiction. The buzzing urge to kill was so overwhelming that, were he to be denied the opportunity, he honestly believed his body would be ripped apart by the build-up of pressure inside him.

So, who to kill? Who would he most *like* to kill? His drunken widower of a father who had never given a sod for him? Mrs Raymond, the vicious old cow of a headmistress who'd expelled him? Sergeant Weathers, who never got off his case, even when he wasn't up to anything? Or how about that stupid bird, Janice Crooks, who had shrieked with laughter when he'd asked her out in the pub a few months ago?

Anyone would do, right now. If an opportunity were to present itself where he *knew* he could kill Carl, his life-long mate, and not get caught for it, he'd do it. He'd kill old women, little kids, babies…

Through the buzzing cacophony of his thoughts he heard the doorbell ring downstairs. Was this it? Was this what he'd been waiting for? Had a victim come to his lair? He scrambled out of bed and ran downstairs, only half-aware that he'd been wearing the same crumpled T-shirt and jeans for several days now, that in all that time he hadn't washed or brushed his teeth or combed the lank, shoulder-length hair that he kidded himself made him look like Charlie George.

He saw the man blink in shock and disgust as soon as he opened the door, saw it in the split-second before he covered it up. Guy was disappointed. The man looked lean and fit, as though he'd be hard to kill if Guy decided to try it, as though he wouldn't go down without a fight.

The frustration gnawed inside him, seemed to awaken the terrible itching that constantly simmered just beneath the surface of his skin. He wanted to tear at his own chest and arms with his fingernails. He gave an involuntary moan and the man looked at him curiously.

'Are you all right?'

'I…' Guy's voice was a croak; his face felt like a loose rubber mask he was trying unsuccessfully to control. With a gargantuan effort he pulled himself together, though his voice sounded slurred and rasping. 'What do you want?'

'My name is Mike Yates,' the man said. 'I'm looking for a Mr Derek Elkins. We have an appointment.'

As the information seeped slowly into his brain, Guy could only stare at him.

'Er… I was told he lived at this address,' the man added helpfully. 'Perhaps I was incorrectly informed?'

Guy knew some sort of reaction was called for. He stepped back, dragging the door open as he did so. 'No,' he mumbled, and nodded at the door on his right. 'There.'

'Thank you,' the man said, stepping inside. He gave Guy an encouraging smile. 'Is it all right to go in?'

Guy could only grunt and nod. The itching was becoming unbearable now. As the man stepped past him, Guy thought about ramming a knife into his guts, slashing his throat. He shuddered and moaned, his hand spasming.

The man gave him another curious look and went into the room Guy had indicated. As soon as the door closed behind him, Guy turned and staggered towards the stairs. He was shaking, his head pounding, his body full of a desperate need. The itching was so bad it was like his skin was being torn by tiny hooks.

He was stumbling like a drunk by the time he reached his room. He fell to his knees beside the bed and scrabbled beneath it. His hand closed around the jar and he yanked it out, almost salivating at the sight of the clear, jelly-like substance inside. He unscrewed the lid, put the jar shakily down on the floor and tore off his T-shirt.

His chest and arms were covered with tiny black quills that had sprouted from his skin. He fingered them for a moment, shivering at the ripples that coursed through his body. He was fascinated and awed and oddly proud of the transformation he was undergoing. He picked up the jar with his left hand and delved into it with his right, scooping out a lump of the jelly. Without hesitation he smeared the stuff on his arms and chest where the itching was most concentrated. Instantly the gel acted like a balm, cooling and soothing his inflamed skin. Guy crooned like an animal and sank to the floor. Soon, when the itching had subsided as much as it was going to, he would go out and find something to kill.

'There's something he's not telling us,' said Tegan. 'I just know it.'

'Feminine intuition?' Turlough smirked.

Tegan flashed him one of her dangerous looks. 'Don't make fun of me, Turlough.'

'I'm not,' Turlough said contritely. 'I just think you're reading something into the situation that isn't there.'

Tegan glanced anxiously across the hotel foyer at the Doctor, who was standing at the reception desk booking rooms for them all. 'You don't think he's behaving strangely?'

'No stranger than usual.'

'You don't think he's being... secretive? Evasive?'

Turlough sighed. 'The Doctor's always secretive. You might as well face up to it, Tegan. You're never going to be privy to his innermost thoughts.'

She glared at him. She still wasn't sure whether Turlough *meant* to belittle her when he spoke like this or whether it was just his way. Whichever, his condescending manner was like a flame to her all-too-short fuse. 'Well, I've known him a lot longer than you have,' she snapped, 'and I reckon he's up to something.'

It had started in the fairground, this vague and distracted manner of the Doctor's, which Tegan felt certain meant there was something rather substantial on his mind. It couldn't still be the events on Sea Base Four which were disturbing him, could it? Tegan knew that the Doctor abhorred violence and regarded violent death as a senseless waste, but he had seen so many tragedies, so many atrocities in his long lives that he tended to put them aside quickly, sometimes forgot them within minutes of re-entering the TARDIS – or so it had always seemed.

No, Tegan felt certain it wasn't that. So, what was it? Maybe Turlough was right. Was she simply looking for trouble where there wasn't any?

Her anger evaporated and she sighed as doubt crept in to replace it. The thing was, travelling with the Doctor had made her *expect* trouble wherever she went. If she hadn't been captured or shot at within ten minutes of arriving somewhere she became suspicious. Which, to be honest, was no way to be, was it? Perhaps she ought to think about getting out before she became so battle-hardened that her encounters with death became no more distressing than... than breaking a fingernail or stubbing a toe.

The Doctor strode back across the hotel foyer, oblivious to the strange looks he was attracting, and dangled room keys in front of each of his companions' faces. Turlough took his, but Tegan looked up at the Doctor with a frown and asked, 'Why are we staying here?'

The Doctor looked surprised. 'You don't like it?'

'It's not a case of like or dislike. It's...' She paused a moment to collect her thoughts, which gave Turlough the opportunity to insinuate himself silkily into the conversation:

'Tegan thinks you have a hidden agenda, Doctor.'

She went puce with fury, but the Doctor simply looked baffled. 'Hidden agenda? Whatever do you mean?'

Turlough smirked in the face of Tegan's anger and pressed the fingertips of his hands together. Speaking as though she was biting off each word and spitting it out, Tegan said, 'I just want to know what we're doing here, that's all.'

'Doing?' said the Doctor, still baffled, or feigning it. 'We're having a holiday. I told you, I thought we could all do with one.'

Tegan was irritated by his presumption, but decided not to pursue it; she was more concerned with the matter in hand. 'But why here? We've got our rooms in the TARDIS.'

'What's the point of going on holiday but staying at home?' said the Doctor.

Tegan sighed again. She was getting nowhere fast. Maybe there was nowhere *to* get. 'All right, I'll buy it,' she said. 'But you would tell us if there *was* something wrong, wouldn't you, Doctor?'

'If I thought we had any cause to worry, I'd certainly inform you of the circumstances,' he assured her.

The key to the room he had booked for Tegan was still looped over his forefinger. She took it and picked up the bag he had told her to pack in the TARDIS after their afternoon at the fun-fair.

As they waited for the lift, the Doctor rocked back on his heels, hands in pockets, and commented on the architecture. Turlough nodded but remained silent. Tegan merely grunted.

Their rooms were on the fourth floor. Tegan had 404, Turlough 408 and the Doctor 418 at the end of the corridor.

'See you later,' he said with a brisk smile outside the door to Tegan's room and turned to stride away.

'When later?' she called after him.

'Dinner at seven,' he replied without turning back.

She made an exasperated face, which Turlough, fitting the key into the door of his own room, responded to with what might have been construed as a sympathetic raising of the eyebrows. Tegan went into her room and shut the door. Looking around, she huffed out a sigh, though in fact it was a very pleasant room, spacious and airy with butter-yellow walls and a deep-mattressed double bed. She dumped her bag on the armchair beside the dressing table and strode across to the large window flanked by flowery curtains on the far wall. She opened the window wide and, sticking her head, out closed her eyes and took several deep breaths.

Immediately, she felt calmer. The combination of warm sunlight on her face and the salty tang of sea air filling her lungs was a soothing panacea. The cries of gulls, though raucous, were familiar and comforting, transporting her back to a happy weekend she had spent in Brighton with Aunt Vanessa not long after arriving in England, and to days sailing off the south coast with her grandfather.

With a guilty start she remembered that the last time she had seen her grandfather he had been about to move house and she had promised to visit him just as soon as she returned from Amsterdam. However it was in Amsterdam that she had met up with the Doctor again. She wondered now how her grandfather had taken her apparent disappearance – he was bound to be worried about her.

She pulled her head back in through the window, then blinked. Of course! The solution was so blindingly obvious she was a dolt for not having thought of it straight away. All she had to do was ask the Doctor to take her to visit her grandfather *before* he had cause to wonder where she was.

Tegan had never been one to let the grass grow under her feet. She believed in striking while the iron was hot, acting on impulse. Of course, this attitude had got her into trouble many times, but she knew she would never change.

She almost ran across the room and pulled open the door, only remembering at the last moment to go back and snatch up the key from the bed before yanking the door shut behind her. She marched down the corridor and rapped on the Doctor's door. There was no answer. She knocked again, put her ear to the door, and called out, 'Doctor? Doctor, are you in there?'

Still no reply. Was he sleeping or just ignoring her? Frustrated, she pounded on the door with her fist and shouted, 'Doctor, will you please answer me? I need to talk to you!'

A door further down the corridor opened and Turlough popped his head out. 'What's the matter?'

'What does it look like? I want to talk to the Doctor, but he won't answer.'

Turlough wandered up and put his ear to the door. 'Perhaps he's not there.'

'Well, where is he then?'

He raised his hands as if to protect himself from her anger. 'I only said perhaps. I don't know any more than you do.'

'This is ridiculous,' she muttered, and marched down the corridor and through the half-open door into Turlough's room. Polite applause from the cricket match on the TV greeted her as she entered. The carpet bag that the Doctor had lent Turlough was open on the bed, though he had not yet removed any of its contents. Tegan snatched up the phone on the bedside table and dialled the Doctor's room number. Receiving no reply, she banged down the phone, then immediately picked it up again and dialled '10'.

'Reception,' said a woman's voice.

'Hello, this is Tegan Jovanka from room 404. I'm trying to get in touch with a friend of mine in room 418, but there's no reply.'

'Dr John Smith?' said the woman.

'Er... yes, that's right.'

'Just a moment please, Miss Jovanka.' There was a brief pause, then 'I'm sorry, Miss Jovanka, but Dr Smith left the hotel about ten minutes ago.'

'Left?' exclaimed Tegan, her previous suspicions re-awakening. 'Did he say where he was going?'

'I'm afraid not, Miss Jovanka, but I believe he left you a note... Ah yes, here it is.'

'Could you read it please?'

'Certainly, Miss Jovanka.' There was the sound of rustling paper, then the woman said, 'Dear Tegan and Turlough, I've had to pop out for a while. Things to do. See you soon. The Doctor.'

'That's all?'

'Yes, Miss Jovanka.'

'Thank you,' said Tegan, tight-lipped, and put the phone down.

The Doctor sniffed the air like a bloodhound but could detect nothing unusual. He appeared nonchalant as he strolled along the promenade, hands in pockets, though in fact his mind was attuned to the slightest trace of the telepathic link he had briefly established earlier.

It was an alien mind he had made contact with, of that he was certain. But as to where it had come from, he had no idea. His gaze roamed along the rows of seafront shops and hotels and boarding-houses; he peered up into the diamond-blue sky and watched the gulls wheeling and screeching; he scanned the busy stretch of dun-coloured beach where people were sunbathing, playing football, flying kites, building sandcastles, paddling in the shallows or bobbing among the waves; he stared out to sea, which shifted and rippled and swelled constantly, as if a myriad pulses were beating at random beneath its blue and glassy skin.

He ordered a '99' from an ice-cream van and asked the heavily sideburned proprietor whether he had seen anything unusual in the town recently.

'Only you, mate,' said the man with a grin.

'Me?' said the Doctor, taken aback. Then he smiled and touched the stick of celery attached to his lapel. 'Ah. Yes, I suppose my attire is a little anachronistic.'

The man chuckled as if the Doctor had made a joke and leaned forward, elbows resting on the counter of the van's serving hatch. 'You'll have heard about the palaver down by the harbour earlier.'

'Will I?'

'I thought everyone had.'

'I'm new to town,' said the Doctor, licking his ice-cream.

The man nodded wisely, then winked and glanced right and left as if about to impart confidential information that he didn't want overheard. 'Aye, well, they sealed the whole place off.'

'Who did?'

'The police.'

'Really? Any idea why?'

'They reckon there was a fishing boat found this morning, just floating out at sea. Everyone on board dead. Murdered, they reckon.'

The Doctor stared at the man for a moment, then thrust the half-eaten '99' into his hand. 'Thank you, you've been most helpful,' he said as he spun away.

'Oi!'

The Doctor halted in mid-spin. 'Hmm?'

'Are you going to pay for this or what?'

'Yes, of course.' The Doctor rammed his hand into his coat pocket and produced a dozen or so glittering purple shells which he scattered across the small counter in front of the man. The man gaped at them in astonishment, then spluttered, 'Hey, wait a minute.'

But the Doctor was already half-way down the road, hurrying in the direction of the harbour. 'It's all right, keep the change,' he called back over his shoulder.

The earlier excitement had died down by the time the Doctor reached the police barrier. There was a smattering of curious onlookers, though with nothing much to see. On the jetty, a couple of hundred yards beyond the makeshift cordon of yellow tape, a lone uniformed policeman stood guard beside a trawler whose deck was covered by several tarpaulins.

'Excuse me,' the Doctor shouted, raising a hand in an attempt to snag the policeman's attention. Unsuccessful, he cried out more loudly, 'Ahoy there!', but again the policeman either didn't hear or chose to ignore him.

The Doctor sighed in exasperation, ducked beneath the barrier and strolled nonchalantly towards the boat. The policeman stepped into action. He hurried forward to intercept the Doctor, his face red with exertion and anger.

'What the hell do you think you're doing? I could have you arrested for crossing a police line.'

'Good afternoon,' said the Doctor, offering his most winning smile. 'I don't want to cause any trouble. I'd simply like to speak to whoever's in charge.'

'You would, would you? And which backstreet rag do you represent then?'

'Oh, I'm not a journalist. I work for UNIT. In an advisory capacity, of course. I have a pass here somewhere.' The Doctor rummaged frantically through his pockets, then all at once his face cleared and he grinned. He removed his panama hat to reveal a square of laminated card perched on the top of his head. He nodded and the card fell neatly into his palm.

He held it out to the policeman, his forefinger concealing the photograph of his third incarnation, then replaced it deftly in his pocket. 'I understand you have something of a mystery here,' he said, striding towards the trawler.

'Aye, but then your friend will have told you all about that.'

The Doctor stopped and turned so abruptly that the policeman almost walked into the back of him. 'Friend?'

'The other UNIT feller.'

'Yes, of course. You didn't happen to catch his name by any chance?'

The policeman frowned. 'Aye. The DI called him… Bates, I think it was.'

'Mike Yates?' supplied the Doctor.

'Aye, that's it. How many of you people are here then?'

'Oh, several,' said the Doctor vaguely, then clapped the policeman on the arm. 'Tell you what,' he said as if it had suddenly occurred to him to do this man a great favour, 'why don't *you* tell me exactly what happened here?'

'Your friend not fill you in then?' said the policeman drily.

'Different departments,' bluffed the Doctor. 'Mike Yates is the military liaison officer, I'm in the scientific research team. Our paths don't cross all that often. Besides, I've always been a great believer in getting the facts from the horse's mouth, so to speak.'

The policeman raised his eyebrows, but seemed convinced enough of the Doctor's credentials to fill him in on the fate of the *Papillon*'s crew. The Doctor listened hard, then gestured towards the boat. 'May I?'

The policeman shrugged. 'Be my guest. Not much to see now, though, bar a few bloodstains. All the remains were taken for forensic examination a couple of hours ago.'

The Doctor jumped nimbly down to the deck of the trawler and hauled the first of the heavy tarpaulins aside. He spent several minutes examining the boat, alternately squatting on his haunches and jumping up to range about as if searching for something specific.

Finally he leaped back up on to the jetty. 'Thank you, Constable,' he said. 'Most enlightening.' He swivelled on his heels, briefly scanning the holidaymakers toing and froing on the promenade. 'Tell me, have there been any strange occurrences in the town recently? Anything at all out of the ordinary?'

'Well, no, not really, sir. Oh, apart from Elkins's light, of course.'

'Elkins's light?'

'Yes, sir. I thought you knew about all that.'

'Remind me.'

The constable gave him a curious look, but dutifully recounted the story.

'Very interesting,' said the Doctor, staring distractedly into the middle distance. Abruptly he snapped out of his semi-trance and said, 'Anything else?'

'No, sir, not really. There's been a higher level of violent incident than is usual for even this time of year around the Sands these past couple of weeks, but that's most likely a sign of the times than anything.'

'Most likely,' echoed the Doctor. 'Well, thank you for your help, Constable.'

'Not at all, sir.'

The Doctor half-turned away, then something seemed to occur to him and he smiled. 'Oh, one final thing. I don't suppose Mr Yates left a contact address by any chance?'

The first day of Charlotte Maybury's holiday had not been a good one. Despite the sunshine and the change of scenery, her parents had continued to bicker and her brother to mooch sullenly along in their wake.

By 6 p.m. Charlotte was exhausted, her stoically cheerful veneer close to cracking. She felt as if she had spent the day holding at bay two combatants who were determined to rip chunks out of each other. Her various suggestions – Sea Life Centre, crazy golf, beach – had been met with a distinct lack of enthusiasm from her mum and dad and a sort of contemptuous indifference from Chris. In the end they had simply shuffled aimlessly from one location to another, forcing down ice-creams and fizzy drinks and cups of tea at regular intervals merely because it seemed the thing to do. Now they were meandering back to the boarding house and Charlotte was looking forward to a warm bath and a bit of peace and quiet in the privacy of her room.

They were walking past a fish and chip restaurant called The Happy Plaice when her dad, Tony, halted. 'Who fancies haddock and chips?' he said.

Imogen shot him a disdainful look. 'Don't you ever say anything sensible?'

Tony rolled his eyes. 'What's your problem now, woman?'

'Apart from you, you mean?' She sighed and as if speaking to a child said, 'We'll be having an evening meal at the B 'n B.'

'Says who?'

'What do you mean, says who? We've paid for it, you stupid sod.'

'So what? We're on holiday, aren't we? We can splash out a bit.'

'Oh yeah? What with?'

'Don't start going on about that again. For God's sake, woman, a plate of fish and chips is hardly going to break the bank, is it?'

Imogen thrust out her jaw and said through gritted teeth, 'But I don't *want* fish and chips.'

'Well, I *do*,' sneered Tony, thrusting his face close to hers.

Charlotte felt the familiar tension squeezing her lungs. She was so exhausted by their arguing that she felt like screaming at them to stop, felt like grabbing each of them by the scruffs of their necks and banging their heads together. But she knew that anger on her part would do no good. It was her lot to be the conciliator.

Wearily, all thoughts of a warm bath slipping away from her, she said, 'Why don't we just pop in for a cup of tea? We've still got plenty of time before dinner.'

Chris snorted and looked away as if he thought her attempts at arbitration pathetic.

Her dad rounded on her. 'I don't *want* a cup of tea. I want fish and chips.'

'Well, you *have* fish and chips,' she said reasonably. 'Mum and I can have a cup of tea and Chris can have... whatever *he* wants.'

Her brother mumbled something. Imogen snapped her head towards him. 'If you've got something to say, just say it.'

Suddenly Chris was glaring at her, the cheekbones of his spotty face flaring with colour. 'I said what I want is to get away from this bloody family. I don't know why I had to come on this stupid holiday, anyway. I wish you'd all just get stuffed and leave me alone.'

Charlotte looked around. They were starting to attract the attention of passers-by.

Imogen stepped towards him. 'Don't you *dare* speak to me like that!'

'Oh yeah, or what will you do? Smack my bum?'

'*She* might not, but I will,' growled Tony.

Chris took a step back, but his stance was aggressive, defiant. 'I'd like to see you try.'

'Right,' said Tony and lunged forward, face red, eyes bulging. Chris hopped sideways and threw a clumsy punch, which connected with his father's face more by luck than judgement.

Quite a crowd was gathering now. Charlotte rushed forward to position herself between Chris and Tony, her composure crumbling. 'Stop it! Stop it!' she shouted. She tried to grab her dad's arm to pull him back, but he swung out to shrug her off and his hand struck the side of her face, sending her reeling. She stumbled off the kerb and her legs gave way beneath her, dumping her unceremoniously on the ground.

'*You bloody animal!*' Imogen screamed at Tony, but Tony ignored her, advancing on Chris.

'Come here, you little sod!' he roared, but Chris darted into the crowd of onlookers, which parted before him.

When he was a safe distance away, he shouted, 'I hate the lot of you. I wish you'd all just bloody drop dead.' Then he turned and loped away. A group of lads, who had been watching what was going on with grins all over their faces, cheered and clapped.

'And you lot can bloody shut up,' Tony roared, stomping towards them.

The lads ran off, laughing and making V-signs as they retreated.

Tony clumped to a halt. He was red and sweating, the side of his face already purple where Chris had hit him. His eyes bulged and there was froth at the corners of his mouth. For a moment he looked confused, as if he had no idea what to do next, then he swung towards the restaurant. 'I'm off for some fish and chips,' he muttered. 'You two can do what you like.'

Charlotte, still sitting in the gutter, aware that she was being stared at like some curious exhibit in a museum, allowed her head to sink into her trembling hands to hide the tears that were running down her face.

'Right,' said Tegan as soon as she had put the phone down, 'I'm going out.'

'To find the Doctor?'

She gave Turlough a withering look. 'You really think I'm that desperate?'

He shrugged. 'Do you want me to come with you?'

'No, thank you.'

'Well... where *are* you going?'

'For a walk. To get some fresh air.'

Turlough raised his eyebrows dismissively. 'Right... well, I'll see you later.'

'Much later,' snapped Tegan and marched out.

For a while she stomped through the streets of the town, the exasperation inside her blinding her to her surroundings. Eventually, she calmed down, and moving into the town centre, away from the seafront, spent a pleasant hour window-shopping. She grimaced at the seventies' fashions, wondering how she could ever have found such clothes trendy in her teenage years, and marvelled at how cheap everything was. Thinking of money made her remember how the Doctor had insisted on vetting the cash in the little shoulder bag she'd packed – and which she was now carrying with her – to ensure she wasn't about to hand over coins that were yet to be minted. Her throat and stomach tightened again. The Doctor was her friend, she trusted him implicitly, but if he treated her more like an adult she wouldn't have cause to fly off the handle so often, would she?

She spotted a pub, The Captain Cook, and decided to pop in for a drink. She couldn't remember the last time she had sat quietly by herself on her own planet in (more or less) her own time while life drifted by around her. Since Amsterdam, her life had been a whirlwind of exotic locations and life-shattering – sometimes planet-shattering – events. 'Strictly no aliens allowed,' she murmured to herself as she pushed open the pub door and entered.

Predictably, the landlord of The Captain Cook had opted to give his pub a nautical theme. The dark-wood walls were decorated with framed photographs of fishing trawlers and their crews, and with various sea-faring paraphernalia: a ship's wheel, a barometer, an anchor. Above the bar was a huge stuffed marlin in a glass case.

Tegan stood beneath the marlin as she ordered a glass of dry white wine. The barman, whose stringy hair was plastered carefully over his balding scalp, tried to engage her in conversation, but she rebuffed him as politely as she could and took her drink to a table in the corner.

It was still early evening, only just opening time, and Tegan was The Captain Cook's first customer. Within minutes, however, the door banged open and a group of men in their early twenties bustled loudly in. They wore tight T-shirts and jeans so flared they flapped like sails as they walked. Each and every one of them had a helmet-like mop of shoulder-length hair. One of the men spotted her and nudged his companions and they turned with leering smiles.

'All right, darling,' said one.

'Drinking alone, love? Why don't you come and join us?' invited another.

Tegan sighed. 'No thanks,' she replied curtly.

'What's the matter, love? Don't you fancy us?' asked a man

with a pockmarked face and a scrubby blond moustache.

'Not much, no.'

'Ooh, too good for us, are you?'

'Here,' said a man, whose thick dark fringe almost covered his eyes, 'where you from? You an Aussie, are you?'

Tegan looked the man squarely in the eye and said, 'Look, I just came in for a quiet drink, so I'd appreciate it if you'd all go away and leave me alone.'

Her words were met with a barrage of comments:

'Playing hard to get, are we, darling?'

'Tie me kangaroo down, sport.'

'Hey, you know what they say about Aussie birds.'

The blond man with the moustache and the pock-marked face leaned forward, resting his knuckled fists on the edge of Tegan's table. In a voice that was quieter and more threatening than his friends' he said, 'We only want to buy you a drink, lady. We're only trying to be polite.'

Tegan's temper flared. She couldn't help it. 'No, you're not,' she snapped. 'You're a bunch of annoying little boys, all trying to act the big macho man in front of your mates.'

She saw the blond-haired man's face change, a strange blankness come into his eyes, his lips curl aggressively. Astonished she watched as he drew his arm back, his hand closing into a fist. She had no doubt that he intended to punch her in the face.

At that moment she was aware of someone barging through the crowd of youths, and a split second later the blond man's head jerked up and he was yelping in pain. The man who had grabbed her would-be assailant's wrist and twisted it behind his back ignored the threats from around him, and leaned over the blond man's shoulder so that his mouth was positioned directly beside his ear.

'Get off on attacking women, do you, sonny?' he said. 'That about your level, is it?'

'Let me go,' the blond man cried through the pain.

'Or what?' said the newcomer. 'Will you tell your mummy?'

'I'll tell the police you attacked me. I've got witnesses here to back me up.'

'I *am* the police,' said the man, thrusting an ID card into the blond man's face.

The way the others melted away from the scene, some of them sidling over to the pool table on the far side of the pub, a couple even sneaking out through the door, almost made Tegan smile.

The last vestiges of defiance drained from the blond man's voice and he became whiny, craven. 'I didn't do anything,' he said. 'We were just messing about.'

'Well, I don't think the lady found it very funny. Do you?'

'Er... n-no, probably not.'

'So what do you say?'

'Er...'

'I think an apology is called for, don't you?'

'Oh. Oh yeah. Sorry, officer.'

'Not to me, you moron, to the young lady.'

'Oh... er... yeah. Sorry... er, miss.'

Tegan snorted and rolled her eyes.

The policeman said reflectively, 'Now, what shall we do with you? I think a night in the cells might make you think twice about throwing your puny weight around, don't you?'

The blond man quailed. 'No... no, don't, please. I mean, I've... I've learned my lesson. I've never been in trouble before, honest. I won't do it again.'

The policeman was silent for a moment, making the blond man sweat. Finally he said, 'You know, I really can't decide what to do, so I think I'll ask the young lady here. Miss, would you like to press charges against this... er... gentleman?'

Again, Tegan had to fight hard not to smile. She stared coldly at the blond man, who gazed back at her pleadingly. After a leisurely sip of her wine she gave a dismissive shake of the head. 'He's not worth it.'

The policeman abruptly released his captive, who sprawled across her table, his legs splaying in a way that reminded Tegan of Bambi on the ice. Wincing from the pain in his arm, he pushed himself groggily to his feet. When he turned he found himself almost nose to nose with the thicker-set policeman, who grinned and said, 'It's just lucky for you that this lady has such a generous nature and that I'm off-duty. Now make yourself scarce.'

The blond man looked for a moment as though he wanted to say something, but didn't have the courage. Finally he gave a short nod and stumbled away. Rather than joining his friends over by the pool table, he headed straight for the door and lunged outside, his cheeks burning with humiliation.

The policeman watched him go, then turned to Tegan. 'Are you OK?'

'Fine,' said Tegan. 'I might not have been, though, if you hadn't showed up. I really think he intended to punch my lights out.'

'Can I get you a drink?' he said. 'Calm your nerves? I just popped in for a quiet one myself, believe it or not.'

'Sure,' she said and held up her glass. 'Same again, thanks.'

'Coming up.' He walked over to the bar.

Tegan watched him ordering the drinks. He was attractive in a seventies' sort of way. He was around thirty and, perhaps like many policemen of his era, obviously modelled himself on George Carter from *The Sweeney*. Certainly his hair was the same style, albeit darker, as were his clothes: kipper tie worn loosely, cuffs of his shirt turned up in a way that she always thought looked faintly ridiculous when she watched re-runs. He was not as rugged as Carter, though; his face was boyish, pleasant-looking, seemingly never far from a smile. He was broader-shouldered too, stocky but certainly not fat. He came back with another glass of wine for her and a pint of bitter already half drunk for himself. 'There you go,' he said.

'Thanks.' She drained the remains of her first glass and picked up her second. 'Cheers.'

'Cheers,' he responded. They chinked glasses and drank. After a few moments he said, 'Perhaps we'd better introduce ourselves. My name's Andy Weathers.'

'Is that PC or...'

'Sergeant,' he said with a grin.

'Tegan Jovanka,' said Tegan, thrusting out her hand for him to shake. He looked faintly surprised at the gesture, but shook anyway.

Nodding at the group by the pool table, he said, 'So, do you know that crowd?'

'Do I look as though I'd hang around with creeps like that?' She smiled to soften her indignation. 'No, I was just sitting here when they came in and started giving me hassle. When I told them where to go, Prince Charming decided to thump me.'

He shook his head. 'Toerags. I ought to arrest the lot of them.'

'I'm OK. I've handled a lot worse than them, believe me.'

'So what brings you to the Sands?'

She smiled teasingly. 'How do you know I'm not a local?'

'If you are, that's a very convincing Australian accent you've got there. So, come on, what brings you to this part of the world? Are you here on holiday?'

'Got it in one.'

'So which part of Australia are you from?'

'Brisbane. But I don't live there at the moment.'

'No? Whereabouts do you live?'

'So many questions!' she said. 'No wonder you became a policeman.'

He took another sip from his glass and leaned back with a smile. 'Sorry. Just making conversation. I don't want you to think I'm coming on too strong.'

'No, that's OK,' she said. 'I'm enjoying just sitting here, talking. I can't remember the last time I did this with anyone.'

'Really?' he said, visibly brightening, and leaned towards her again. 'Why's that?'

'I guess because my life's so hectic.'

'Why? What do you do?'

'I used to be an air hostess, but now I just... travel.'

'Seeing a bit of the world, eh?'

'Something like that.'

'Isn't it a bit dangerous,' he said, 'a girl travelling around on her own?'

Tegan realised she was going to have to tread warily here. She didn't want to get embroiled in a tangle of lies, but neither could she tell Andy exactly what her life entailed. 'Oh, I'm not alone,' she said. 'I travel with a couple of friends.'

'And where are they tonight?' he asked.

'One decided to stay back at the hotel and the other one's gone off on his own somewhere.'

'"His"?' said Andy casually. 'They're not both girls then?'

Tegan knew where this was leading, but found that she didn't mind. Equally casually she said, 'No. As a matter of fact they're both blokes.'

'Really?' he said, raising his eyebrows. 'Sounds like an interesting arrangement.'

'It's not what you think. They're just friends,' she said, and added teasingly, 'Not that it's any concern of yours anyway.'

'Course not,' he said innocently, swiftly draining the last of his pint. 'Fancy another?'

Tegan laughed. 'Are you trying to get me drunk?'

'Course I am. Get the tourists drunk and have our evil way with them. That's what we do in this town.'

When he returned from the bar, Tegan asked him to tell her about himself. Andy grimaced and said there wasn't much to tell. He'd been born and brought up in Tayborough Sands, and came from a long line of fishermen. 'I decided to break tradition and become a copper,' he said. 'There's no future in fishing any more for little family businesses like ours. The big factory trawlers are taking over.'

'How does that make you feel?' asked Tegan. 'Pretty bitter, I bet.'

He shrugged. 'Not so much bitter. A bit sad, maybe. But it's progress, isn't it? Time moves on. You can't do anything to stop it.'

'No,' Tegan said, 'you can't. So what's it like being a policeman in a place like this?'

'Seasonal. Quiet in the winter, hell in the summer.'

'I bet you hate tourists, don't you?'

'Some of them.' He smiled. 'To tell you the truth, I don't mind being busy. These last few weeks, though –' he frowned and shook his head – 'the whole place has gone crazy.'

'Really? In what way?'

'Well, what happened to you tonight was a good example. I mean, this time of year we get a lot of incidents relating to alcohol – fights in discos, people pulled in for drunk and disorderly, criminal damage, that sort of thing. But this year violent incidents have doubled, if not trebled.'

'What do you think's causing it?' asked Tegan.

'I don't know. The heat maybe? It *has* been hotter than usual this year. And violence, when it starts, tends to spread.'

Tegan sipped her wine and said reflectively, 'That guy tonight… just before he drew his arm back to hit me, his eyes went sort of blank. It was weird.'

Andy nodded thoughtfully, then smiled. 'Anyway… Look, you're here on holiday. I shouldn't be sitting here telling you what a terrible place this is. The last thing I want is to scare you off.'

'Oh, you won't scare me off,' said Tegan. 'I'm a pretty tough cookie.'

'All the same, I hope you'll let me walk you back to your hotel.'

'Course I will. But let's have another drink first, eh? My round.'

In fact, they had two more drinks. Tegan didn't realise how much the alcohol had affected her until she stood up. Her head started to spin and she had to concentrate hard to stop herself from stumbling.

'Oh, rabbits,' she murmured.

'Are you all right?' asked Andy, concerned.

'A bit woozy,' she admitted. 'I can't remember the last time I had this much to drink.'

'Come on, take my arm,' he said. 'A bit of fresh air will do you good.'

The pub had filled up with people and smoke since Tegan had entered a couple of hours ago. They manoeuvred their way to the door, Tegan holding on to Andy's arm, and went outside.

At first the fresh breeze blowing through the narrow streets made her head spin even more. She staggered as if the breeze was strong as a hurricane. Andy slipped his arm around her waist to steady her.

'Whoops,' she said. 'I bet you didn't bank on being lumbered with a drunken Aussie.'

'I've got no complaints about the company.' He grinned. 'Can you walk in a straight line?'

It was a beautiful night, the air warm, the sky clear and pinpricked with stars. Despite the violent picture Andy had painted, the streets of Tayborough Sands were quiet. They walked down to the seafront, Tegan still holding on to Andy for support. To anyone else they must have looked like lovers sharing a romantic stroll after dinner. They listened to the rushing, gravelly roar of the sea as it swarmed triumphantly over the shore before retreating with a sigh. There were no lights on the beach, and the only way they could distinguish sand from water was by the glittering shards of the moon's twin bobbing on the sea's black surface.

As they meandered along the pavement to the Lombard Hotel, Andy said, 'Can I see you again?'

Tegan felt a slow smile stretching her lips, but she tried to keep her voice casual. 'If you like.'

He hesitated, then plunged in. 'How about tomorrow? We could spend the day together. I'm not on duty till six.'

Tegan found herself wondering briefly what the Doctor's plans for the next day were, then immediately quashed the thought. 'Sounds great.'

'Ok, I'll pick you up from Reception about... nine?'

'I'll be there.'

They lingered at the hotel steps, unsure how to end it. 'Well... goodnight,' Tegan said at last, and abruptly thrust her hand out again. 'Thanks for being my knight in shining armour.'

'My pleasure.' He took the hand, but this time instead of shaking it he kissed the back of it gently. 'Until tomorrow,' he said softly.

'Until tomorrow,' Tegan repeated, trying desperately not to blush.

Several hours earlier Mike Yates had opened the door of his attic room to find a complete stranger standing there. The stranger was wearing odd clothes: a cricketing jumper and a long cream coat with a stick of celery attached to the lapel and funny striped trousers. Despite the heat the man looked cool and fresh. As soon as he saw Mike, a huge and delighted grin spread over his face.

'Mike Yates!' he exclaimed. 'How wonderful to see you again!'

Mike frowned, puzzled and a little wary. 'Have we met

before?'

'Oh, many times,' said the stranger as if he was enjoying himself hugely, 'though not since I regenerated.'

'Regenerated? You don't mean… You're not the Doctor?'

'Yes!' cried the man as if Mike was a rather dim pupil who had just grasped a basic mathematical formula.

Both the Doctor and the Brigadier had explained the fundamentals of regeneration to him, but Mike had not realised how drastic the change could be. 'But you're… so different,' he said weakly.

'Oh, I'm still the same old Doctor underneath,' the Doctor said airily. 'May I come in?'

Mike was about to step back and pull the door wide when he paused. 'How do I *know* you're the Doctor? How do I know you're not trying to trick me?'

The Doctor blinked. 'Why would I want to do that?'

'I don't know. Maybe you want to get to the real Doctor through me. You could be the Master for all I know.'

The Doctor flinched and his voice became a little high-pitched with indignation. 'Please! I've never been so insulted.'

'I'm sorry,' said Mike. 'It's just… you're so different. You don't seem as…'

'Arrogant? Overbearing?'

Mike shrugged embarressedly. 'You said it.'

'Yes, well,' said the Doctor, non-plussed, 'when one matures, one irons out these little foibles.'

'Matures?' said Mike. 'But you look so much younger!'

'Appearances can be deceptive, you know.'

'My point exactly,' said Mike triumphantly.

The Doctor sighed. 'The thing about regeneration is that it's something of a lottery. But whatever I look like, I'm still fundamentally the same underneath. How can I convince you of that?'

Before Mike could reply, the Doctor's eyes widened. 'What

date is it?' he asked.

Puzzled, Mike told him.

The Doctor gazed into the middle distance as if looking back through time. 'So you've not been back on active duty for long. You've been recovering from the events at Llanfairfach.'

Mike frowned. 'Go on.'

The Doctor snapped out of his semi-trance. 'How are you feeling now, Mike?'

'Fine.'

'No ill-effects?'

'No, I don't think so.'

The Doctor looked at him strangely, reached out and patted him on the forearm. 'You're a good man, Mike. I've always thought so.'

'Thanks, but I don't –'

Breathlessly the Doctor said, 'BOSS took you over. I brought you back with a blue crystal from Metebelis Three. I sent the crystal to Jo for a wedding present.' His hand dipped into his pocket and he produced a small card which he handed to Mike. 'My UNIT pass. Now I wouldn't let this fall into the wrong hands, would I? The Brigadier would have my guts for garters.'

Mike took the card and looked at it perfunctorily before handing it back. Smiling he said, 'All right, Doctor, let's say I believe you.'

The Doctor grinned. 'Splendid. Then we can get down to business.'

Mike ushered the Doctor in, then crossed to the bed and sat down. The Doctor wandered around the small room as if restless, hands in the pockets of his striped trousers. 'So what caused you to regenerate?' Mike asked.

The Doctor swung round from his contemplation of a rather poorly-executed print of a sailing yacht hanging above the dressing table. 'Hmm?'

Mike repeated his question.

'Ah,' said the Doctor, and crossed the room to sit in the armchair beneath the alcoved window. 'It's rather complicated. You see, since you last saw me I've regenerated twice. But that doesn't mean you've seen the last of the me that you know. I'm just popping in while I'm away, so to speak. The next me to arrive will be the old me with no knowledge of the new me – presuming that none of the other mes drop in in the meantime, of course.'

Mike looked at the Doctor deadpan for a moment, and then said, 'Thank you. That makes everything perfectly clear.'

His ironic tone seemed lost on the Doctor, who looked at him keenly. 'Tell me about the light that Mr Elkins saw.'

'You know about that?' said Mike.

'I've been doing some investigating.'

Mike pulled a dismissive face. 'Load of rubbish, if you ask me. The man's an old soak. Probably fell asleep and dreamt the whole thing.'

'Hmm,' said the Doctor thoughtfully. 'You saw the bodies on the fishing boat?'

'Yes.'

'I understand their injuries were rather severe?'

Mike raised his eyebrows. 'That's putting it mildly. Apart from one chap who looked as if he'd had half his throat torn out, there were only bits left behind.'

'Indeed,' said the Doctor thoughtfully. 'And what could cause that degree of damage, do you think? An aquatic mammal, perhaps?'

'Well... I don't know. The police seem to think one of the men went berserk and killed the others.'

'Is that possible? Given the injuries you saw?'

Mike looked dubious, but paused before replying. 'Those men were torn apart, Doctor. Not cut or chopped. *Torn*. If one of the crew *did* kill the others, he did it with his bare hands.'

'Interesting,' said the Doctor. 'In which case a much more likely supposition would be that the men were killed by whatever came out of the vessel that Mr Elkins saw land in the sea. Wouldn't you agree?'

Mike pulled a face. 'The thought had crossed my mind. But old Elkins seems such an unreliable witness I'm reluctant to involve the Brigadier until I've got more evidence. I don't want to haul half of UNIT up here only for them to find they're faced with nothing but an old drunk and a local squabble. You know, first day back on the job and all that.'

The Doctor nodded his understanding and said slyly, 'Is it really necessary to involve UNIT at all? I've never been overkeen on the military marching about, upsetting everyone. I'm sure if we put our heads together the two of us could sort this matter out without any fuss.'

'I'm sorry, Doctor,' said Mike, 'but I'm answerable to the Brigadier. I have to inform him about what's going on.'

For a moment the Doctor looked like a little boy who has been refused a packet of sweets. 'Well, if you must, you must,' he said. He thought of the alien mind he had briefly touched earlier that day, and sighed.

'Is something the matter?' asked Mike.

'I think I just might have the extra evidence you need,' the Doctor said.

Tegan didn't realise she was still angry until the Doctor popped his head out of the door of his room as she was unlocking hers.

'You missed dinner,' he said, the note of indignation in his voice immediately causing her to bridle.

'I wasn't hungry,' she replied tersely, determined that he wouldn't spoil what had turned out to be a lovely evening.

He wandered along the corridor towards her. 'Turlough and I were concerned. We missed your company.'

'I'll bet,' she muttered.

'Have you eaten?' he asked.

She swung round on him, still feeling a little dizzy from the alcohol. 'Since when have you cared about my welfare?'

He looked taken aback, hurt. 'I care a great deal!'

Realising she had overstepped the mark, but too proud to apologise, she mumbled, 'Anyway, who are you to ask me where *I've* been? Where did *you* disappear off to this afternoon?'

All at once he looked evasive. 'Catching up on an old friend.'

'What old friend? Doctor, what's going on?'

He sighed. 'Nothing's going on.'

'Yes it is. As a Time Lord you may have strange and unusual powers, but you're a rotten liar. Tell me, Doctor.'

He raised his eyes heavenward. 'All right.' He told her about the light in the sky; the trawler; the alien mind that had briefly touched his upon their arrival.

Tegan saw her holiday evaporating before her eyes. 'Why didn't you tell me all this earlier?'

'I didn't know about most of it earlier. Besides, you and Turlough are supposed to be on holiday, recuperating from recent traumas.'

'So are you!'

'My powers of recuperation are considerably greater than yours.'

'So you keep us in the dark, treat us like children!' she snapped.

'Only because you often behave like one,' retorted the Doctor.

She glared at him for a moment, then abruptly turned and walked away down the corridor, back towards the lifts.

'Tegan!' he called.

'Drop dead!' she shouted.

The Doctor spun on his heels in exasperation – and came

face to face with Turlough, who had been standing silently in the doorway of his room, watching the exchange.

Turlough raised his eyebrows in apparent sympathy and said, 'Shall I go after her?'

'You do what you like,' the Doctor muttered, and stalked back to his room.

Perhaps if she hurried she could catch up with Andy, though what would follow from there she really had no idea. She wouldn't want him to think she was throwing herself at him, and however much she liked him she knew that there was no future in their relationship. She supposed she just wanted someone to talk to, someone neutral, normal, sympathetic – though how she could explain what was on her mind without telling him about the kind of life she led was anybody's guess.

When the lift doors opened on to the reception area she half-expected to see the Doctor standing there, waiting for her, having beaten her to the ground floor via the stairs. When he wasn't she felt a strange mixture of disappointment and relief. She hurried across to the main doors and out into the night.

Andy was nowhere to be seen, but maybe that was a good thing, after all. Tegan had enjoyed the sheer *normality* of the evening they'd spent together, but perhaps what she really needed right now was time to think, time to sort out the confusion in her mind.

Should she leave the Doctor and try to pick up the threads of her life again? Rather than simply taking a holiday, or visiting her grandfather, should she break her ties with him once and for all? There was a part of her that craved the kind of normal human interaction she had experienced tonight, and a part that told her she should grasp her once-in-a-lifetime experience of life aboard the TARDIS with both hands and wring from it what she could. She was travelling around the universe in a time machine, for Christ's sake! She was seeing and experiencing things that the vast majority of people could only dream about! In that respect she was mad for even contemplating giving it all up. But wherever they went they found trouble, danger, death…

She walked along the promenade until she came to a flight of stone steps that led down to the beach. She descended carefully, holding on to the metal railing at her side, the roaring of the sea increasing like some vast animal excited at her approach. She knew she had reached the bottom only when her feet met a surface that was softer, more giving, than stone. Despite the fat yellow moon and the craning, pumpkin-orange light of the street lamps on the prom above, it was too dark to discern where the sand ended and the sea began.

The wind ruffled her hair as she began to walk and made her shiver slightly. It was chilly, but at least it might help clear the remnants of the alcohol which still befuddled her thoughts. It was unwise to make any decisions about her future now; she would sleep on it, think about it again in the morning. One conclusion she did come to, though, was that whatever was happening here, she would let the Doctor deal with it on his own. She had no intention of breaking her date with Andy tomorrow.

She came to a halt, wondering whether she ought to head back to the hotel. How long had she been gone? Ten minutes? It wasn't much of a statement, was it? About five hundred yards away, moonlight was washing across a set of caves, their yawning mouths pooled with shadow. She would walk as far as the caves and then slowly back, she decided.

Her ears filled with nothing but the foaming rush of the sea, she trudged unhurriedly towards them.

Deep in the shadows at the back of the largest cave, something stirred. Its spiny flesh rasped the stone wall it had been slumped against as it emerged from its fevered sleep. The smell that had roused it – coppery, pungent, and oh so deliriously, unbearably *sweet* – made it salivate, tremble and jerk with excitement. It hauled itself forward to the cave mouth, its stertorous breathing audible only to itself beneath the constant frothing hiss of the waves, and peered out.

A woman was approaching along the sand, the wind plucking at her hair and clothes, her outline backlit by the moon. It was her blood that the creature could smell; it was beating off her in waves. As she drew closer, so the smell intensified, until the creature was almost crazed by it. Slowly it levered its body up on its eight legs, tensing itself for the kill...

Part Two
Breaking Out

Turlough shouted her name again, but Tegan didn't respond. Either she was willfully ignoring him or she couldn't hear him above the crashing of the waves. He made an exasperated sound and resumed his shambling run. He had always hated physical exercise; if you had to exert yourself to get something you wanted, then it probably wasn't worth getting in the first place.

He shouted her name a third time, and on this occasion, to his relief, she stopped and turned round.

'What do you want?' she asked discouragingly as he drew near.

He thumped to a halt and bent double, hands on his knees, out of breath. After a moment he gasped, 'I came... to see... if you were all right.'

'Did the Doctor send you?' she asked suspiciously.

'No. But I do think you ought to come back and talk to him. Clear the air.'

Obstinately she folded her arms. 'Why?'

'Well, because... because you and the Doctor are the only friends I've got. I don't like ill-will between any of us.'

She snorted. 'That's rich, coming from someone who was trying to kill him not so very long ago.'

He looked shame-faced, hurt. 'You know I was tricked by the Black Guardian. Besides, that's all in the past now. I'm doing my best to make amends.'

'Is that so?'

'Yes! Look, I don't suppose I can blame you for not trusting me, but we got each other out of Sea Base Four alive, didn't we? There'll be no more lies, I promise.'

'We'll see,' said Tegan, though her voice was softer now.

Turlough extended a tentative hand towards her. '*Please* come back to the hotel.'

Tegan sighed and glanced towards the Lombard. She could see the lights in its windows glowing some distance away, up beyond the promenade.

'He treats us like children,' she said. 'He doesn't tell us what's going on.'

'He's not like that all the time,' said Turlough.

Tegan gave him a sharp look. 'Why are you defending him?'

'I'm not. It's just…' He sighed. 'I think you're being a little hard on him, Tegan. He just wanted us to have a holiday, to relax after what happened on the Sea Base.'

Now it was her turn to sigh. 'I know. I don't like him making decisions for me, that's all. I'm old enough to make my own.'

Turlough smiled wryly. 'Not in his eyes. Though if you manage to live for the next four or five hundred years, you just *might* get a little respect.'

She laughed and took the hand he was still holding out towards her. 'All right,' she said resignedly, 'let's go back.'

'And you'll talk to the Doctor?' said Turlough.

'I'll try. But I can't guarantee it'll be a *civilised* conversation.'

As the two figures turned and walked away, the creature in the cave snarled and writhed in frustration. The smell of their blood, carried on the wind like musk, was sending it wild with the urge to tear and rend and devour. But just when its feast was almost within reach, it seemed it was to be cruelly denied it. Desperately, the creature moved forward to the cave entrance, but as soon as the moonlight touched it, it shrank back.

Despite its craving, an overriding instinct compelled it to remain in the shadows. Very soon it would not matter, but for now it was important that the creature not draw attention to itself. Blood-lust pounded through its veins; a desire so powerful that the creature's eight legs twitched and jerked in involuntary spasms, scraping against the walls and gouging out great ruts and scars of stone.

After saying goodnight to Tegan, Andy Weathers decided to call in at one of his favourite haunts, The Blue Falcon, for a nightcap. He was feeling good, still buzzing from Tegan's company, and he didn't feel like heading home just yet. One or two of the lads might be in the Falcon – it was a favourite police haunt – but it wouldn't bother Andy unduly if he had to drink alone. Besides, it would give him the chance to plan his day with Tegan tomorrow.

The first thing he noticed when he pushed open the door was that there was a rowdier than usual crowd in tonight. The lads from the force could get a bit loud, especially on a Friday when the landlord employed a couple of strippers to bolster trade, but this lot was different: young lads and lasses, holidaymakers probably. As he made his way to the bar, Andy realised that the atmosphere was not merely rowdy, it was downright threatening. He glanced quickly around, but the hostility did not seem to be directed at him in particular. It was simply there, as thick as the cigarette smoke that curled around the room in swirling grey patterns.

The landlord, Bob Walker, moved down the bar to serve him, and immediately Andy saw the tension on his face.

'Evening, Bob,' Andy said.

Walker gave a brief nod. 'Andy.'

'Something going down tonight, is there?'

Walker's gaze flickered nervously around the room. 'So you feel it too, do you? It's been like this all week,' he said quietly.

'Any trouble?'

'Nothing serious so far, but I have this horrible feeling that it's only a matter of time.'

'Same mob every day is it?'

'No, that's the odd thing. There are some of the same faces, but nearly everyone who comes in looks as if they're spoiling for a fight. Even –' he faltered.

'Even what?' Andy said.

Walker looked uncomfortable, embarrassed. He lowered his voice even more. 'Now, don't take this the wrong way, Andy. I don't mean to be insulting or anything. But I've even noticed it in some of your lot.'

Andy frowned. Walker's words had served to crystallise some of his own recent concerns. 'I've noticed it too,' he admitted. 'For a week or two now I've had this feeling that… that we're sitting on a powder keg.'

Walker pulled a pint of bitter without being asked and placed it on the bar. 'Any idea what's causing it?'

Andy shrugged. 'Not really. The hot weather maybe.'

He paid for his beer and went to sit down. As he drank he glanced around, covertly watching the pub's customers. The majority, he noticed, were scowling, standing with their fists clenched, turning to stare at strangers as if inviting confrontation. At the bar, people were barging through without care or apology, causing a number of heated exchanges, and several snapped threats.

He had been in the pub for ten minutes when, seemingly apropos of nothing, a pint glass flew across the room, beer arcing from it, spattering the crowd.

The glass smashed against the bar, spraying a woman with crystal splinters. She screamed, her hands flying up to her lacerated face. The man beside her turned, enraged, and launched himself at the nearest target, an elderly, bespectacled man who was standing with his wife, sipping whisky. He bore the man to the ground, punched him in the face, smashing his spectacles. The elderly man's wife slammed a wine glass on to her husband's assailant's head, cutting her hand, and then, astonishingly, spun like a dervish and began to viciously pummel the young man in the leather jacket who was standing next to her. The young man retaliated, kicking and bludgeoning the woman to the ground. As if the sudden flurry of violence had snapped their own fragile threads of inhibition, other people abruptly turned to launch unprovoked attacks on those standing close to them. These tinders of violence escalated into a forest fire with such astonishing speed that within half a minute of the catalyst of the exploding glass the entire room was in uproar.

The chain of events was so swift that Andy, like many others, could only gape at first, his beer glass clutched almost forgotten in his hand. He had been involved in violent situations before and quickly realised that what was happening here did not conform to the usual patterns. Brawls and riots generally looked more frightening than they actually were, most of those involved content simply to make up the numbers, to get caught up in the excitement whilst staying out of trouble. Here, though, things were different. Here, the majority rather than the minority seemed eager to get in on the action.

Women were screeching and clawing and kicking; men were punching, head-butting, picking up whatever they could find to use as weapons. The violence was intense, random, senseless, frenzied. People were simply inflicting pain on others for the sheer crazed joy of it, fighting with whoever was closest to hand, regardless of age or gender.

Andy had only a second or two to take this in before a big guy with a thick moustache and a look of glazed madness in his eyes lunged towards him. Andy jumped up from his seat and instinctively threw his beer in the man's face. As the man blundered on, momentarily blinded, Andy dropped his beer glass and in one movement stepped forward and punched the man right in the centre of his face, poleaxing him. Before anyone else could zero in on him, Andy ran across to the door at the back of the bar, shot through it and slammed it behind him.

The corridor behind the bar, at the end of which was a staircase leading up to the living quarters, was deserted. To Andy's immediate right was a fire exit door, which he slammed through without hesitation. He found himself in a cobbled back yard that narrowed to an alleyway that ran along the side of the building. The noises coming from inside the pub made it sound as if a wild party was taking place in there. Andy took out his walkie-talkie and put a call through to the station. By the time the police arrived, three minutes later, the violence had spilled out into the street.

Andy stayed out of sight at the end of the alleyway until he heard the sirens and saw the flashing lights of four panda cars and a Black Maria. When he emerged into the glass, debris and body-strewn street, the doors of the police vehicles were opening and uniforms were piling out. Though he was grateful for the back-up, Andy still couldn't help feeling uneasy. A good number of his colleagues looked as itchy for a fight as most of the people in the pub had been, and Andy didn't think their eager, yet oddly blank expressions could simply be put down to adrenalin.

As the uniformed PCs and the pub combatants clashed, Reg Stafford, a fellow sergeant and a friend of Andy's, got out of the front passenger seat of the leading panda car and hurried across. 'What the hell's been going on here, Andy?' he said.

'All hell broke loose in there, and I don't just mean a few blokes throwing punches,' Andy said. 'Someone chucked a glass, and next thing I knew everyone was going at it hammer and tongs – men, women…' He tailed off, shaking his head.

'Right,' Reg said, and even his eyes were glittering a little, 'I'll follow my boys in, see what the damage is. You coming?'

'Wouldn't miss it for the world,' Andy said without enthusiasm.

Reg and Andy followed the uniforms through the open double doors. Inside the pub, which had been comprehensively wrecked, PCs had drawn their truncheons and were setting about their task of breaking heads. Andy tried to avoid watching them too closely, not because he was squeamish, but because he didn't want to see how undisciplined his colleagues had become; didn't want to see the glee on their faces as they brought their truncheons cracking down on skulls. Instead he concentrated on tending to those who had been bludgeoned and beaten out of the fight.

Most of them had relatively minor injuries – scratches, bites, broken noses, missing teeth, black eyes. Others were injured more seriously: there were broken limbs and ribs and gashes to the head, some of which were quite deep.

Almost every one of those who had been too badly injured to continue fighting seemed dazed, confused, as if they had emerged from a hypnotic trance. Several of them asked Andy what was happening; one or two even seemed to have difficulty remembering where or who they were.

Andy made as many of them comfortable as he could, assured them that ambulances were on their way, then moved deeper into the mêlée. The police were getting on top of the situation now, hauling people outside. Some battlers still struggled furiously as they were dragged away, whereas others became quiescent, the blank-eyed fury on their faces giving way to a sleepy bewilderment. Glass crunched beneath Andy's feet and the floor was strewn with debris. A large wooden table-top, cracked and splintered, was lying on the ground, the legs smashed off it, no doubt used as weapons. Andy lifted the table-top aside, intending to prop it against the wall, help to clear the way for his colleagues. As he did so he froze. Beneath the table was a man lying in a very large and still spreading pool of blood.

'Over here!' Andy shouted, shoving the table-top aside and dropping to his knees. He grabbed the man's wrist and felt for a pulse. It was there, but it was flickering, erratic. He saw almost immediately what had happened. The man had been stabbed several times in the stomach and chest. The points of entry were ragged as though something other than a knife – a broken glass perhaps? – had been used. Andy hoped that this meant the wounds were not too deep, though the amount of blood that was still gushing from them seemed to suggest otherwise.

Andy and two uniformed constables tried to stem the bleeding as much as they could, first with beer towels taken from the bar and then, after Bob Walker had risen dazedly from his hiding-place, with bigger, thicker towels from the airing cupboard upstairs. It was not long, however, before the towels were saturated and the men's hands and clothes covered in blood.

It seemed to take an age for the ambulances to arrive, but eventually two paramedics in yellow jackets were there beside Andy.

'He's been stabbed several times,' Andy said, moving aside for them. 'His pulse is very weak.'

'All right, let's take a look,' said one of them, a balding man with a darkly stubbled chin, who exuded an air of calm efficiency.

He produced a small scalpel, which he used to slice open the front of the man's blood-soaked shirt. Pulling the shirt open, he instantly recoiled. 'Jesus, what the hell's that?' he exclaimed.

His colleague, Andy and the two policeman stared in horror and disbelief at what had been revealed. All over the man's chest, shoulders and upper arms were masses of small, black quills.

Through her open window came the susurrating rhythm of the sea stroking the shore. Her eyes closed, curled up on her bed, Charlotte wondered whether this was what it was like in the womb. How nice it must be, she thought, to be in the warmth and the dark, soothed by the sound of a mother's internal tide – the pumping of a heart, the ebb-and-flow of life-giving blood. How wonderful to have no cares, no fears, no thoughts. She would have found it easier to relax into the idea if her own cares had not been eating her up inside, denying her sleep.

She sighed, rolled over and opened her eyes. As she sat up, the weight of her anxieties sank like ballast inside her. Mum had gone to bed two hours ago, exhausted with weeping, but Charlotte had lain sleepless ever since. It felt as though her life was coming apart. What had she done to deserve it? Why was she being punished in this way?

She looked at her clock. It was five past two in the morning. For almost five hours her mother had wailed and clung to her, declaring that her life was over. Charlotte had done her best to console her, even though she too had felt like weeping. They had had no dinner, but even now Charlotte felt too sick to eat.

The evening had been punctuated by emergency sirens whooping outside, police cars and ambulances racing by. Soon after, round about 11.30 p.m., they had heard Dad come back. He had been drunk, stumbling and muttering, making so much noise as he tripped up the stairs that Charlotte felt sure it would bring Mrs Macau swooping down on him like a vampire bat. It was the only time that night when her mother had stopped crying. She and Charlotte had clung to each other, staring fearfully at the closed door.

Thankfully he had blundered past, opening and then

slamming the door of the room he was supposed to be sharing with Mum. After that they had heard nothing. He had probably collapsed on to the bed and instantly fallen into an alcohol-induced sleep.

At midnight, Mum had announced that she too was going to bed. Before turning in she had tearfully wondered about calling the police to report the fact that Chris still wasn't home. Charlotte, though, had managed to dissuade her. 'Don't worry, Mum, he'll come back when he's ready.'

'But he's only a baby,' Imogen wailed.

'Don't let *him* hear you say that,' Charlotte said, trying to keep her voice light.

Mum clutched her hand and looked imploringly into her eyes. 'He *will* be all right, won't he?'

'Course he will.'

'Promise me.'

Charlotte licked her lips uneasily. 'I promise.'

Mum had seemed pacified by that, had kissed Charlotte goodnight and gone to bed. Charlotte had offered to let her have *her* bed and to sleep on the floor, but Mum had waved the offer away.

'*I'll* be all right. Your dad's too drunk to argue and I'm too tired.'

'Well, if you want anything I'll be here,' Charlotte had told her.

Mum's eyes had filled with tears. 'I know you will, love. I don't know what I'd do without you. Goodnight.'

That had been two hours ago and it had not been a good night. It had not been a good night at all.

As far as she was aware, Chris had still not returned to the boarding house. She got out of bed and went to the window, sticking her face between the gap in the curtains. She couldn't see much. Aside from the nimbus of orange light emanating from each street lamp and pooling on the ground beneath it, the tarmacked road and stone-flagged pavements, and even the beach, looked not only black but composed of the same substance. Only the sea looked different, the shards of white moonlight on the waves giving it the appearance of rippling black plastic.

She shivered, despite the warm night air, and left the window. She crossed to her suitcase, which was sitting open on the floor beside the wardrobe, only partially unpacked. Delving beneath her clothes she found a cardboard box, similar in size and shape to that which might contain a toothpaste tube.

She sat down on the bed, cross-legged, her back supported by a pillow jammed against the headboard, and stared at the words in blue on the box's white surface: PREGNANCY TESTING KIT. Her hands were shaking. She wondered whether she ought to put the kit back and wait for a better time. But the house was quiet and everyone was asleep. What better time could there be? If she didn't do it now then she probably never would.

Opening the box, she tipped its contents on to the bedclothes. The equipment for this potentially life-changing event was singularly unimpressive. A strip of plastic with a window of white paper in the centre. Even though she knew how to use it, she studied the instructions again, buying herself a little time. Finally, with a sigh of annoyance, she snatched up the plastic strip. Her stomach performing slow, queasy somersaults, she tiptoed along the creaking corridor to the bathroom at the far end.

Two minutes later she was back in her room, waiting for the results. If a blue line appeared, bisecting the square of paper, the test was positive; if it remained white, it was negative.

The few minutes she had to wait were excruciating. Unable to bear holding the strip of plastic in her hand, she placed it on top of the chest of drawers and sat on her bed, watching the clock.

Finally it was time. Despite the warmth of the summer night she felt cold inside. She picked up the strip of plastic, looked at it.

She exhaled, making a low sound somewhere between a sigh and a groan. there was a bright blue line bisecting the square of white paper.

Within minutes of lying down on the beach, Chris began to shiver with cold. It was a balmy night, but the chill seemed to seep up from the sand, into his bones. He sat up, hugging himself, his head whirling so much that he felt he was still sitting on the Spinning Spider at the fun-fair. He felt sick from drinking the six cans of Special Brew he had asked an older kid to buy for him from an offy on the seafront, and every time he tried to walk it seemed as if the ground was pitching and tossing like the deck of a boat on a stormy sea.

He had run straight to the fun-fair after his fight with Dad, and had stayed there until the place closed down for the night at 10 p.m. He had gone on tons of rides – all the big stuff of course, none of the little kids' rubbish – and had eaten so many hot dogs that by the end of the evening the smell of them made him want to puke.

Yet although he had had a good time, his family and their stupid problems had always been there, lurking at the back of his mind. He hated the way his mum and dad argued all the time; it made him feel as though his head was being squeezed in a vice. Charlotte was OK, but she got on his nerves by not standing up to them, not saying or doing anything to stop their rows. She just tried to be nicey-nicey, to pretend nothing was happening, but it didn't work. It was just pathetic.

Chris was sick of it all. He wished he never had to see any of them ever again. He had even asked a couple of blokes who were working on the rides if there were any jobs going on the fair, but they had just looked at him and laughed as if he was some stupid little kid.

Fed up, he had finally wandered down to the promenade and drunk himself into near-oblivion. All he wanted to do now was sleep, but he needed somewhere warmer than the beach. He had a warm bed at the guesthouse, but he would rather freeze to death than go back there tonight.

All the same he had to find somewhere. He rose unsteadily to his feet and stood swaying for a moment, taking deep breaths in the hope that fresh air would rid the urge to throw up. He looked around, moving his head slowly. There were bus shelters on the promenade, but he would feel too vulnerable there.

His gaze drifted further, finally alighting on a block of craggy darkness at the far end of the beach. Chris vaguely remembered seeing the caves that afternoon and wondered whether they would be warm enough. They ought to be. It wasn't as if it was a cold night, after all. It was only the breeze coming off the sea that was making him chilly and the caves would provide shelter.

He weaved along the beach. As he blinked at the gaping caves they seemed curiously insubstantial. Their blackness seemed to divide and sub-divide, to spin like a vortex, increasing his nausea. Abruptly he stopped, leaned forward and vomited hot dogs and beer all over the sand. His stomach spasmed and he threw up again, so violently that tears were squeezed from his eyes. After that he felt a little better. He stumbled the last two hundred yards almost blindly, desperate to sleep.

The largest of the cave mouths seemed to suck him in. As he stepped into the cave, lulling darkness wrapped around him. The solid walls muted the gnashing of the sea and provided a barrier against the snapping sea-breeze. Chris sighed, half-way to sleep, though not too far gone to notice a curious smell in here. It was strong and fishy, like spoiled crab-meat, but also... musky, hot, animal-like. Horse-sweat and cowsheds and the lion enclosure at the zoo.

He moved deeper into the cave... and started at a stealthy scraping from the murk in front of him. It sounded like someone dragging a sharp, metal implement across granite. He imagined a ragged figure with wild hair and wild eyes lurking in the darkness, clutching a meat cleaver. He tried to lick his lips, but they were gummed together with curd-thick saliva. He instinctively took a step backwards.

And something flew at him from the darkness, its reverberating screech transfixing him with utter terror, echoing at crazy angles from the cave walls.

Chris caught a brief, terrifying impression of black, spider-like eyes, and jointed, chitinous, razor-edged legs. Then unbelievable pain ripped through him and turned his world a brilliant, scorching red.

'Good lord,' said the Brigadier wearily.

The Doctor grinned. 'Lethbridge-Stewart, my dear fellow. How are you?'

'Same as ever, Doctor. Unlike yourself.'

'Didn't Mike explain?' the Doctor asked, glancing at the Brigadier's number two, who was standing between his commanding officer and the burly frame of Sergeant Benton, still wearing his civvies.

'Well, er, I tried,' Mike said with a grimace of apology.

'I'm sure you did a sterling job,' said the Doctor breezily, turning to address him before swinging to face the Brigadier again. Suddenly sombre, he said, 'Now, where's this body you called me in to see?'

'Through here,' the Brigadier said, indicating with his swagger stick. He led them through a small, scrupulously clean anteroom containing a set of lockers, two large sinks and various items of medical equipment, to a set of double doors at the far end, which he pushed open.

The mortuary was a large well-lit room whose main wall was composed of rows of big square metal drawers, each of them numbered. A small, balding, white-coated man with a scrubby moustache and thick spectacles scurried forward to meet them. 'Brigadier Stewart?' he enquired.

'Lethbridge-Stewart,' corrected the Brigadier severely.

The little man quailed and glanced at the clipboard he clutched in his hand. 'Ah yes, of course. You've come to view number thirty-two, I understand?'

'If that's the stab victim who was brought in last night, then yes we have,' said the Brigadier.

'Of course,' said the man again. 'This way.' He led them over to the wall of metal drawers and tugged at the handle of drawer 32. It rolled open with a metallic rumble.

Mike Yates gasped involuntarily. Sergeant Benton murmured, 'Blimey.'

The Brigadier regarded the body grimly for a moment, then glanced up. 'What do you make of it, Doctor?'

The Doctor was already leaning over the body, a concentrated frown on his face. After a few seconds he looked up at the little man, who was hovering on the periphery of the group. 'Do you have any surgical gloves, Mr...'

'Booth,' said the man. 'Yes, sir, I'll just get you some.'

He scuttled away and returned moments later. The Doctor thanked him, pulled on the gloves and began to examine the dead man more closely, touching the spines on his chest and arms, prodding the surrounding flesh. 'I understand the man died of blood loss due to his injuries?'

'Yes, sir. He was stabbed four times.' Booth indicated the now bloodless purple-black slits in the man's abdomen.

'Hmm. Was anyone else involved in this incident treated for injuries at this hospital?'

'Yes, sir. Several people.'

'And did they exhibit similar... afflictions?'

'I'm not sure, sir. I could find out for you.'

'I'd be grateful if you would,' said the Doctor and straightened up, looking down at the corpse curiously. 'He seems to be lying rather awkwardly.'

'Yes, sir,' said Booth. 'He's a hunchback.'

'Do you mind if we have a look?'

'No, sir. I'll give you a hand.'

They heaved the corpse over on to its side. Now they could all see the peculiar double-hump, almost like vestigial wings, on the man's back.

'Interesting,' breathed the Doctor.

'Well, Doctor?' said the Brigadier. 'What do you think?'

The Doctor looked round at the three UNIT men. 'Metamorphosis,' he said.

'Meta-what?' said Benton.

'The people of Tayborough Sands are changing, Sergeant,' the Doctor replied. Then he looked thoughtful and his voice dropped an octave. 'The question is – into what?'

The ringing of the telephone jerked Edith Perry from a dream about her long-dead husband Harold and his pigeons. The pigeons had been changing into little trains with wings, and Harold had been waving his fists in the air and ranting, 'It's that boy what's done this. Where is he? I'll tan him, I will.'

The ringing made her heart flutter like a dying bird in her paper-thin chest. She swung her legs slowly from the bed, confused and alarmed, wondering who could possibly be calling at such an hour.

Then she glanced at the clock and saw that it was almost 7 a.m. What was going on? Why hadn't Jack brought her her early morning cup of tea before slipping out to work? Surely he hadn't overslept for the first time in his life?

The sultry night had given way to an already muggy morning, but she shivered as she crossed the room to the dressing-gown hung on the back of her door. In the past five years or so she had become prone to an inner chill that only old people seemed afflicted by. It made her wake each morning with stiff limbs, made her feel as though her blood had congealed to cold jelly in the night.

She pulled her dressing-gown around her bony shoulders, rubbed her aching, arthritic wrists and moved sluggishly out on to the landing. The ringing of the phone went on and on, setting her teeth on edge. 'All right, all right,' she croaked, 'I'm coming.'

She wondered why Jack hadn't been roused by the noise as she picked up the receiver and pressed it to her ear.

'Hello?' she said a little suspiciously.

'Mrs Perry?'

'Yes.'

'Good morning, Mrs Perry. My name's Gordon Cleeve. I'm Jack's boss. I was just calling to find out what's happened to him this morning.'

'Happened to him?' said Edith.

'Yes. I mean, he didn't turn up for work.'

'Didn't he?'

'No, he didn't.' There was a pause, then Cleeve asked cautiously, 'I take it that Jack's not there with you then?'

'He's not with me at this moment, no,' said Edith, 'but I can't say for certain that he isn't in the house. I haven't had the chance to look yet, you see. Your phone call woke me up.'

'Oh, I'm sorry.'

'No, no, that's quite all right. I'm usually a much earlier bird than this. I don't sleep well, you know. Haven't done since my husband died.'

It was evident that Cleeve didn't quite know how to respond to this. 'Um… sorry to hear that,' he mumbled. 'Was it… was it recent? Your husband's death, I mean?'

'Good lord, no! 1959 it was. A stroke, you know.'

'Ah,' said Cleeve. 'Well, if you could get Jack to call me at his earliest convenience, Mrs Perry?'

'I'll go up straight away and see if he's here. Find out what's ailing him. To be honest he has seemed a little off-colour this week. Perhaps he's got a touch of summer flu.'

'I'm sure you're right, Mrs Perry. Goodbye.'

'Goodbye,' Edith said.

She put the phone down and shuffled to the bottom of the stairs. 'Jack,' she called up, her voice high and splintery. 'Jack, are you there?'

There was no reply. Edith frowned and tried to recall the last time she had seen her son. Her short-term memory was terrible these days. She could remember events from ten, twenty, even fifty years ago with crystal clarity, but attempting to place recent events into some semblance of order never failed to get her into a dreadful muddle.

Had she seen him yesterday? Hadn't they sat down together to a supper of baked salmon and broad beans? They usually ate together, so surely she would have remembered if they hadn't? Wasn't it yesterday that he had been quiet, almost surly? Hadn't he left his food untouched, then stumped upstairs without a word?

She began to climb the stairs, slowed down by her aching joints. She hoped he wasn't in trouble. Though what sort of trouble *could* he be in? He never saw anyone, never went anywhere, except for the railway station on a Sunday to help out. He was a good boy, Jack. He had always looked after her. Not that she had asked him to, of course; everything he'd done had always been his own decision.

She reached the top landing, breath wheezing thinly in her throat. Jack's door was closed. She moved across to it and tapped lightly.

'Jack, love, are you all right?'

Silence.

She grasped the handle in both hands and pushed it down. The door opened with a grinding clunk. She stepped into the room – and instantly recoiled. The smell in here was terrible. It was like the fish market on a Friday, but somehow darker, heavier.

She looked towards the bed, across which lay a bar of sunlight from a gap in the curtains. The bed was clearly not empty, but she could not see its occupant. Something was moving beneath the brown sheet which was all Jack had been sleeping under since the nights had turned humid. The movements were slow, almost sinuous, making her think of coiling snakes. Wrinkling her nose against the awful smell, she took another step into the room.

'Jack?' she said uncertainly. 'Jack, is that you?'

The figure in the bed stopped moving, but it neither responded nor emerged from beneath the sheet.

Edith felt a little tic start up at the side of her eye and a nervous curling in her stomach. She wanted to retreat from the room, but a part of her was concerned for her son.

'Jack, please come out from under there,' she pleaded.

Still no response.

'Right,' she muttered, and with a flash of irritation she hobbled across the room, grasped the bed sheet and yanked it away.

Jack was sitting, naked, cross-legged, eyes closed, hands dangling loosely in his lap. Yet despite his apparently relaxed stance there was something terribly wrong with him. His fleshy, usually hairless chest, chubby arms and rounded shoulders were covered in tiny black spines which made him look like a human cactus. Even more alarming were the humps on his back, which were *moving*, as if something was alive in there.

'Oh, Jack,' Edith said, her voice little more than a whisper.

He opened his eyes. They were as black as tar.

Edith tried to scream, but could manage nothing more than a squeak. She stumbled backwards, nearly fell. Jack turned his head and *hissed* at her.

The hump on his back *surged*, and abruptly, with a wet tearing sound, it split open. Before Edith's horrified gaze, six large, long, jointed, crab-like legs unfurled themselves. They probed blindly at the air for a moment before finding purchase on the walls and bed. Pain flared in Edith's chest; she was finding it hard to breathe. Jack gave a savage grin and, using his newly-hatched limbs, scuttled across the room towards her.

The Doctor wanted something to thump, but the lab benches were smothered with a complex array of delicate scientific equipment, so he had to be content with spinning on his heels and smiting his brow in frustration. Three hours ago he had thought that analysing the cell samples taken from the dead man in the hospital mortuary would be a relatively simple task; he had even been blithely confident of coming up with an antidote to the metamorphic processes unleashing themselves on Tayborough Sands's inhabitants. But the cell samples, despite his best efforts, were stubbornly refusing to identify themselves. He'd tried everything he could think of, using the technology of countless civilisations.

Now, temporarily defeated, he glared at the eclectic jumble of equipment beeping and whirring around him, and hoped that his more long-term endeavours would provide the breakthrough he was looking for. He perfunctorily checked a multi-rack of test tubes in which samples of the infected man's blood had been mixed with a variety of potential neutralising agents, and a row of petri dishes in which various cultures were growing, then he trudged out of the laboratory and out of the TARDIS, and remained lost in thought and almost oblivious to his surroundings until he reached the Lombard Hotel.

'Where've you been?' Turlough asked a little plaintively, throwing open his door before the Doctor had finished knocking on it.

'Here and there,' said the Doctor briskly. 'Where's Tegan? She didn't answer my knock.'

'She's gone out, again,' said Turlough, as if he disapproved.

'Out? Out where?'

'She said she had a date.'

The Doctor stared at Turlough as if searching for signs of duplicity. Turlough shrugged, looking sulky. 'Someone she met last night apparently. She said she'd be back later.'

'I see,' murmured the Doctor, looking concerned. 'I do hope she'll be careful.'

Turlough raised his eyebrows. 'I'm sure Tegan is quite capable of looking after herself, Doctor.'

'Oh, I'm sure she is, in the normal run of things,' the Doctor said, 'but there are some dangers that are not immediately apparent.' Abruptly he bustled past Turlough and into his room. Crossing to the dressing table, he pulled open the top left-hand drawer and began rooting through it.

Turlough looked indignant and, despite himself, somewhat guilty. 'What are you looking for?'

'Nothing incriminating,' said the Doctor pointedly. 'Ah!'

Turlough was still blushing at the oblique reference to his past as the Doctor pulled out a sheet of writing paper and a pen, both emblazoned with the hotel's name. His hand moved in a blur as he applied pen to paper. Even as Turlough was opening his mouth to ask, 'What are you doing?', the Doctor was folding the sheet neatly in half and striding back to the door.

'Come along, Turlough,' he said before his companion could

speak.

Turlough spluttered a little, then his voice became plaintive again. 'Where are we going?'

'I've an appointment with some old friends of mine.' The Doctor offered a disarming grin. 'One of them's an old friend of yours too.'

Turlough hated these manic bursts of energy that gripped the Doctor sometimes. All he could do was scurry along in his wake, wishing he knew what was going on. By the time he had reached the ground floor – the Doctor having bounded down the stairs ahead of him, of course, too impatient to wait for the lift – Turlough was wheezing and gasping like an asthmatic.

In the reception area, the Doctor's straight, blond hair whipped about his face as he looked quickly around. Seconds later he was striding towards a trio of payphones in an alcove beside the main doors. As the Doctor made a call, Turlough took the opportunity to recover his breath. He dabbed at the sweat on his forehead with a white handkerchief as he watched the Doctor speak rapidly into the phone, put it down, cross to the reception desk and hand the receptionist the folded sheet of paper before re-joining him.

'Why all the subterfuge, Doctor?' Turlough protested.

The Doctor looked puzzled. 'Subterfuge?'

'Why won't you tell me what's going on?'

'No time for explanations,' the Doctor said. 'If we're to prevent an epidemic we need to make good use of every available second.'

'An epidemic?' said Turlough, baffled. 'An epidemic of what?'

'I don't know yet,' the Doctor admitted sombrely, then abruptly perked up again. 'Come along, we'll wait outside.'

Turlough gave a groan of exasperation as the Doctor strode off once more, heading for the main doors. He descended the wide stone steps to the pavement two at a time, then prowled back and forth in front of the hotel like a caged tiger, scrutinising the oncoming traffic.

Turlough sat down on the low wall outside the hotel and folded his arms. He watched the Doctor for a couple of minutes, then said, 'So what exactly are we waiting for now?'

'Transport.'

'Transport to *where*?'

The exasperated plea in his voice prompted the Doctor to halt, and join Turlough on the wall. 'Have I ever mentioned my days with UNIT?'

'The Brigadier and all that,' said Turlough, nodding. 'Yes, once or twice.'

'Hmm. Well, that's who we're going to see now. In this time zone the Brigadier is still UNIT's commanding officer.'

Turlough looked at him. 'Isn't that going to be rather awkward?'

'In what way?'

'Oh, just that in a few years time, I'm going to turn up as a pupil at the school where he teaches maths. Which rather raises the question: why didn't he recognise me when I arrived?'

The Doctor squinted up at the sky where gulls wheeled and soared as though engaged in some arcane ritualistic dance. 'I wouldn't worry about it,' he said vaguely. 'Time has a way of dealing with these things.'

Turlough raised his eyebrows. 'I don't see how it can. Though I suppose I *could* always wear a hat and some dark glasses.'

'There'll be no need,' said the Doctor with a grin. 'You'll see.'

Turlough regarded him thoughtfully. 'And you're absolutely certain of this, are you?'

'One should never be certain of anything,' said the Doctor and abruptly jumped up. 'Here's our car.'

A blue Ford Escort was pulling up in front of the hotel. The Doctor returned the cheery wave that Mike Yates gave him.

Mike leaned across and pushed open the passenger door. 'Hop in quick, Doctor.'

The Doctor climbed into the passenger seat, Turlough got in the back and the car sped away.

Mike Yates drove the Escort, which had been seconded to him from the army car pool, the same way he drove his own red Spitfire – fast but skilfully. The Doctor seemed unperturbed, but Turlough clutched the seat, his face pale, tight-lipped. He hadn't been in a car since he had crashed the Brigadier's beloved Humber Tourer and he had no wish to repeat the experience. When the Doctor introduced him, he could manage no more than a stiff nod and a curt 'Hello.'

Their destination was UNIT's temporary HQ at the local naval base five miles down the coast. Some four dozen UNIT troops had been billeted there, having arrived late last night.

'It won't be long before the Brigadier will have them performing manoeuvres on the beach – re-enacting the D-Day landings I shouldn't wonder,' the Doctor said, tempering his rather caustic humour with a grin.

Mike gave a vague smile, tactfully avoiding being drawn into the fun that the Doctor was poking at his commanding officer. A little reproachfully he said, 'It's always been UNIT's policy to keep a low profile until circumstances dictate otherwise, Doctor. You know that.'

'Do I?' said the Doctor, still grinning. 'Must have slipped my mind.'

The naval base, HMS Bilford, was made up of a complex of grey blocks surrounded by high chain-link fences topped with barbed wire. Mike drove up to the main gates and showed his UNIT pass to an armed Naval rating, who stared suspiciously at the Doctor and Turlough for a moment before Mike told him that their presence here could be vouched for personally by Brigadier Lethbridge-Stewart. The Naval rating retreated to his sentry box to make a phone call, reappearing a few moments later and grudgingly waving them in. Mike parked the car. 'This way,' he said, heading across a quadrangle to a long low blockhouse that annexed the main building.

Just like school, Turlough thought, as Mike pushed open several sets of reinforced glass doors and led them along a number of featureless corridors. Eventually they stopped outside a door numbered 106. Mike tapped on it smartly and the unmistakable voice of the Brigadier called, 'Come in.'

The room they entered was indeed a classroom, complete with desks and chairs and a blackboard at one end. There were two men drinking coffee – a burly man in a green army sweater, combat trousers, boots and a beret, and of course the Brigadier, albeit a younger, trimmer version than Turlough was used to.

The Doctor made the introductions with a twinkle in his eye, then he and Turlough helped Mike Yates to stack a couple of rows of desks at the side of the room, creating a space in the centre of the floor. When Benton had provided them all with fresh coffee, they sat down, facing each other on a rough circle of chairs.

Never one for unnecessary preamble, the Brigadier said, 'Any new theories on the situation, Doctor?'

'Yes. I believe the answer lies in whatever Mr Elkins saw land in the sea.'

'In what way, Doctor?' Mike asked.

'Well, my theory is that the object is causing some kind of water-borne contamination.'

'Chemical warfare?' suggested Benton.

'Perhaps. Or maybe the object is simply a piece of space debris whose impact with the earth cracked it open, releasing an alien pollutant.'

'Charming thought,' said the Brigadier. 'As if we haven't got the effects of our own pollution to worry about.'

'Quite so,' said the Doctor.

'So you reckon the only people affected will be those who've been in contact with the water?' Benton asked.

'Not necessarily. Anyone who has eaten fish or seafood since the object came down could be at risk too.'

'Then we may have a problem,' said the Brigadier. 'The Royal Navy kindly laid on a rather splendid fish supper for us all when we arrived last night.'

The Doctor raised his eyes heavenwards. 'Marvellous. And how about you, Mike? Have you eaten fish too?'

'As a matter of fact, no I haven't.' Mike gave a tight smile. 'Pity. I was looking forward to a nice bit of haddock tonight.'

Sunning herself on the beach, Tegan wondered what would happen if she stayed here with Andy. She'd carry on getting older, whilst in several years' time a younger version of herself would blunder into a police box on the Barnet bypass. Eventually the Doctor would bring her here, where she would meet Andy and the whole cycle would begin again. It made Tegan's head spin thinking about how tangled up in time you could become if you really put your mind to it.

She would never be able to travel to London to meet herself, of course, because as the Doctor was always telling her, there were rules against that sort of thing. So if she did stay here, she wouldn't be able to save Aunt Vanessa from being murdered by the Master in a few years' time. That alone – aside from the practical limitations – was reason enough why she *couldn't* stay.

'You OK?' asked Andy, lying on the towel beside her.

Tegan opened her eyes. Everything looked bleached, not quite real. 'Fine,' she said. 'Why?'

'You looked fed up all of a sudden. I just wondered if something was wrong.'

She turned and smiled at him. 'I was just wishing I could stay here for ever – but I can't.'

'Why not?' he asked casually.

She sat up, drawing her knees towards her and wrapping her arms around them. 'I just can't. In a few days or a few weeks I'll have to move on. You wouldn't understand.'

'Thanks,' said Andy.

'No, I didn't mean it like that. It's complicated.'

'Wanderlust,' said Andy.

'Pardon?'

'You've got wanderlust. I understand that all right. You're a free spirit. You don't like to be tied down.'

She laughed. 'If only it were that simple.'

'Well, if it isn't wanderlust, what is it?' He paused. 'You're not on the run, are you?'

She laughed even harder. 'You've got it! I'm a desperate fugitive. That's why I'm spending my day with a policeman.'

He smiled 'Maybe you like to live dangerously.'

Tegan looked out over the ocean and said, almost to herself, 'I do that all right.'

Andy looked perplexed. 'You know, I've never met anyone quite like you.'

'Isn't that a bit of a cliché?'

He shrugged. 'Maybe. It's true, though.'

They lapsed into silence, both of them watching the sea charging at the shore, kids playing, dogs barking as they frolicked at the water's edge. If she was going to enjoy her day with Andy, Tegan knew she would have to stop dropping subtle clues that there was more to her than met the eye. She didn't *mean* to do it, but she couldn't help it somehow. It was as if a part of her wanted him to find out who she was, where she came from. Maybe, rather than her staying here, Andy could come with *them* in the TARDIS. Then the Doctor could hop forward, say, eight years and they could both simply pick up their lives again...

No, what was she thinking of? She hardly knew the bloke, for goodness sake! Why couldn't she just concentrate on enjoying the day ahead? Morning on the beach, lunch in a nice pub, a walk in the countryside – why look beyond that?

'Are you *sure* you're OK?' Andy asked, breaking her out of her reverie.

'Yes, I'm fine. I was just thinking.'

'You don't want to do that, you know,' he told her. 'Makes your brain hurt.' He leaned closer to her, propping himself on one elbow. Tegan could smell the suntan lotion on his shoulders and chest. His voice became softer, more serious. 'Look, Tegan, I just want us to have a nice day together. I reckon if you've got stuff to tell me, you'll tell me in your own time. I don't want to come over all heavy on you. My philosophy is, enjoy life while you can. You might not be here tomorrow.'

'Very comforting,' said Tegan.

He grinned. 'Come on, let's go for a swim. Get rid of some of those cobwebs.'

He jumped to his feet and held out his hand to her. Tegan laughed. 'You're not going to get me in there.'

'Why not? Can't you swim?'

'Course I can swim. But the sea back home is like a warm bath compared to that!' She nodded disdainfully at the grey water.

Still grinning, he grabbed her hand and hauled her to her feet. 'Bracing is what it is. Come *on*, Tegan.'

She put up only token resistance as he dragged her, laughing, down to the water's edge.

'Urgh, what's this stuff?' she said, side-stepping what looked like a lump of colourless jelly that had been carried in by the tide.

He shrugged, unconcerned. 'A melted jellyfish? Maybe the heat of the sun was too much for it.'

'It's all over the beach,' she exclaimed, noticing mounds of it scattered along the shoreline.

'Don't worry about it. As long as you don't step in it, you'll be all right.'

Ten yards from the water, he let go of her hand, ran at full-pelt down to the sea and plunged in. Tegan saw a wave crash over him and then a few seconds later he surfaced, coughing and spluttering.

'You're mad!' she shouted.

'Come on in,' he replied. 'It's lovely.'

'Not likely,' she said, though she walked down to the water's edge and allowed the tide to swirl in around her feet. She was right. Despite the heat of the day, the water was freezing. Within a minute her feet were aching with cold right through to the bone.

Andy stood up and waded towards her. Tegan couldn't help thinking how great he looked in his tight blue trunks, water trickling through the wiry hair on his chest, dappling his broad shoulders. Suddenly, five feet from her, he leaned forward, scooped up two great handfuls of water and drenched her.

She leaped back, gasping. 'You beast!' she shrieked when she managed to get her breath back. She kicked water at him, but it was no more than a token gesture. Andy was laughing so much that he fell backwards into the water anyway.

At HMS Bilford the Brigadier's brainstorming session was continuing apace.

'Could this infection be transmitted from person to person, Doctor?' Turlough asked.

'It's possible,' the Doctor said. 'I'll know more once I've pinpointed its exact nature. So far it's proving impervious to analysis.'

'We could set up a lab for you here, Doctor, if that TARDIS of yours doesn't carry the necessary equipment,' the Brigadier said with the trace of a smile.

The Doctor raised his eyebrows. 'Thank you, Brigadier, but I don't think that will be necessary.'

'It's not a bad invasion plan… if it *is* an invasion plan,' Benton said, then reddened when everyone looked at him. 'What I mean is, well it's sneaky, isn't it? Coming in by the back door, so to speak. And somewhere like this, well it's the obvious place. Lots of people coming and going all the time. You could pick up the infection here, then go back to, say, London or Glasgow or Birmingham and spread it on there. It could be all over the country in no time.'

'It *is* a feasible scenario, sir,' Mike Yates said.

'Alarmingly so,' the Brigadier agreed. 'How long before this infection begins to take effect, Doctor?'

'A matter of days, it seems, though I suspect it rather depends on the individual and the level of contact. Our young friend in the mortuary had been in the town only four days, you say?'

Mike nodded. 'He arrived last Wednesday.'

'Hmm. Then a solution must be found quickly.'

'I'll leave that up to you if I may, Doctor, whilst I concentrate on containing the problem,' said the Brigadier.

'Contain how?' asked Turlough.

'First of all by attempting to get the necessary authority to quarantine the town, close down the beach and ban the sale and consumption of seafood.'

Mike pulled a face. 'With all due respect, sir, I think that might prove difficult. This *is* the height of the season, after all. There's bound to be a huge amount of opposition to your proposal, both locally and nationally.'

The Brigadier was silent for a moment, then he nodded thoughtfully. 'Yes, I do take your point, Yates. I'll just have to convince the chaps at Whitehall that we're facing a national emergency, won't I?'

'Yes, sir. But I still don't think it'll be easy. So far the only evidence we've got that there's anything amiss is the chap in the mortuary, and he alone hardly constitutes the beginnings of an epidemic.'

'What about the other people given hospital treatment after last night's incident?' asked the Doctor. 'Did none of them exhibit similar symptoms to the dead man?'

'Not as far as we're aware, Doctor,' said Mike.

'Perhaps they went out of their way to keep themselves covered up,' suggested Benton.

'Hmm,' said the Doctor. Abruptly he slapped his hands down on his knees. 'Well, whilst you concentrate on containment, Brigadier, Turlough and I will attempt to get to the heart of the matter.'

'How?' Benton asked.

'By setting the TARDIS co-ordinates for the area in which Mr Elkins saw the object come down.'

'Won't that be rather dangerous?' Turlough asked, trying to conceal his alarm.

'Not at all,' said the Doctor airily. 'The TARDIS has an in-built ability to seek out the nearest safe landing spot – which is why she never materialises inside solid objects or underwater. If there is a solid, hollow object – a spacecraft, for instance – on the ocean bed, you can rest assured the TARDIS will find it.'

Charlotte had never had a harder night to get through. She had finally drifted off around 5 a.m., just as it was getting light. When she had seen the result of the test she had begun to shake – not just her hands or her arms, but her whole body, as if someone had started a powerful motor chugging inside her belly.

Dropping the strip of plastic she had rushed to the toilet and thrown up. So violent had the reflex been that she had been terrified the foetus might be harmed, and yet there was a part of her that thought that losing the baby at this early stage would maybe not be such a bad thing. She had thrown up twice more, and each time she had felt certain that if it happened again it would turn her inside out. When the urge finally subsided, she sank to the toilet floor, trembling and weeping.

How long she sat there she wasn't sure. She might have been there all night if it wasn't for the thought that Mum – or even worse, Dad – might wake up at any time, needing the loo. Though she felt drained of energy, she pushed herself to her feet, flushed the toilet and stumbled back to her room. She flopped on to her bed, curled into the foetal position, and dragged her bedclothes over her legs.

She lay like that for a long time, her mind full of rushing thoughts. Before she had known she was pregnant, she had decided that she was going to keep the baby, but now she didn't really know what to do. She felt sick and lost and frightened.

Finally, around dawn, exhaustion overtook her and she slipped into a sleep that was ragged and fitful with half-remembered dreams. It was the sound of someone banging on the door that dragged her out of sleep.

She opened her mouth to shout 'Hang on', but the sound that emerged was, 'Nu-arrn.'

'Charlotte, it's Mum. Are you up?'

Her mother's voice crystallised her thoughts, cut through the last clinging threads of sleep. Sitting up, she called in a cracked voice, 'Hang on a minute, Mum.'

She took several deep breaths in an attempt to rouse herself and tried to rub the tiredness from her eyes before realising it was deeply ingrained in her body. She was halfway across the room, when something on the carpet tugged at the edge of her vision. She looked down and saw the pregnancy testing kit. She scooped it up and shoved it into her suitcase, beneath her underwear. When she opened the door seconds later her smile belied her crashing heart.

'Hi, Mum,' she said, speaking quickly to hide what she felt sure was a guilty expression. 'Are you OK?'

Though she nodded, Imogen didn't *look* OK. She looked drawn, haggard.

'Not too bad,' she said. 'I was so exhausted I slept like a log at any rate. How about you?'

'Oh… I didn't sleep so well. I had too much stuff on my mind. You know?'

Imogen gave a tight but sympathetic smile and reached out to touch her daughter's cheek. 'I'm sorry to burden you with all our problems – mine and Dad's, I mean. We should sort ourselves out, shouldn't we? Not heap it all on you.'

Charlotte shrugged and tried to make a joke of it. 'You need someone to sort you out.' Then she asked tentatively, 'How is dad this morning?'

'Still snoring. I've left him to it. He'll have a killer of a hangover when he comes round, I shouldn't wonder, and it'll serve him right.'

Charlotte's legs felt wobbly. She crossed back to the bed and sat down. 'What time is it?'

'Gone half ten. We've missed breakfast, I'm afraid.' Imogen gave a watery smile. 'We're not really getting our money's worth out of this holiday so far, are we?'

Charlotte yawned. Her eyelids felt full of grit. 'It's OK. I'm not really hungry anyway.'

'Me neither. I could murder a coffee, though.' Imogen paused, then said, 'Chris didn't come back last night.'

'Didn't he?' said Charlotte neutrally.

'No. I think maybe I should call the police.'

'I'm sure he'll be OK, Mum,' Charlotte said. 'He's probably staying away to punish us.'

'All the same, it would set my mind at rest if the police at least knew he was…'

A peculiar expression, somewhere between distress and confusion, crossed her face, and Charlotte knew her mum had balked at the word 'missing'. She understood why immediately. It sounded too ominous, too final.

'I'll come with you,' she said quickly. 'We'll go downstairs, ring the police, then we'll go out somewhere and treat ourselves to a really nice breakfast. Just give me ten minutes to get ready, OK?'

'Ok. You don't mind if I wait here for you, do you?'

'No problem. I won't be long.'

Though all Charlotte really wanted was to sink back on to her bed, close her eyes and blot out the world, she spent the next ten minutes making herself presentable. She had a wash and brushed her teeth, promising herself that tonight, without fail, she would have that lovely warm bath she'd been so looking forward to. She scraped her hair back into a ponytail. She dressed in shorts and a pink sleeveless top, wondering how long it would be before her bump started to show.

She was desperate to tell Mum about the baby, but she knew this wasn't the right time. She'd know when the moment arrived, she told herself. Everything would come together and she would just *know*.

She was about to announce that she was ready when there came three sharp raps on the door. Charlotte and Imogen looked at each other, Imogen's face a mixture of alarm and hope. Charlotte crossed to the door and opened it. The slight, vulture-like figure of Mrs Macau stood there.

'There are two gentlemen to see you downstairs,' she announced before Charlotte could say anything. She was already turning away when Imogen, still sitting on the unmade bed, stammered, 'What… who… who are they?'

'Police officers,' Mrs Macau said, the disapproval evident in her voice.

Imogen paled. 'Police officers?'

'Did they say what they wanted?' Charlotte asked quickly.

'I didn't enquire.' Mrs Macau looked as if she was about to turn away again, then paused. 'I don't put up with trouble on my premises.'

Charlotte felt her face flush with indignation, but the words that emerged from her mouth sounded like an apology. 'We're not going to cause any trouble.'

'I do hope not,' said Mrs Macau. 'Good day.'

Charlotte turned to her mum. Imogen's eyes were wide and fearful.

'It'll be nothing,' Charlotte said reassuringly, though her insides were fluttering like a moth. 'They probably just found Chris asleep on a park bench. They'll want us to go down to the station to pick him up.'

Imogen nodded eagerly, but said nothing, and the two of them went downstairs. Charlotte expected the policemen to be uniformed, but they weren't. They were waiting in the hallway, looking hot and uncomfortable in their grey suits and ties despite their unbuttoned shirt collars.

They straightened up when the two women appeared, like army privates in the presence of a commanding officer. 'Mrs Maybury?' said the foremost of the two men. Charlotte was about to defer to her mum when Imogen stepped forward, anxiety making her movements and voice jerky.

'Yes, that's me. What's happened?'

'Is there somewhere more… comfortable we can talk?'

'Why? What is it you've come to tell us?' Imogen snapped.

'There's the lounge,' said Charlotte, slipping into the familiar role of arbitrator. 'We can go in there.'

Dusty sunlight streamed through the tall bay windows, enlivening the red flock wallpaper, but seeming to bleach and age the lumpy sofa and pale brown carpet. The sofa rustled when the women sat down on it as though its misshapen cushions were filled not with foam padding but with straw. The senior officer perched on the edge of an armchair facing them, elbows on knees, trousers riding up to reveal fluffy green socks. His colleague, a younger man with fuzzy sideburns and wiry eyebrows that clashed in a tangle above the bridge of his nose, leaned against the wall, arms folded.

'I'm Detective Inspector Worthington,' the seated officer said, and there was something about the urgent compassion in his voice that increased the fluttering dread in Charlotte's belly. 'I'm afraid you're going to have to brace yourself for some distressing news.'

'What is it?' Imogen whispered, and Charlotte could feel her mum trembling beside her. 'What's happened?'

Gently DI Worthington said, 'This morning a body was washed up on the shore several miles from here. We believe it to be that of your son, Christopher.'

In the silence that followed it seemed as though time was coming to a slow, soupy halt. Distantly Charlotte heard a door open and it seemed to give her the momentum to ask, 'Why do you think it's Chris?'

'He was carrying a rail card with his name and address on it,' DI Worthington said. 'Our enquiries led us here. We were given this address by a neighbour of yours.'

'Mrs Ramirez,' said Charlotte dreamily. 'She's looking after our house while we're away.'

DI Worthington nodded. 'I understand what a terrible shock this is for you, but I'm afraid the body must be formally identified, and as quickly as possible. Christopher may have died in suspicious circumstances. We need to carry out a post mortem immediately to ascertain exactly how.'

Charlotte felt light-headed, not quite rooted in reality. She stared at DI Worthington with tunnel vision, oblivious to everything else around her. 'What do you mean, "suspicious circumstances?"'

He shifted uncomfortably in his seat. 'There was extensive… damage to the body. It may have been caused by rocks, but then again…' He clasped his hands together and gave a grimace of apology, sympathy, discomfort.

All at once Charlotte was jolted back to reality by her mother's scream. It was a terrible scream, like an animal in intense pain. Charlotte jumped, then sank back, shaking, as her mum dissolved into tears beside her.

The grief was frightening in its intensity, emotion so raw it seemed to possess an awful destructive power that Charlotte felt sure would tear around the room like a hurricane if unleashed. Suddenly everything seemed too stark, too real. Charlotte saw DI Worthington cross the room and drop to his knees in front of her mum, trying vainly to comfort her. She saw the tall man she'd bumped into on the doorstep yesterday enter the lounge, to be immediately confronted by Worthington's colleague, who peeled himself from the wall and held up his hands as if to physically repel the man back into the corridor.

'I'm Captain Mike Yates from UNIT,' she heard the man say, raising his voice above Mum's hysterical wailing. 'I'm afraid I couldn't help overhearing what your colleague said, and I think it might have some bearing –'

Charlotte lowered her head, squeezed her eyes tight shut and pressed her hands over her ears. She didn't care what the men were talking about; she didn't care about anything. Chris was dead, and there was an unwanted baby growing inside her, and Mum and Dad hated each other, and her whole world was falling apart. At that moment, she realised, she envied her brother more than she grieved for him. She wished with all of her heart that she could be dead too.

The Brigadier slammed the phone down in frustration. Surely those idiots in Whitehall ought to realise by now that he asked them for aid and co-operation only when absolutely necessary? He'd saved them from getting a considerable amount of egg on their faces over that Global Chemicals business, and how did they repay him? By continuing to put barriers in his way.

He hadn't even managed to get through to the Prime Minister this time; no doubt the fellow was too embarrassed to speak to him following his misjudgment over the Llanfairfach incident. He had left it to one of his minions to inform the Brigadier that quarantining the town would be tantamount to martial law and therefore out of the question.

Martial law! Did the fellow have no inkling of how UNIT operated, of how many times the planet had been saved from invasion or annihilation by the Brigadier's small but highly trained force? Given UNIT's track record they ought to be allowed *carte blanche* to take whatever steps they deemed appropriate in any situation.

But no. Still the Brigadier had to put up with government fat cats droning on about 'public interest' and 'civil responsibility', knowing all the while that the only responsibility they felt was to themselves and to the retention of their parliamentary seats. Actually they were less like cats and more like turtles, retreating into their shells, unwilling to stick their necks out, refusing to acknowledge that if they continued to decline to untie the Brigadier's hands every time he asked for a little leeway, then sooner or later their gutless reaction might well lead to some hostile alien force or devastating home-grown threat reducing them and their precious parliament to so much turtle soup.

The Brigadier opened his clenched fists in an effort to release his rage, but it didn't work. He tried to focus on the positive aspects of the discussion he had just had, which were pitifully few, but better than nothing. The oily-voiced cretin had promised him that the government would 'look into' the alleged connection between seafood and illness and that they would encourage – though not order – the local authorities to put up signs warning people that there was a danger of pollution along the coastline and that bathing was inadvisable.

Unless something happened that required a military response – and no one wanted that because it would mean that things were getting quickly out of hand – the Brigadier was therefore stuck in the familiar situation of twiddling his thumbs and waiting for the Doctor to come up with something. He thought about the fish he and his men had eaten last night and hoped that this new fellow was up to the job. If not, then before very long they might all be in a great deal of trouble.

'Nothing,' said the Doctor dejectedly, his eyes scanning the results scrolling down the screen in front of him. 'Nothing at all.'

'You can't find an antidote?' said Turlough, hovering at the Doctor's shoulder.

The Doctor spun round. 'Worse than that. I can't even identify the infection.'

'But I thought you said you had some of the most sophisticated equipment in the Universe in here?' Turlough reminded him.

'Oh, I do. But the infection is continuing to prove impervious to analysis. It appears to have no physical characteristics whatsoever.'

Turlough looked irritable, as if the Doctor was being deliberately obtuse. 'But that's impossible.'

'Yes,' said the Doctor thoughtfully. He pivoted slowly on his heels, eyes roving around the vast laboratory as if searching for something specific. 'I wonder.'

'What –' Turlough began, but the Doctor was already off, striding along the aisles between the cluttered benches, cream coat flying behind him. Turlough caught up with him beside a pair of double doors, which he had assumed led deeper into the TARDIS. They were made of some heavy dark wood, each one carved with the stylised representation of a shaggy tusked beast rearing up on its hind legs. The Doctor threw the doors open with such force that Turlough had to jump back to avoid being hit in the face.

When he recovered he saw not the expected corridor, but a large cupboard. Though Turlough had never seen spiders in the TARDIS, the jumble of scientific equipment heaped haphazardly on the shelves was festooned with cobwebs.

'Aha!' the Doctor cried, and dropping on all fours crawled into the cupboard, dipping his head to duck beneath the bottom shelf. He reached in and grabbed something, then backed out, hauling the object with him.

It was a green metal cabinet with a panel of buttons on the front and a small screen inset at an angle into the top. The cabinet was on castors and the Doctor pushed it gently in Turlough's direction. 'Look after this for a moment, would you?' he said, then plunged back into the cupboard again.

Turlough stopped the trundling cabinet with his hand, grimacing at the sticky dust that adhered to his fingers. The screen was cracked and there was a mess of multi-coloured wires hanging out of an open panel at the back.

The Doctor back-shuffled out of the cupboard again, this time dragging what appeared to be a large green hair-dryer on a tall metal stand. It was only when he had pulled the object fully out into the light that Turlough realised it was a rather more sophisticated piece of equipment than he had first thought. The exterior of the cone-shaped helmet was studded with lights that were evidently linked to a maze of circuitry within the helmet itself. Like the cabinet, the 'hair-dryer' was covered in dust and cobwebs – as indeed, by this point, was the Doctor himself.

'What is this thing?' Turlough asked, prodding at the cabinet with his foot, sending it trundling a few inches across the floor on its squeaky castors.

'It's an Image Reproduction Integrating System – IRIS machine for short. It translates thoughts into pictures.'

'Does it work?' Turlough asked.

'Oh yes. But the only time I used it, someone died. I haven't tried it since.'

Turlough looked dubiously at the two pieces of equipment, battered and covered in grime like so much scrap. 'Will it still work?'

'I don't see why not,' said the Doctor, plucking threads of cobweb from his hair. 'All it needs is a bit of spit and polish. Come on.'

He bent and picked up the 'hair-dryer' and carried it – its jointed metal stand scraping the floor behind it – over to his main area of operations. Turlough followed, pushing the cabinet on its squealing castors. The Doctor placed the 'hair-dryer' on a clutter-free work bench, took a large maroon handkerchief from his pocket and wiped away the worst of the grime. He handed the handkerchief to Turlough, then pored over the interior of the cone, prodding connections, 'hmm'ing and 'hah'ing as he worked. Turlough half-heartedly wiped dust from the cabinet, grimacing all the while as if the task was beneath him. He had almost finished when he heard a familiar sound.

'Doctor, listen.'

The Doctor looked up, strands of cobweb still clinging to his fringe. 'Hmm?'

'We're materialising.'

The Doctor's face cleared. 'So we are. I wonder where.'

Leaving the IRIS machine for later, he hurried out of the lab, Turlough scurrying behind him. They crossed a courtyard with a white marble fountain in the shape of a cherub, and strode along a narrow cobbled street reminiscent of Victorian

England, complete with what appeared to be a starry night sky overhead, before finally emerging in one of the TARDIS's innumerable, identical corridors. The Doctor halted, raised a finger as if to point right, then abruptly spun to the left. Several twists and turns later they reached the console room.

The Doctor dashed inside and began to scamper around the console, making all the necessary checks. Turlough stood to one side, arms folded, but turned his head when the Doctor operated the scanner to see what awaited them outside.

It looked neither encouraging nor welcoming. They saw metal support girders, covered in rust, trickling with moisture. Part of a wall, part of a bulkhead, the whole thing soaked in brownish, penumbral light. That was all.

'Are we inside what landed in the sea?' Turlough asked doubtfully.

The Doctor continued to stare at the screen for a moment as if he could see something that Turlough couldn't. Then he said, 'Let's find out, shall we?' and operated the door lever.

Two things struck Turlough as soon as they stepped outside: the cold and the smell. The chill was motionless and permanent, like the inside of a refrigerator. The smell was worse than the cold, though. It was like too many bad things all rolled into one. Rotting fish, rancid meat, large sweaty animals, the dankness of decaying vegetation.

He took a fresh handkerchief from his pocket and held it over his nose and mouth. He glanced at the Doctor, who seemed unaffected by the stench. The Doctor was looking around the vast, high-ceilinged area, which appeared to be some kind of cargo bay (or perhaps shuttle bay, although there were no shuttles to be seen) with a mixture of caution and keen interest. Turlough said, 'What is that awful smell?'

The Doctor sniffed the air as if he couldn't detect it otherwise. 'It smells like putrefaction,' he said matter-of-factly, 'but I don't think it is. I suspect it's some kind of musk.'

'Musk?' said Turlough, looking around nervously. 'You mean there are animals down here?'

'Or were,' said the Doctor. He moved across to a bulkhead door on the far side of the room, some two hundred yards away, his feet reverberating hollowly on the metal floor.

Rusty water dripped from above. When a spot landed on the Doctor's head, he stopped, glanced up ruefully, then unfolded his hat from his pocket and put it on. Reluctant though he was to leave the protective confines of the TARDIS, Turlough stuffed the handkerchief into his pocket and followed, glancing around nervously, all but wringing his hands. He kept thinking he glimpsed movement in the clotted brown areas of shadow, but each time he turned to look there was never anything there.

He caught up with the Doctor by the bulkhead door. The Doctor had perched a pair of half-moon spectacles on the end of his nose and was engrossed in an examination of the control panel beside it. Half-turning, he said, 'What do you make of this?'

Turlough looked, though without much enthusiasm. The panel was a mess; the cover had been prised off and a mass of trailing wires linked the unit to a greenish component that looked more like a spiny shell than a piece of technology. This in turn was linked to what appeared to be some kind of circuit board, which had various other bits and pieces attached to it.

'It's a bit of a mish-mash,' Turlough said, shrugging. 'So what?'

The Doctor looked at him, a little pained by his lack of interest. 'What if I were to tell you that there are at least… oh, seven separate technologies evident here?'

Turlough feigned interest and asked, 'Is that significant?'

'It means that whoever these visitors are, they're very resourceful,' said the Doctor. He paused for a moment, then added, 'I don't think they crashed. I think they landed here deliberately.'

'So their intentions *are* hostile?'

'Not necessarily. They may be quite unaware of the effect their presence is having on the indigenous population.'

'Some kind of chemical leak?' suggested Turlough.

'Possibly. Let's find out, shall we?'

The Doctor ran his fingers deftly over the various component parts of the panel and, despite its haphazard appearance, the bulkhead door slid smoothly open. 'Technology assimilation,' he said. 'It may not look pretty but it certainly works.'

As they passed through the door, Turlough asked, 'Have you any idea what kind of ship this is, Doctor?'

'Morok battle cruiser,' the Doctor replied without hesitation, and indicated a row of embossed metal symbols running along the length of one wall. Turlough couldn't decide whether the symbols were intended to be ornamental, instructional or functional. The Doctor's voice became thoughtful as he added, 'However, somehow I don't think the Moroks are in charge any more.'

'What makes you say that?'

'The Moroks are a very proud race. They certainly wouldn't use alien technology to improve, or even patch up, their existing systems. They'd rather die than admit that any technology is superior to their own.'

'So who are we dealing with then, Doctor?' Turlough asked, his voice quavering with nerves.

The Doctor pressed his lips together in contemplation, as if Turlough had posed nothing more than an intellectual question. 'A crew of mercenaries recruited from the far-flung corners of the galaxy?'

'Oh, is *that* all?' replied Turlough heavily. 'And I thought I had cause to be worried.'

'I could be wrong,' the Doctor admitted. 'A man who is never wrong is rarely right.' He smiled cheerfully and strode on. 'In my experience, people are usually friendly enough if you show them you mean them no harm.'

Turlough gave him an incredulous look and followed. Over the course of the next ten minutes the two of them passed through a vast air filtration and water treatment plant, the systems humming and chugging efficiently away despite their apparently decrepit state; a food-producing area where the plants had withered and the fruit and vegetables had been allowed to bloat and rot in their artificial environments (leading the Doctor to comment that the dietary requirements of whoever had taken over the ship were evidently very different from those of the Moroks'); and finally a derelict recreation area whose facilities suggested that the emphasis was not so much on pleasure as on physical fitness.

Leading off from the recreation area in one direction were the mess hall and kitchens. In the other direction, like spokes protruding from a vast wheel, were numerous corridors inset with evenly-spaced doors, a different symbol – which Turlough took to be either names or numbers – emblazoned on each.

'Crew quarters,' the Doctor said, and selecting a door at random began to tap in a sequence on the control panel beside it. He stopped almost immediately, however, fingers poised in midair. 'No power.'

'This place is falling apart,' commented Turlough.

'On the contrary. Essential systems appear to be running at maximum efficiency. This area is obviously superfluous to requirements.' The Doctor shoved his hands in his pockets and rocked back on his heels. 'What happened to the crew, I wonder.'

'I'd rather not think about it,' Turlough said.

'Hmm,' mused the Doctor, then abruptly he slapped Turlough on the arm. 'Oh well, onward and upward.'

They moved deeper into the ship, the smell growing

stronger as they neared what the Doctor said was the command centre. Turlough produced his handkerchief again, covered his mouth and nose with it and tied it at the back of his head. He felt miserable, cold, sick and scared, and barely listened to the Doctor, who had started jabbering away like a tour guide about the austerity of Morokian architecture, its lack of colour, its over-reliance on dense metals.

Suddenly the Doctor stopped in mid-sentence. His eyes widened and he delicately pressed the fingertips of his right hand to his forehead. Then all at once his face creased in pain and he staggered, dropping to his knees as if he had been shoved hard in the back.

Turlough watched in horror, then glanced quickly around in an effort to ascertain where the attack had come from. Seeing nothing, he squatted beside the Doctor and called his name. The Doctor groaned; his eyelids flickered. Terrified of the prospect of the Doctor passing out and leaving him alone to face whatever had taken up residence on the ship, Turlough shook his friend roughly by the shoulders and shouted into his face, 'Come *on*, Doctor! Please wake up!'

To his relief the Doctor's eyes opened. They were a muddy blue, their vacancy matching the Doctor's slack, expressionless face.

'Are you all right, Doctor?' Turlough said desperately. '*Please* be all right.'

The Doctor's eyes focused suddenly. He closed his mouth and Turlough saw his throat move as he swallowed.

'We have to get back to the TARDIS,' he said, his voice thick.

'What?' said Turlough. 'I... I don't understand. What happened?'

The Doctor tried to climb to his feet. Turlough helped him, then held on to his arm to keep him steady.

'I made contact,' the Doctor said. 'They know we're here.'

'This doesn't sound encouraging,' Turlough said bleakly. 'Go

112

on.'

'I sensed... hostility. Raw and savage. Beyond reason.' He looked at Turlough earnestly, and with not even the faintest trace of fear in his voice he said, 'If they find us, they'll tear us apart.'

Turlough's ice-chip eyes widened, his face drained of what little colour it had. He plucked at the Doctor's sleeve with trembling fingers, and in a voice wavering up and down the scale, he pleaded, 'Please, Doctor, let's hurry.'

They did. Back through the crew quarters and the recreation area. Back through the agricultural section with its slimy rot. All the time they were running, Turlough fancied he could hear sounds around them: scurrying, scuttling, clattering sounds, as if there were giant insects moving behind the walls.

Happily they reached the cargo bay without incident and burst through the bulkhead doors to see the dark, shadowed block of the TARDIS waiting for them two hundred yards away – stoical, dependable, reassuring. Turlough's breath was rattling in his chest and he felt as though his head was pulsing with a hot, juicy rhythm in tandem with his heart. All the same he was making ready to sprint across to the TARDIS when the Doctor stayed him with a hand on the arm.

'Listen.'

Turlough listened. He could hear nothing except the drip of water and the muffled thumping of blood in his ears, and told the Doctor so.

'That's just my point,' the Doctor explained. 'The sounds in the walls have stopped.'

Turlough looked at him, appalled. 'You mean you heard them too?'

'Of course,' said the Doctor, looking surprised.

'I thought I was imagining them,' Turlough murmured miserably, then corrected himself. 'I *hoped* I was imagining them.'

'Brave heart,' the Doctor said, patting Turlough on the arm. 'Come on, we'll keep together and take it slowly.'

They began to creep towards the TARDIS, Turlough's eyes darting everywhere, his imagination making him believe that each dense patch of shadow was a hiding place for something that would come whirling and screeching towards them. His footfalls, and those of the Doctor's, were the faintest of clangs on the metal floor, yet Turlough gritted his teeth in agony with each step, his senses so heightened that he felt as though they might as well be continually banging a gong to announce their presence.

They got half-way there, then three-quarters, then suddenly they had no more than twenty paces to go. It was still quiet, the coldness welcome now on Turlough's hot skin, his face running with sweat beneath the handkerchief that he wore over his mouth and nose. They came to a momentary halt, a natural pause before the final push for home. The Doctor took the TARDIS key from his pocket, gave Turlough a brief nod and they stepped forward again.

A shadow loomed from behind the TARDIS. Turlough faltered, gripping the Doctor's arm, but the Doctor merely patted him absently on the hand and took another step forward.

And then all at once, away to their left, a section of metal wall, some twenty feet square, crashed down like a drawbridge.

Turlough's heart gave such a lurch that he thought he was going to drop dead on the spot. He all but leaped into the Doctor's arms, who himself swung round, instantly alert.

Dust was spiralling up from the section of collapsed wall. Beyond, there was only blackness.

The shadow behind the TARDIS bulged again, and suddenly something was emerging from it. Turlough couldn't help it – he screamed. The creature now scuttling into the semi-darkness of the cargo bay was like something from his worst nightmare. Its torso was roughly the size and shape of a bull's – powerful and huge-shouldered, packed with muscle. However it moved on eight jointed, black, crab-like legs, and from the tip of its hind-quarters a massive scorpion-like tail curled upwards into the air like a giant black question-mark. Its face, bristling with the quills that covered the rest of its body, was studded with bulging black eyes like those of a spider. As it moved forward with a hideous balletic grace to position itself between the two time travellers and the TARDIS, Turlough became aware that more of the gigantic arachnids were scurrying from the square of blackness where the section of wall had fallen down, moving forward to surround himself and the Doctor. Turlough was petrified, but the Doctor calmly doffed his hat and said, 'Good morning.'

The creature that had emerged from behind the TARDIS raised itself up on its legs so that its face was a good eight feet above the ground, opened a flap-like mouth beneath its myriad eyes and made a furious hissing sound, like water dumped on a pan of hot fat.

Part Three
Falling Prey

The creatures advanced slowly, tightening the circle around the two time travellers. As they moved, the bristles that covered their bodies rustled like wind through dry leaves, and their 'feet' clicked on the metal floor like tap shoes. The hot, musky stench of them was almost overwhelming. Turlough, already light-headed with fear, felt certain he was going to pass out. He only managed to avoid it by clutching tightly to the Doctor's arm. He glanced at the Doctor and saw that his eyes were closed, his face serene. What did that mean? Had he already accepted his fate and put himself into some kind of self-induced trance – perhaps so that when the creatures began to tear them apart he wouldn't feel a thing? If so, it was grossly unfair. Why should Turlough have to suffer alone?

He squeezed the Doctor's arm as hard as he could. Then, when that didn't work, he shook him. He tried to speak the Doctor's name, but his saliva had thickened to a gum that glued his tongue to the floor of his mouth. He tried to close his eyes, to blot everything out as the Doctor had done, but terrible though it was, he couldn't not watch what was going to happen. Any moment now, he expected the creatures to rush forward, making that awful hissing sound. The only thing he felt he could hope for was that his demise would be mercifully quick.

All at once the legs of the creature that had first appeared, the one blocking the way to the TARDIS, seemed to buckle slightly. The creature staggered sideways as if drunk, its legs scraping and clattering on the ground as it tried to right itself. It cocked its head in a curiously dog-like way and this time its hissing sounded like an expression of bewilderment. Turlough stared at the creature, dumbfounded, then gradually became aware that the others were behaving the same way. They were blundering against one another like cattle in the dark, hissing confusedly. One, at the outermost edge of the circle, was barged by its tottering fellows with such force that it crashed sideways to the ground, black legs pedalling frantically at the air.

The Doctor's eyes popped open so suddenly that it seemed to snap his head back. For a moment he stared straight ahead as if hypnotised, then he blinked and his features relaxed. He looked around him with an expression of mild curiosity. 'Interesting reaction,' he murmured.

Turlough, his mouth still too dry to speak, gripped the Doctor's arm even tighter. The Doctor winced and looked at him. 'Would you mind not doing that.'

With a gargantuan effort, Turlough tore his lips apart and tried to speak. The pressure made him feel as though his head was about to burst, but he managed to croak out the word, 'TARDIS.'

His companion's lack of urgency made Turlough want to shake him. The Doctor glanced around once more, then nodded slowly. 'In the circumstances, that might be the most prudent course of action.'

He walked unhesitatingly forward towards the giant arachnid, which looked utterly disorientated now, stumbling around in a drunken circle, as if chasing its huge, swaying tail. The Doctor gave the creature a wide berth, Turlough cringing behind him, clutching the sleeve of his coat like a small child hanging on to its mother's skirts. Calmly the Doctor fitted the key into the lock and opened the door. As Turlough plunged gratefully inside, the Doctor turned back briefly, raised his hat and said, 'Sorry, must dash.' Then he followed Turlough inside.

Once inside the console room, Turlough tore the sweaty

handkerchief from his face, slumped against the wall, then sank to the floor in a quivering heap, roundels pressing uncomfortably into his back. Shudders of reaction flowed through his body as the Doctor pottered around the console like an old man in his garden shed, making minor adjustments with little nods and grunts of self-satisfaction. Turlough allowed his head to droop into his cupped hands and for a while he simply sat there, eyes closed, waiting for the reaction to run its course. At last he opened his eyes and raised his head, and saw the Doctor standing with his hands in his pockets, regarding him patiently. Feeling that the onus was on him to speak, Turlough swallowed and said, thickly, 'Those things out there... what were they?'

The Doctor removed his hands from his pockets and put them on the edge of the console, leaning forward like a speaker at a lectern. 'I haven't encountered them before,' he said, 'but I'm almost certain they were Xaranti. They're a species of intergalactic scavengers with no particular technological or cultural identity of their own. They move through space in the hijacked vessels of other species, perpetuating their own race by subjecting the crews of the ships they capture, and the populations of the planets they invade, to an infection so aggressive that it forces their victims' bodies to transform. As they absorb other species physically, so they absorb their knowledge too.'

'They're parasites, in other words,' Turlough said.

'Precisely.'

Turlough shuddered. 'Those things didn't look capable of piloting ships. They seemed so... savage.'

'Oh, there's far more to the Xaranti than those creatures out there. They're simply the hunter-gatherers. The brains behind the operation will be at the heart of the community, well hidden and well protected. When a member of a particular species becomes a Xaranti, they don't so much lose their knowledge and their memories as *store* them. In effect, their new bodies become processing plants for the information they store, and once processed the Xaranti secrete this information as a kind of… colourless gloop. These various secretions, which are quite literally knowledge and memory given physical form, merge to form a separate living, thinking entity, a controlling intelligence for the creatures who spawned it.'

Turlough was frowning, struggling to grasp all this. 'So you're saying these creatures create their own queen?'

'Exactly!' the Doctor cried with an air of triumph, as if Turlough had finally grasped a concept that had been eluding him. 'The Xaranti warriors are not themselves designed to use the knowledge they absorb, so instead they create a giant, communal mind which assimilates all the information fed to it and which controls and directs their actions. It's a perfect symbiotic relationship.' He beamed, as if he himself was the one responsible for such an extraordinary genetic feat.

Turlough shook his head in wonderment. 'It's very clever,' he said.

'Clever?' said the Doctor indignantly. 'It's staggering!'

'I suppose so,' said Turlough dryly, beginning to regain a little of his composure, 'though what the Xaranti do is only the biological equivalent of other species building computers to solve problems that they're unable to solve themselves.'

'Not at all. Any old fool can build a computer. This is more like mentally-deficient parents purposely creating a super-intelligent child to take charge of their lives.'

Turlough raised his eyebrows as if he couldn't be bothered to argue, and nodded towards the doors. 'So what happened to those creatures out there?'

'I was only trying to communicate with them,' said the Doctor, as if he was being accused of something. 'I think my message must have interfered with their instructions and confused them.'

Turlough pushed himself to his feet, approached the console, and after a moment's hesitation turned on the scanner screen. The Xaranti were still milling about outside, though looked to be getting themselves back together again now, their movements more co-ordinated. He shuddered at the sight of their spiny bodies, and the legs – like huge inverted black Vs – that supported them, and switched it off again. 'Where are they from, Doctor?' he asked, trying to sound brisk, business-like.

'Originally from an unnamed planet in the Tau Ceti system, but that was destroyed several centuries ago in their war with the Zygons. Both races are nomadic now, but no doubt the conflict will continue until one or both of them have been wiped out.'

He shook his head sadly. Turlough said, 'The Xaranti are on a recruitment drive then?'

'Perpetually,' said the Doctor.

'Then I suppose we'll have to stop them, won't we?'

The Doctor looked at Turlough, his face giving nothing away. 'What do you suggest?'

Turlough tried to look confident. 'From what you've told me, they must be vulnerable through their queen. Couldn't you pilot the TARDIS directly into the queen's lair and destroy it?'

The Doctor shook his head. 'She'll be heavily protected, and she won't allow her warriors to be caught out telepathically a second time.'

'Well... why not simply blow the ship up then? Humans have got nuclear technology, haven't they?'

'We're inside a Morok battle cruiser,' the Doctor pointed out.

'So?'

'It has reflective melganite shielding. A nuclear warhead would not even so much as dent it.'

Turlough scowled, irritated. 'Well, if there's nothing we can do, we might as well just get out of here and leave the Xaranti to it.'

The Doctor blinked at him in astonishment. 'Who says there's nothing we can do?'

'Are you sure you're all right?' Mike asked gently.

For almost half a minute Charlotte didn't answer. She sat in the front passenger seat, staring unseeingly at her sandalled feet, hands resting slackly in her lap. Mike waited patiently, and at last she slowly raised her head. She was a pretty girl, but even the first time he had met her, Mike had noticed tell-tale signs of strain around her mouth and eyes. Now she looked haunted. The skin around her eyes looked bruised, the eyes themselves like bore-holes into her wounded soul. The wound was fresh now, and though Mike knew that in time it would heal, he knew also that the scar of it would always be with her.

'Yes,' she whispered as though it was required of her.

'What would you like to do now?' Mike asked, and immediately thought how inappropriate his question sounded. He imagined Imogen Maybury, Charlotte's mother, leaning forward from the back seat and snapping, 'What do you suggest? The fun-fair? The beach? Or perhaps we should take in a show?'

Mike glanced at Imogen, and although she showed no sign of doing or saying anything of the sort, he felt an urge to modify his question. Almost stumbling over his words he said, 'Would you like me to take you back to the... the boarding house?'

Charlotte paused, then gave a single nod. It looked as though it was taking her a great deal of effort even to communicate and Mike felt ashamed for imposing on her. He should be taking charge, not putting the onus on her to make decisions. She was what... seventeen, eighteen? And yet Mike had observed that between mother and daughter, it was Charlotte and not Imogen who took on the natural role of protector. It was Charlotte who had – eventually – spoken to the policemen and to Mike; she who had accepted Mike's offer of support; she who had put her arm around her mother's shoulders and walked with her to the car.

It was Charlotte, too, who had walked across the car park with Mike to the ominous, antiseptic environment of the police mortuary and identified her brother's body. Mike had seen many victims of violent death in his military career, but Charlotte's presence had made this experience one of his worst. The morticians had done their best to hide the gruesome nature of Chris Maybury's injuries, but the way they had pulled the white sheet almost primly up to his nose so as to hide the fact that his bottom jaw had been all but ripped from his skull, made it worse, somehow, than seeing the full extent of what had been done to him.

When Mike looked at Charlotte to see how she was coping with it all, he saw that her face was almost as white as her brother's. Crossing her arms tightly beneath her breasts as if for protection, she edged right up to the viewing window and gazed with vacant eyes into what they could see of Chris's dead face.

A man wearing a surgeon's gown and cap, his mask resting on his chest like a small bib, was standing in the white-tiled room beside the trolley. He watched Charlotte's impassive face through the glass for a little while, then stepped forward and bent towards a microphone.

'Miss Maybury,' he said gently, 'can you confirm that this is the body of your brother, Christopher John Maybury?'

Charlotte gave no sign of having heard the police surgeon. Mike reached out and touched her bare arm.

'Charlotte,' he said. 'Is it Chris?'

Apart from her lips, no part of her body moved. 'It doesn't look like him,' she said bleakly.

'So it's not Chris –' began Mike.

Her head snapped round and the expression on her face was awful to see. Part anger, part confusion, part horror, but all of it for the moment mostly repressed, crushed down by numbing shock. 'No,' she said, her voice rough and exhausted as if she was close to breaking, 'it *is* him. It just… doesn't… look like him.'

Her face crumpled and she bowed her head. She looked to be weeping tearlessly and soundlessly. Mike reached out again and this time put his hand on her back. Feeling her bra strap beneath her pink top he withdrew it immediately, flushing with embarrassment.

Annoyed at himself, he glanced at the police surgeon, nodded and raised his eyebrows, silently asking the question: *Is that all you need? Can we go now*? The police surgeon nodded back and Mike said, 'Come on, Charlotte, let's get out of here.'

Charlotte blinked up at him, then looked blearily at her dead brother through the glass once again. 'What will they do with him?' she asked plaintively.

'Nothing,' said Mike, caught offguard by the question.

'Will they look after him?'

'Of course they will. Come on.'

Charlotte had to sign a couple of forms and then they were outside, blinking in the sunshine. As Mike drove her and her mother back to the boarding house, he had to fight down a constant urge to apologise for all the people they could see enjoying themselves. There were kids eating ice-creams; couples walking hand in hand on the promenade; shrieks of delight accompanying the blare of music from the fun-fair; groups of rowdy young men sitting outside pubs, drinking beer.

By the time they pulled up in front of Ambrosia Villa, Mike felt as if he was sweating not from the heat but the silence. He cut the engine and looked at Charlotte, who had either fallen asleep or merely closed her eyes to blot everything out for a while. Glancing into his rear-view mirror, he saw Imogen sitting stiffly in her seat, staring into the distance.

'Mrs Maybury?' Mike said quietly. When there was no response he raised his voice a little. 'Mrs Maybury, we're here. Would you like me to come with you while you speak to your husband?'

Imogen's eyes flickered as if with fear. 'I can't,' she whispered.

Mike was considering how to respond when Charlotte murmured, 'I'll do it.'

Mike looked at her. She hadn't moved, but her eyes were open. 'Charlotte, you've done enough,' he said gently.

'I'll do it,' she said more fiercely. 'I'll do it now.'

Mike was naturally mild-mannered, but he couldn't help feeling a flash of irritation towards Imogen Maybury. He understood how utterly devastated she must feel, but all the same surely she should not continue to allow the full burden of responsibility to fall on the shoulders of her teenage daughter. He glanced again at Imogen in the rear-view mirror, but she failed or refused to meet his eye.

'Look, Charlotte, are you sure you want to go through with this?' he asked after a moment.

She nodded, her face set, giving nothing away. 'I'm sure.'

'All right,' Mike said. 'I'll come with you then – that's if you want me to, of course.'

The smile she gave him was stiff, but full of gratitude. 'I would,' she said. 'Thanks.'

'Right,' he said. 'If you don't mind, I'd better just tell the Brigadier what's going on first or he'll be wondering where I am. Is that OK?'

Charlotte did her utmost to look brave, grown-up, mature. 'Of course,' she said.

* * *

It was only when the Brigadier switched off the RT that he realised he had hardly taken in a word that Mike Yates had said. He had conducted the conversation on autopilot, had presumably made all the correct responses – but to what information he had no idea. His mind felt like a landscape wreathed in fog, grey and vague and difficult to negotiate. He forced himself to concentrate hard, pressed his fingertips into his forehead and closed his eyes until eventually a phrase swam up through the murk. Just before putting the phone down, he remembered himself saying, 'All right, Yates, I'll get the Doctor on to it straight away.'

But on to what exactly? What *was* it Yates had told him? Something about… about… No, it was no good. He could recall the sound of Yates's voice, but his Captain might as well have been talking in double Dutch for all the sense it had made.

The Brigadier was appalled. He prided himself on his decisiveness, on being able to think quickly in tough situations. Healthy body, healthy mind and all that. Perhaps he was simply tired. Overwork. But he had never allowed it to effect him like this before. No, this one went on till he dropped. Hundred per cent commitment. Always been the case, always would be. There was something… something at the back of his mind. Oh, damn it! What was it now? Think, man, think!

Something. Something the Doctor had said. Something about fish?

Absently the Brigadier rubbed at his shoulder, which had begun to itch and prickle.

'Are you all right?' Tegan asked.

Andy blinked and puffed out a deep breath, shook his head quickly like a character in an old black and white comedy who has been bopped with a frying pan. 'Yeah, I'm fine,' he said.

'Just feeling a bit woozy all of a sudden.'

'Too much sun,' Tegan said decisively. 'Do you want to sit down?'

'No, honestly, I'll be all right in a minute.'

They were by the meat counter in Asda, shopping for the picnic they planned to eat up in the hills behind the town. Just as Tegan had been asking him what he wanted in his sandwiches, Andy had staggered as if he'd had one too many, and had put his hand out to the glass counter to steady himself.

'You don't look too well,' said Tegan. 'You look a bit peaky.'

Suddenly he frowned and abruptly snapped, 'I said I'm fine, all right? Stop fussing.'

Tegan was too taken aback to get angry herself, besides which as soon as the words were out of his mouth, Andy was apologising for them.

'Sorry, that was uncalled for. I don't know what came over me.'

'That's all right,' Tegan said guardedly. Then, not wishing to sour the lovely morning they had had, her voice became playful. 'Just don't do it again, all right? I'm enough of a hothead for both of us.'

He grinned, though Tegan couldn't help but detect a certain weariness in his expression. *I hope he isn't getting bored with me,* she thought before she could help it. 'Are you sure you still want to go on this picnic? We don't have to if you don't feel like it.'

He looked genuinely alarmed at the thought of not going, which reassured her. 'No, of course I want to go,' he said. 'Don't you?'

'*I* want to.'

'Well, then, let's get on with it.'

They bought some corned beef and ham at the meat counter and moved on to the bread aisle. Although this was less than ten years before the time she had last left 'her' Earth with the Doctor, she was amazed at the lack of choice available and had to bite her lip to keep from saying so. There was no vegetarian section, very few speciality or ethnic foods, no vegetables that couldn't be grown in the British Isles, no New World wines, and only a tiny amount of brown bread amongst the loaves of Nimble and Slimcea and Mother's Pride.

Tegan chose some crusty white and Andy grabbed a packet of jam tarts. They were at the checkout, a thin-faced girl with freckles and lank red hair grumpily running their purchases through, when Andy groaned and slumped forward as if he was about to be sick.

Everyone nearby stopped what they were doing and stared as he stumbled backwards, clutched at the edge of the checkout, missed, and thumped gracelessly down on to his backside. Some people tittered, others stared at him aggressively, as if they thought that by drawing attention to himself he was challenging them in some way. The checkout girl barely suppressed a snigger as she raised herself to peer over the end of the checkout desk; it was clearly the most fun she'd had all day. Tegan would have bitten her head off if she hadn't been both discomfited by the all-pervasive atmosphere of hostility and concerned for Andy. She crouched down and placed a supporting hand on Andy's back.

'Are you all right?' she asked for the second time in the past ten minutes.

Andy looked at her, but seemed to be having trouble focusing. 'Feel so weird,' he said muzzily. 'Dizzy and sick.'

Behind the checkout a narrow aisle led to the exit, plastic chairs for pensioners and the footsore lined up along the wall. 'Come on,' said Tegan, 'let's get you on to one of these.' With Andy helping as much as he could, she hauled him to his feet and dumped him on one of the chairs.

'Is your husband all right, madam?' said a voice from behind her. Tegan turned and saw a balding, fussy-looking man in a blue suit and flowery tie, his expression hovering somewhere between professional concern and disapproval.

'He's –' Tegan was about to say 'not my husband', but decided she couldn't be bothered to add fuel to the man's prissy little fire – 'got some sort of virus. Sunstroke maybe. Would you mind bringing him a glass of water?'

Mr Prudom – his name written on the rectangular badge affixed to his breast pocket above the words STORE MANAGER – looked slightly put out by her request, but nodded. 'Certainly, madam.' He turned and clicked his fingers at the gawping checkout girl. 'Janice, bring this gentleman a drink of water, would you please?'

Janice looked disgusted, but muttered, 'Yes, Mr Prudom,' and wandered off on her errand.

'And would you mind calling us a cab?' Tegan asked.

Mr Prudom glanced around, but the other checkout girls were all busy. He looked momentarily trapped by his inability to delegate, then his shoulders slumped. 'Certainly, madam,' he said again. 'I'll see to it myself.'

The water arrived and Tegan made Andy drink it. 'I feel such an idiot,' he said. 'Nothing like this has ever happened to me before.'

'You must have picked up a bug,' Tegan said. 'I'm going to take you back home to bed.'

'Sounds promising,' he said, managing a tired grin.

'Don't push your luck,' Tegan replied, but she was smiling too. 'I'm going to tuck you in, then I'm going to head back to my hotel. We'll go on our picnic another day.'

He sighed. 'Sorry about this.'

She rubbed his shoulder. 'Don't worry about it. It's not your fault.'

A few minutes later the cab arrived. 'Can you walk?' Tegan asked.

'I think so.' Andy stood up, then immediately had to clutch at her for support. 'Whoa, my head's spinning.'

'Just hold on to me,' Tegan said. 'We'll take it slowly.'

They were heading out of the door when Mr. Prudom scuttled up behind them. 'Madam,' he said, 'your shopping.'

Tegan glanced back. Half of what they were going to buy for their picnic had been stuffed into a plastic bag, half was clustered at the bottom of the checkout conveyor belt.

With a wicked sense of glee which she did her best to conceal, Tegan said, 'You might as well put it all back. We won't be needing it now.'

Prudom's Adam's apple bobbed as he swallowed. 'Yes, madam,' he said.

As soon as he saw Tegan framed in the opening lift doors the Doctor hastily said his goodbyes to the Brigadier and put down the phone. He hurried across the hotel foyer with a grin on his face, calling out her name as if she was the person he most wanted to see in the entire universe.

Then he noted how unhappy she looked, saw how tightly she was clutching his message in her hand, and his face fell. 'Oh dear,' he murmured, managing to inject such gravity into his voice that Turlough, who was behind him playing catch-up as usual, felt his heart sink.

Tegan held up the note, looking at the Doctor almost accusingly. 'Alien contamination?' she said. 'What kind of alien contamination?

'Turlough, would you be so kind as to order some tea?' the Doctor asked. He took Tegan's arm gently and drew her aside. 'Let's sit down, shall we?'

At first Tegan looked as though she might protest, but then she nodded glumly and allowed herself to be led. The Doctor escorted her over to where he had been sitting, a seating area bordered by tall, white pillars. The seats were all black squishy leather with chrome frameworks, the coffee tables low and glass-topped. Harry Nillson was piping from the speakers, lamenting that he couldn't live if living was without you. Didn't that guy know any other songs? Tegan thought irritably.

They sat, the Doctor leaning forward to rest his elbows on his knees, his legs slightly splayed, white-booted feet turned inward. To Tegan he looked like a little kid who'd been told to sit quietly, but who really wanted to run off and play.

His eyes, however, were alert, full of wisdom, windows to the awesome complexity of his thoughts.

'Which was it?' he asked gently.

'What?'

'Did you swim in the sea or eat the fish?'

'Oh. I swam in the sea. Or at least I paddled. What's going on, Doctor?'

The Doctor sighed, and as Turlough meandered across to join them, began to tell her exactly what *was* going on. He had just finished when their tea arrived.

'Ah, tea!' the Doctor exclaimed as if it was the answer to all their problems. As the waiter departed the Doctor reached for the teapot. 'Shall I be mother?'

'What's going to happen to me?' said Tegan miserably. 'Am I going to turn into one of these Xaranti things?'

The Doctor glanced at Turlough as if urging him to remain silent. 'I'm sure it won't come to that,' he said reassuringly.

She didn't look convinced. 'First the Mara, now this. I'm sick of being taken over by aliens.'

'Yes, the novelty does wear off after a while,' the Doctor remarked dryly.

Tegan glared at him. 'Are you making fun of me?'

'Of course he isn't,' said Turlough.

Tegan thought that one day she ought to tell Turlough that being nice didn't suit him. Whenever he tried it, he simply ended up sounding oily and insincere. 'Isn't he?' she said curtly.

'Of course not. In fact, he's working on a cure even as we speak.'

'No he's not,' said Tegan. 'He's eating chocolate bourbons.'

The Doctor popped the remainder of his biscuit into his mouth a little guiltily and reached into the inside pocket of his coat. He withdrew a square, grey object that resembled a powder compact, though when he flipped open the lid with his thumb, Tegan saw that it looked more like a miniature laptop. 'There are various diagnostic programmes running in the TARDIS,' he told her. 'I can analyse the data on this. It gives me up-to-the-minute reports.'

He demonstrated by pressing a pinhead-sized button and producing a scroll of figures and symbols across the screen.

Tegan held up a hand. 'All right, all right, I believe you.' Suddenly the look of irritation on her face changed to one of dawning horror. 'Oh my God!'

'What is it?' asked Turlough.

'I've just realised what might be wrong with Andy.'

'Andy?' enquired the Doctor.

'Someone I met. My date. I've got to make a phone call.'

She leaped up and ran to the pay phones beside the main doors. The Doctor watched her with an intent expression as if he was trying to read her lips.

Two minutes later she was back, looking anxious.

'What's wrong?' Turlough asked.

'It's Andy. He's not answering his phone. You don't think...' She couldn't go on.

The house seemed empty, though somewhere a radio was playing so faintly that Mike couldn't make out the song. The Mayburys' accommodation was on the landing below Mike's attic room. He and Charlotte passed the room that Chris Maybury had never even slept in, and on to the one at the end

134

of the landing that Charlotte's parents shared.

Before knocking, Mike offered Charlotte a brief, reassuring smile. She twitched her lips back at him, though her eyes still retained that haunted, sunken look. He turned and rapped authoritatively on the door.

'Mr Maybury,' he said, 'Mr Maybury, are you in there?'

There might have been a groan, a vague movement. Mike imagined Charlotte's hungover father turning over in bed.

'Mr Maybury,' he repeated, raising his voice, 'my name is Captain Mike Yates of the United Nations Intelligence Taskforce. I have your daughter, Charlotte, here with me. We have something very important to tell you.'

This time there was a definite series of groans, though Mike got the impression that they were being made regardless of, not in response to, him. He turned again to Charlotte. 'I think we'd better go in.' Charlotte nodded and Mike pushed the door open.

He recoiled immediately. The smell was worse than the army changing rooms at the end of the annual rugger tournament. He looked around for its source, but could see nothing. Behind him Charlotte gagged and Mike said, 'I'll open a window.' Taking a deep breath, he plunged into the room.

As he threw open the curtains and fumbled with the window catch, he was only peripherally aware of Tony Maybury as a hunched shape beneath crumpled, twisted covers, tossing from side to side in his bed. The man was moaning as if in pain, and it occurred to Mike, as the catch came free and the bottom section of the casement window rattled upwards, that Charlotte's father may have more wrong with him than a simple hangover.

Gratefully Mike gulped in several lungfuls of air that seemed as fresh as any he had ever tasted, then turned back into the room. From outside came the ubiquitous cries of gulls and the distant jingle of an ice-cream van.

'Dad,' Charlotte said uncertainly, taking a step forward, 'Dad, are you OK?'

Tony gave no indication that he was even aware of their presence. Charlotte glanced pleadingly at Mike, and he strode forward from the window to the head of the bed.

All he could see of Tony Maybury was his hair, a dark, sweaty clump poking out from beneath the sheets. Mike leaned forward. 'Mr Maybury,' he said loudly and clearly, 'can you hear me?'

Still no reply. Mike raised his eyebrows at Charlotte, who was standing at the foot of the bed, watching her father's writhing form with a mixture of deep concern and anxiety. Then he reached forward and started to pull the sheet from the upper half of the man's body.

It did not come easily. It seemed to snag on the man's skin, and as Mike tugged harder he actually felt it tear in several places. Remembering the man in the mortuary, Mike suddenly knew what he was going to see before he saw it. He allowed the sheet to fall back over Tony and turned to Charlotte. 'Perhaps it might be better if –'

He got no further. At that moment the figure in the bed sprang to its feet with an agility that seemed unnatural. It whipped the sheet from its body and hurled it aside. As the sheet fluttered to the floor, Charlotte screamed.

Tony Maybury had transformed to such an extent that he looked terrifying, despite the ridiculous pale blue Y-fronts he was wearing. His entire body, including his face, was covered with quills identical to the ones Mike had seen on the man in the mortuary. Although he moved with the quick, predatory movements of a striking spider, Maybury was hunched over, two large, grotesquely shifting growths bulging on his back between his shoulder blades. His eyes were no longer human, but completely black, his eyelids peeling back from them, making his eyes look as if they were in danger of popping from their sockets.

Mike did not even have time to reach for his gun before the creature was upon him. It sprang at him, clamping fingers that had elongated to taloned claws around his throat. Hit by its full weight, Mike stumbled and fell backwards, banging his head on the floor. A white burst of light and pain exploded behind his eyes, and for a moment he felt as if he was sinking into a treacly black liquid, unable to do anything but wave his arms in feeble protest as the creature straddled his chest and rammed fingers like knife blades into his Adam's apple.

At first the creature's dead-fish smell was pungent in his nostrils, its slavering, hissing breath and the rustle of its quills echoing in his head. But as consciousness ebbed away, so Mike's senses seemed to recede, leaving only blackness to fill the gaps.

Mike's first conscious thought when he came round was that there was no longer a weight on his chest. His throat felt thick and dry, but when he tried to swallow, sharp, hot pain lanced up into his head and down his gullet, hitting his breastbone and fanning out across his chest like heartburn.

At least the pain brought him back to life. He sat bolt upright, and saw the creature writhing on the floor beside him, growling and holding its head. Standing above it was Charlotte, looking shell-shocked and clutching a hefty-looking standard lamp in both hands.

Mike had barely registered this before the creature twisted, rose in one fluid motion and smashed the lamp from her hands. It flew across the room, shattering against the corner of the dressing table. Before Charlotte had time to react, the thing was upon her, hands clamping around her neck, bearing her effortlessly to the ground.

Horrified, Mike leapt to his feet, reaching for the gun in its holster beneath his jacket. 'Leave her alone or I'll fire,' he yelled

– or tried to; pain sawed through his vocal cords like a rusty blade and his voice emerged as a croak. The creature that had been Tony Maybury either didn't hear him or chose not to. Hissing like an enraged snake, it bore down savagely on Charlotte's throat, as if he was trying to crush the fine bones in her neck.

Mike aimed at one of its outstretched legs and fired. As the bullet struck, bone and flesh parted in an eruption of evil-smelling blood so dark it was almost black. The creature threw back its head and howled in rage and agony, then its head whipped round with a look of pure hatred. Mike braced himself for the attack, but after glaring at him for a second or two – marking him – the creature turned back to Charlotte.

Charlotte had neither made a sound nor moved. She lay pinioned, arms and legs splayed and limp. Either she was dead, or unconscious, or simply too traumatised to fight back.

'Let her go!' Mike croaked again, but the creature ignored him.

Calmly Mike raised his gun for the second time and shot Tony Maybury through the back of the head.

Black lumpy stuff flew in all directions, spattering the bed, the carpet, the wall, the mirror of the dressing table. The corpse toppled forward on to Charlotte's prone body with the floppy gracelessness of a tailor's dummy.

Immediately Charlotte began to make breathy little screaming sounds, her arms and legs pistoning frantically as she tried to push her father's corpse off her body. Black ichor-like fluid from its shattered cranium drooled on to her white skin and stained her pink top like melted liquorice.

Mike crouched down and shoved the corpse to one side. It rolled slowly over on to its back, quills rattling and rustling. Charlotte scrambled out from beneath it, eyes bulging, her mouth a quivering *moue* of panic. She looked like an animal, terrified almost to the point of insensibility.

Mike grabbed her and held her tightly. 'Everything's all right now,' he whispered over and over, and gradually he felt her shaking subside. Cautiously he relaxed his grip a little and was about to say, *Let's get out of here*, when all at once she doubled over in pain as if someone had punched her in the stomach.

'What's wrong?' Mike asked in astonishment.

Charlotte looked at him with frightened eyes, her face suddenly deathly pale, almost grey. 'My baby,' she whispered. 'Help me *please*...'

Then she passed out in Mike's arms.

It was nice to get a break from the kids, but ever since arriving here on Friday June Goldsmith had felt nervous. There was a funny atmosphere in the town; everywhere she looked people seemed unaccountably aggressive. It was the way they stood, the way they stared at you – as if you'd done something to offend them. And it wasn't just her imagination either – she had witnessed a fight between two men in a restaurant, had watched people (both male and female) squaring up to each other on the beach. There'd been some sort of incident on a fishing boat out in the bay as well; no details had been released, but the rumour was that everyone on board had died in mysterious circumstances. And last night there had apparently been a riot in a town-centre pub in which one man had been stabbed to death.

The kids – Freddie, who was nearly five, and Dana, two and a half – ran her ragged, but secretly June would be pleased when the weekend was over and she and Terry were in the car, heading back to Sheffield. Terry had done his best to reassure her, to convince her that whatever weird thing was going on in the town had nothing to do with them, but June could tell the tension was getting to him, too; he'd become more irritable as the weekend had progressed, and had developed a rash on his upper arms which he kept scratching, much to her own irritation.

They were walking hand in hand along the beach now. A last stroll along the sand, Terry had suggested, before heading back to the hotel to pack. June had wanted to pack straight after lunch and reach her mother's in time to give the kids their tea and put them to bed, but she didn't want to get Terry's back up again this weekend so she had smiled and said, yes, that would be lovely.

Only it wasn't lovely, was it? It was every bit the ordeal she had been expecting. She gripped Terry's hand tightly, avoided eye contact with each person staring at her as she walked past, and concentrated on putting one foot firmly in front of the other.

Making a conscious effort to appear casual, June looked at Terry, who was walking closest to the water's edge, gazing out to sea. They had met ten years ago when they were both twenty-six, in a disco in Sheffield. It had been her best friend Millicent's hen night, and June had been very drunk. The following morning she had not been able to remember much about Terry, even though it had been the start of a relationship leading eventually to marriage, to their own house, to two beautiful children.

Ten years on, and looking at Terry now, June realised that she had never once regretted writing her phone number on a beer mat and thrusting it into his hand at the end of that riotous evening. Too many business lunches had thickened his girth and doubled his chin, and the thick dark hair that had once grown on his head now seemed to have chosen to sprout from his nose and ears instead, but none of that altered the fact that she loved him as much now – if not more – as she ever had.

She squeezed his hand, and when he didn't respond she murmured her pet name for him: 'Terribubble.'

He looked round, face slack.

'Hmm,' he said, managing to sound like the village idiot on a go-slow.

'I'm sorry,' she said playfully, 'was I keeping you up?'

'I was just… just… just thinking,' he slurred. Then a slight frown crinkled his forehead. 'What do you want?'

Part of her wanted to snap, 'Oh, never mind!', but it would be a shame to end the weekend on a sour note. 'I just wanted to tell you I love you,' she said.

There was a pause as if he was waiting for more. Then he said, 'Thanks. I love you too.'

She sighed, though not loud enough for him to hear, and they walked on. A couple of minutes later she said, 'Do you know what's strange?'

Again that slow reaction: 'Hmm? What?'

'It's a boiling hot day and yet most of the people on this beach are covering themselves up. I wonder why.'

He shrugged as if he couldn't see what she was getting at. A few moments later he answered, 'Maybe they don't want to get sunburned.'

'No, I don't think it's that.' She frowned for a moment, lips pursed, then raised her eyebrows in a facial shrug. 'Oh, what does it really matter? We'll be home soon. This is just a peculiar place, that's all.'

They were near the end of the beach now, most of the holidaymakers behind them. June began to relax a little, even though they would have to run the gauntlet again on their way back. A little further along the sand gave way to jutting rocks, seaweed-slimy rock pools and the silently howling mouths of cliff caves. There were few people around here. The whispering of the tide sounded like a secret that the sea would reveal only to them.

June stopped and looked out at the water, fascinated and soothed by the shifting mosaic of green, blue and grey, coins of golden sunlight bobbing and sparkling on the waves. Terry let his hand slip from hers and moved on slowly. He clambered up over the first of the rocks, stepped carefully around a few pools with his flip-flopped feet, and ambled aimlessly towards the nearest cave, a dark, vertical gash in the sun-drenched cliff.

June watched him go, then turned back to the sea, enjoying her moment of communion with it. If she hadn't felt so nervous of her fellow human beings, she could have sat on a rock and gazed at it for hours, intermittently dozing, allowing the rhythmic liquid breath of the tide to transport her to another place.

Despite her state, the sea managed to weave its mesmerising magic. June was certain she had remained conscious as the sea's never-ending patterns kaleidoscoped in front of her eyes, yet suddenly she was jerking not so much awake as *aware*, with no idea how long she had been standing there. She looked around, hoping to catch sight of Terry pottering among the rock-pools, but there was no sign of him. She almost called out but didn't want to attract attention to herself.

He couldn't be too far away. If she didn't see him when she climbed up on to the rocks, she'd no doubt find him poking about in one of the caves, looking for interesting stuff that had been washed ashore by the tide. She sidestepped a great swathe of clear jelly at the base of the rocks and headed towards the caves.

The rocks were relatively dry, though the mossy seaweed that provided them with a furry green coat was still damp and slippery underfoot. As she stepped down from a jagged crest of rocks on to a relatively flat area, the nearby entrance to the first of the cliff caves gushed with light.

It was sunlight, of course. She must have looked at the cave at the exact moment that the sun inched far enough across the sky to flood the entrance and drown the shadows inside.

Not that the shadows had been hiding anything interesting. The sand in the cave, still damp from the lack of sunlight to bake it dry, was strewn with bladderwrack, an old blue fishing net, pop bottles, driftwood and more blobs of the jelly-like stuff that the sea seemed to have coughed up like phlegm.

She walked past the cave and stopped outside the next one. The entrance was four feet high at its apex and she had to crouch down to peer inside. There was nothing to see. The interior was no bigger than a teepee. On to the next one, and still no sign of Terry. She glanced back the way she had come. Surely she was now far enough away from the people on the beach to be out of earshot? She walked towards the next entrance, calling her husband's name – and was rewarded almost immediately by what sounded like a rustle of movement.

She smiled and all but skipped the last few steps to the mouth of the cave. She was immediately struck by an unpleasant smell – like dead fish and rotten vegetables – but she took a step inside. Instantly the stench wrapped itself around her like a winding sheet, making her gag. She clamped her hands over her mouth and nose and took a hasty step backwards. The stench was pungent as ammonia; her eyes began to water, her surroundings dissolving into a blur of watery shadows. Something must have died in here, she thought. There was no way that Terry would have lingered here.

Without any warning a figure stepped into view from behind a shelf of rock in front of her, making her jump. In the dim light its head was a bleached skull, its hands held out before it, palms up. As it moved towards her June's heart skipped a beat and then she gasped as she realised that it was indeed Terry, after all. His sunglasses and her blurred vision had made his eyes look like nothing more than dark, empty sockets. She blinked to clear her vision, and was only partially successful. Terry's outstretched hands looked dirty, but as he stepped forward into the sunlight she saw that they were not black, but red.

'Blood,' he said before she could speak.

There was a beat of silence as she took this in, then, 'My God, what have you done to yourself?'

He frowned as if he didn't understand the question, and shook his head. 'Not mine. It's all over the wall.'

She glanced behind him, fighting off the smell. 'My God,' she breathed. 'Terry, we've got to tell someone.'

Then the interior of the cave erupted.

June's first thought was that a bomb had gone off. All at once sand was geysering up and out of the cave in a great plume, covering them both. June felt it blasting through her hair, stinging her eyes, crunching grittily between her teeth. She was thrown backwards, on to her knees, swiping at her face as if she was being attacked by bees. She coughed, sneezed and spluttered, her eyes streaming.

She straightened bolt upright, however, when she heard Terry begin to scream.

The first, a terrible, wrenching scream of mortal agony, was rapidly followed by a succession of others. June felt every muscle clench at the sound, felt a bolt of coldness tear through her stomach. Despite the stinging pinpricks of sand in her eyes she forced herself to open them. When she saw *why* Terry was screaming, she forgot her own discomfort in an instant. Her eyes widened in terror and disbelief.

The thing that had erupted from beneath the sand was an impossibility. Part bull, part spider, part scorpion, it was massive, its jointed, spiny legs at least eight feet long. Even its bristling, multi-eyed head, which looked tiny in relation to its muscle-packed abdomen, was substantially bigger than June's. It was tearing apart the figure pinned to the ground between its two front legs. Blood was gushing out over the sand as it feasted, trickling down the rocks, swirling around June's feet like a sticky incoming tide.

Within seconds Terry had stopped screaming. His body jerked spasmodically. His mouth was open and full of blood. His sunglasses had fallen off and his eyes had rolled up into his head.

The scene was so appalling, so unbelievable, that June was numbed almost to the point of inertia. But acting with an odd, distant composure, she stepped out of her flip-flops, turned from the scene and walked away. She moved carefully as she picked her way across the rocks, taking pains not to slip. It was only when she reached the edge of the formation and she had jumped over the blobs of jelly nestled in the crook between rocks and sand that she began to run, heading back the way she had come.

She had progressed no more than a dozen yards when she heard a scuffle-clatter of movement behind her. Breathing hard, she glanced back over her shoulder. The creature had evidently finished with Terry and was now scurrying unevenly across the rocks towards her.

In an instant the fragile veneer that had shielded June from her emotions shattered. Gut-wrenching terror surged through her like an electric shock. Her legs took up the challenge, doubling their pace, and as she ran she let out a piercing scream that seemed to tear her throat, releasing the taste of blood into her mouth.

Now she didn't care that the people on the beach were looking at her. Rather, it urged her to cry out for help, her voice raw and ragged. However, no one came to her aid. The people either stood transfixed – some of them with gleaming, hungry eyes – or screamed and turned tail.

Seconds later the stink of dead things overwhelmed her and she fell, struck from behind. It was only when she saw her own blood spilling on to the sand that she realised she'd been sliced open. She tried to roll over, to get back to her feet, but it was no use. She tried to crawl but her limbs wouldn't let her.

Then it was upon her and there was only the scuttling, stinking blackness of its body. Her last thought was of her children, miles away in Sheffield, excitedly awaiting their parents' return.

The Brigadier took off his cap and leaned forward in his chair until his forehead was touching the desk. The hard surface was cool, comforting. Not for the first time that day he closed his eyes and allowed himself to drift.

It was proving increasingly difficult to hold on to his thoughts. He remembered speaking to Yates on the RT and arranging a UNIT clean-up team to deal with… with some sort of incident at the guest-house where Yates was staying. And more recently he had spoken to the Doctor, hadn't he? But not *his* Doctor. The younger chap he'd met earlier, the one in the cream coat. What was it this new Doctor had told him? It was something about the threat that was facing them. He'd said a word – *Xaranti* – that, even though the Brigadier was sure he'd never heard it before, nevertheless seemed to resound in his head like some newly-roused memory.

He was not too far gone to realise that whatever was wrong with him was something rather more serious than mere stress-fatigue or overwork. Perhaps he ought to relinquish his post, declare himself unfit for duty, hand over the mantle of command to Mike Yates. To do so, to admit to any kind of weakness, was anathema to him, but he was nothing if not a realist. He knew he couldn't go on like this. For the first time in his military career he simply had no idea what to do next. And if he couldn't make proper, informed decisions then he might very well end up endangering the lives of his men – not to mention putting the country, or even the entire planet, at risk.

He raised his head wearily from the desk and was reaching for the RT – first of all pausing to scratch the infernal itching that had started on his shoulder and was now spreading down his arm and across his chest – when the door opened and Benton blundered breathlessly in.

The Brigadier jerked upright as if he had been caught napping and for a moment his mind cleared. 'Benton,' he snapped, 'don't you know to knock before entering a superior officer's... er... office?'

If Benton noticed the Brigadier's moment of confusion he didn't let on. In fact, he looked a little confused himself. 'Sorry, sir. It's just that... well, there's a monster on the beach, sir.'

'A monster?' repeated the Brigadier scathingly. 'Can't you be a little more precise, Benton?'

'Sorry, sir.' Benton looked as if he was concentrating hard. 'The local police have just rung in. They say there's a large, insect-like creature running amok on Tayborough Sands beach. Quite a few fatalities already it seems, sir.'

'Right, Benton,' said the Brigadier, not quite with relish, but certainly galvanised – however temporarily – by the prospect of action. 'Get the men ready to move out in force. And try to get hold of the Doctor, let him know what's going on.'

'He probably knows already, sir. His hotel is right on the seafront.'

'Is it, by George?' said the Brigadier, wondering whether he already knew this. 'Well, try and get hold of him anyway. Tell him not to go near this dratted creature until we get there.'

'I'll *tell* him, sir...' Benton said, clearly implying that if the Doctor was set on a separate course of action, then nothing Benton could do or say would make a blind bit of difference.

The Brigadier flapped a hand, acknowledging the fact that the Doctor was a law unto himself. 'Just do your best, Benton. I'll put a call through to Captain Yates, get him to meet us down there.' The Brigadier again reached for his RT and glanced up at Benton, who was hovering by the desk, as if waiting to be dismissed. 'Well, jump to it, man. Chop chop.'

White bonnets and yellow faces. Flowers. Daisies. She was surrounded by daisies. Lovely. But there was something wrong with them. They were all identical. And they were in rows. Regiments. Hovering in mid-air. And mid-air was pale green.

Charlotte's eyes focused on the curtain. It was attached to a rail, which, if she wished, she could pull all the way round her bed to conceal herself from the outside world. What that consisted of was a bit of a mystery. Noise, certainly. There were people talking. Footsteps moving rapidly to and fro. Things clanking.

'Charlotte,' said a voice.

Her eyes flickered in the direction of the voice and she saw a man with a look of concern on his thin face, sitting at the side of her bed. Remembering that his name was Mike Yates brought all her memories rushing back. Like a wave, they filled her mouth and throat like sludgy water, and she found herself gasping for breath, struggling to sit up. A band of pain clamped across her stomach and she fell back, head pounding.

'Hey,' said Mike gently, 'take it easy. You're safe now.' He covered her hot hand with his cool one.

The suffocating effect of the memories subsided, but the pain of them did not diminish. 'My dad,' she whispered. 'He's dead. You killed him.'

It was not an accusation, merely a statement of fact. Mike nodded. 'I had to. If I hadn't killed him, he would have killed you.'

She remembered the spines on her father's body, his black, bulging eyes. She shuddered. 'What's happening?' she pleaded, her voice cracking, tears not far away. 'Mike, what's happening?'

'There's some sort of… contamination,' he said carefully. 'It's affecting people. Making them change.'

'Contamination? What do you mean?'

He raised his hands, looked apologetic. 'We don't know yet. That's what we're trying to find out.'

Charlotte's head was buzzing. Her thoughts hurt. There was a dislocated, unreal feeling to all of this. She shifted position in bed slightly, and was once again aware of the pain in her stomach, like a big bruise. Fearful, she said, 'My baby. Is my baby…?'

'It's fine.' Mike smiled back, squeezing her hand to reassure her. 'The doctors say your baby's going to be fine. You just need to rest. You went into shock after the attack.'

Momentary relief washed over her, but then she thought of Chris and her dad again. 'Does Mum know?' she asked. 'About the baby, I mean. I hadn't told her, you see.'

'Not yet. She's under sedation in another ward. Do you want me to tell the doctors not to tell her?'

Charlotte nodded weakly. 'I want to tell her myself.'

'Of course you do,' Mike said.

There was a sudden crackle of static from his jacket pocket and a tinny voice said, 'Greyhound One to Greyhound Three. Are you there, Greyhound Three? Over.'

Everyone in the ward turned their heads to look at Mike. He raised his eyebrows in self-conscious apology and took the RT from his pocket.

'This is Greyhound Three. Would you mind hanging on a minute, sir? I need to find somewhere a little more discreet.' He put the RT back in his pocket and flashed Charlotte another quick smile. 'Won't be a minute,' he told her, then stood up and walked briskly out of the ward.

A few minutes later he was back, his face grim. 'I'm going to have to go,' he said. 'There have been one or two developments.'

Charlotte reached out and grasped his hand. 'You will come

back and see me, won't you?'

'Of course I will. Just as soon as I can.' He leaned down and kissed her on the forehead. 'Now you get some rest, and I'll be back before you know it.'

The seafront was in chaos, police and holidaymakers milling around in confusion. A crowd was standing in the road like sheep, immobilised by shock. Several times the Brigadier had to lean on his horn to encourage the crowd to part enough to allow the UNIT convoy to edge through. On the promenade a dozen or more empty emergency vehicles were parked haphazardly, lights flashing.

The whole situation had a feeling of aftermath to it, which the Brigadier recognised only too well. He knew that the emergency vehicles were empty because their crews were tending to the wounded. This, coupled with the fact that there was no panic among the crowds, merely a sense of stunned incomprehension, was evidence enough that the creature was no longer running loose nearby, but had moved on to pastures new. UNIT's job was to track it and, if possible, contain it. Seeing the Lombard Hotel looming large on his right, he reached for the RT on the passenger seat.

'Greyhound One to...' the Brigadier began, confidently enough, then floundered. Good lord, what was Benton's call sign? Angrily he barked, 'Benton, are you there? Over.'

Benton's voice came back, the caution in it evident despite the tinny reception. 'Er... here, sir. Is everything all right? Over.'

'No, Benton, it is not all right. The police operation is a shambles. I'm stopping off here to pick up the Doctor. I want this area evacuated and cordoned off, and I want to know where that damned creature's got to. Over.'

'Leave it to me, sir. I'll get on to it right away. Over and out.'

The Brigadier nodded in satisfaction and tossed the RT back

on to the passenger seat. There was nothing like a bit of direct action to get the adrenaline going, focus the mind. He ignored the fact that he was still battling to concentrate on the matter in hand. His mind kept wandering, but the Brigadier was determined to keep on top of things even if it killed him.

He parked on the double yellows outside the hotel and marched up the steps into Reception. There was another crowd in the lobby, the air buzzing with speculation, strangers united by the need to share their experiences of that afternoon's astonishing events.

As soon as he spotted the skinny, copper-haired young man with the peculiar eyebrows, the Brigadier recognised him. Had it been yesterday or this morning when they had met? He pushed the thought aside, irritated by his inability to remember, and strode across. He was aware of the looks his uniformed presence was attracting, and deliberately focused on the young man (whose name – *Turlough* – popped suddenly into his mind). Turlough was sitting with his hands between his knees, looking nervous and uncomfortable, like a schoolboy summoned to his headmaster's study to explain some misdemeanour. Beside him, standing with her arms folded, was an attractive young woman in a brightly coloured summer dress, whom the Brigadier barely glanced at until she hailed him by name.

He looked at her, startled. 'I'm sorry, miss, do I know you?'

The young woman looked non-plussed. 'Well, of course you do! I'm... no, hang on a minute. You haven't met me yet, have you? Tegan Jovanka,' she announced, holding out her hand.

'I'm sorry?'

'Tegan Jovanka. That's my name. I travel with the Doctor.'

'I see,' said the Brigadier. 'And where *is* the Doctor?'

'Down on the beach,' said Turlough.

'On the beach? I gave specific instructions –'

'The creature's gone,' Turlough interjected, his quiet voice cutting through the Brigadier's bluster. 'It had gone before we even heard about it.'

'We told the Doctor we'd wait here for you,' said Tegan, a little shame-faced. She glanced at Turlough as if for support. 'Neither of us much fancied going down on to the beach.'

'It's like a battlefield down there,' Turlough said by way of explanation. 'Bodies everywhere.'

'I see,' said the Brigadier, scratching absent-mindedly at his itchy arm before noticing the curious looks of the Doctor's two companions. 'And where is this creature now?'

Turlough shrugged.

'Maybe the Doctor's found out,' suggested Tegan helpfully.

'Hmm,' said the Brigadier. 'Ah well. That creature has got to be found before it does any more damage.'

Tegan hesitated, before announcing decisively, 'If you're going down to the beach I'll come with you.'

Turlough nodded, though he looked unenthusiastic. 'Me too.'

They left the hotel and crossed the road where the crowds were being dispersed by a combined force of UNIT troops and policemen. They weaved through the phalanx of ambulances, army trucks and police cars and headed towards the nearest set of steps down to the beach. The armed UNIT sentry whom Benton had stationed at the top of the steps exchanged nods with the Brigadier and the three of them descended on to what Turlough had termed the battlefield.

It was an apt description. Perhaps three-dozen bodies were strewn on the sand in spatters and trails of blood. So frenzied had the creature's attack been that the dead had had to be left to bake in the sun for the time being so that all efforts could be directed towards preserving the lives of the wounded. As the Brigadier led Tegan and Turlough across the battlefield, Turlough tried not to look too closely at the decimation around him and concentrated instead on the Brigadier's back. On the periphery of his vision soldiers, policemen and paramedics bustled about their business, trying to impose some kind of order on to the chaos.

As two ambulance men cut across their path, bearing a stretcher, the Brigadier stopped and barred their way with an outstretched arm. A young semi-conscious woman was groaning in pain, the bottom half of her face flecked with blood. Nearby, the burly sergeant whom Turlough recognised from that morning's meeting was issuing orders, directing operations. Standing at his shoulder was a glum-looking man with a pock-marked face, hands thrust into the trouser pockets of his baggy blue suit.

The sergeant saluted when he saw the Brigadier.

'What's the situation, Benton?' the Brigadier asked without preamble.

'It seems the creature came out of the caves at the far end of the beach, sir. Fourteen people are confirmed dead, twenty-five injured. Most of the injured have deep puncture-wounds. Eye-witnesses say the creature's got a dirty great sting in its tail, like a scorpion, which it kept jabbing in to people. The Doctor reckons it was injecting them with a more concentrated form of the stuff that we might have been infected by.'

Of course! The fish! The alien contamination! The Brigadier suddenly remembered with a jolt what the Doctor had told him that morning, and which had been eluding him all day. For a moment his head swam; he imagined strange poisons working their way through his system, clouding his mind. With an effort he pulled himself together and asked, 'Where's the Doctor now? And more importantly, where's this damn creature?'

'Well, there's the Doctor,' Tegan said.

The Brigadier followed her pointing finger. The Doctor was crouched by the shoreline as if deeply engrossed in something he had found washed up on the beach. The tails of his cream coat trailed in the sand. His white hat with its red band was jammed on top of his head.

'What's he doing?' the Brigadier said, irritated. 'Collecting seashells?'

Benton shrugged with the air of one who had long ago stopped trying to work out the Doctor's motives for anything. 'He said he was just going to take a look around, sir.'

The Brigadier pursed his lips in disapproval, his moustache bristling. 'Right,' he muttered. 'And the creature?'

'It was last seen heading towards the fairground, sir. I've sent some of the lads after it. I've given them orders to report back if they find it, and to keep it under observation. The Doctor did ask us to avoid harming it if we could.'

The man in the baggy blue suit spoke at last: 'Some of my boys should already be down there, clearing the area. They've got orders to keep away from the thing itself, though. I'm leaving this one up to you lot.'

'And *you* are?' said the Brigadier.

'Detective Inspector Pickard. I'm officially in charge of the investigation into the massacre on the *Papillon* – though now it looks as if one of these creatures was responsible for that.' He looked rueful. 'What *are* these things, anyway? Monsters from outer space?'

'Yes,' Turlough said. 'They're called Xaranti.'

Once again the word seemed to echo like a long-forgotten memory in the Brigadier's head. He looked again at the Doctor, who was straightening up now, and absently began to scratch his chest. When he realised what he was doing, he immediately tried to make it look as though he was brushing imaginary dirt from the lapel of his uniform. To cover up his awkwardness he said to Pickard, 'Can I leave the clearing-up operation in your hands now, Inspector? I'll leave some of my men behind to help, of course, but the rest of us really ought to try and stop this creature causing any more mayhem.'

Pickard nodded, trying not to look as if he was out of his depth. 'You can leave it to me. I'll keep everything running smoothly here, don't you worry.'

'Good man,' said the Brigadier absently and turned to Benton. 'Any idea where Captain Yates has got to, Benton?'

'He's on his way, sir. I spoke to him a few minutes ago.'

'Right, well bring him up to speed, would you, and tell him to meet us at the fairground. And warn him to be careful.'

'Yes, sir,' said Benton, already raising the RT to his mouth to relay the message.

The Doctor had seen them now and hurried up the beach, his lolloping stride deceptively swift. 'Here at last, are you, Brigadier?' he said briskly. 'We've been waiting for you. How are you feeling?'

'Never better,' the Brigadier said quickly.

'Are you quite sure? You'll have to have your wits about you, you know. Even a lone Xaranti can be extremely dangerous.'

'Don't you worry, Doctor. I doubt it can cope with our firepower.'

The Doctor looked pained. 'We're not going to shoot it, Brigadier. We're going to communicate with it. Or at least I'm going to try.'

Surprised, Turlough said, 'Surely you've already tried that on the Xaranti ship? You just ended up confusing them.'

'That was different,' the Doctor said. 'I think what we're dealing with here is a recently transformed human. In which case it may be vulnerable, its thoughts not yet fully integrated into the communal Xaranti mind.'

'You mean it's not quite absorbed, so it may let something vital slip?' said Tegan.

The Doctor looked almost defensive, as if Tegan was questioning his judgement. 'Or I may be able to use it as a mental conduit to the queen, slip in via the back door, so to speak.' He shrugged. 'I'm not saying it'll work, but I think it's worth a try.'

'In that case, what are we waiting for?' said the Brigadier. 'Come on, Doctor, Turlough, Miss Jovanka, we'll use my car. Benton, get two dozen of the men together and follow us down.'

They hurried back across the sands and up the steps to the promenade. As they crossed the road to the Lombard Hotel, the Doctor indicated the double yellows on which the Brigadier's car was parked and chided gently, 'Really, Brigadier, I'm shocked. You might have got a ticket.'

The Brigadier 'hmphed', though not without humour, and unlocked the driver's door. Once all his passengers were inside, he glanced into his wing mirror and pulled out. The roads were almost clear now, the seafront having effectively been cleared and sealed off. The fairground was a two-minute drive away. From here it looked like a cluster of towers and minarets jabbing up into the summer sky around the curve of the bay, just beyond the harbour. Tegan, sitting in the back behind the passenger seat, noticed that the traffic lights were red and wondered why the Brigadier was not slowing down.

Then the ambulance cut across them like a white metal wall and a number of events happened in quick succession.

Tegan saw the Brigadier slumping over his wheel as if in a faint, eyes closed. There was noise: the screech of the ambulance's tyres and the blare of its horn, mingled with her own scream of 'Look out!' as the car shot through the lights and bore down on the vehicle. There was a blur of movement from the front seat of the car and suddenly, impossibly, the Doctor was in the driver's position, the Brigadier slumped semi-conscious and muttering in the passenger seat beside him. Tegan's yell as the Doctor twisted the steering wheel to the left was abruptly cut off as she was slammed against the door, the impact jarring her ribs and knocking the breath out of her. For a split-second the side of the ambulance filled their windscreen, then abruptly it was gone. The Doctor guided the car to the side of the road and cut the engine.

He turned to the Brigadier sitting beside him. 'Brigadier,' he said urgently. 'Alistair, can you hear me?'

The Brigadier groaned, then his eyelids fluttered open. 'Eh, what? What's going on?'

'You passed out, Brigadier,' the Doctor said, regarding him earnestly.

The Brigadier's eyes widened, the outrageousness of the suggestion far more effective than any amount of smelling salts. 'Passed out! Don't be ridiculous. I have never heard such... such...' His voice tailed off and he looked around in confusion.

'How are you feeling, Alistair?' the Doctor asked gently.

'Feeling? Well, fine. I told you.'

The Doctor closed his eyes in brief, quiet exasperation. 'I need you to tell me the truth. This is important.'

The Brigadier looked at him for a moment, pride battling with honesty. Then his shoulders slumped a little and he sighed. 'Yes, well, I suppose I have been feeling a bit woozy,' he mumbled. 'And I've got this... this rash.' He ran a hand across his chest, over his shoulder and down his arm to show the Doctor the extent of it.

'May I see?' asked the Doctor gently.

The Brigadier, clearly embarrassed, said, 'Is it really necessary?'

'You know it is,' the Doctor said.

The Brigadier's sigh was deeper this time. Reluctantly he unbuttoned the jacket of his uniform, loosened his tie and unbuttoned his shirt.

The Doctor eased the shirt apart and his face tightened. At this the Brigadier looked down at himself. 'Good grief!' he said.

All across his chest, the black, tell-tale nubs of Xaranti quills were beginning to poke through his skin.

* * *

A UNIT jeep cruised to a stop beside them. As Benton jumped out of the passenger side, the Brigadier hastily rebuttoned his shirt.

Benton poked his head through the open window beside the Brigadier. 'I thought you were all goners for a moment there,' he said. 'What happened? Is everyone OK?'

'Everyone's perfectly fine, thank you, Benton,' said the Brigadier brusquely.

'A slight miscalculation on my part, I'm afraid,' said the Doctor, giving Benton a meaningful look. 'I overshot the red light. Careless of me.'

'I see,' said Benton hesitantly. 'Well, if you're sure you're all right...'

'Never better,' snapped the Brigadier. 'Now, if there's nothing else, Benton, I suggest we go and tackle this creature before it dies of old age.'

'Yes, sir,' said Benton, jumping almost to attention in response to the Brigadier's tone.

As he left, the Doctor said, 'I think a quiet word with Sergeant Benton might be in order.'

'Going to tell him about my funny turn, are you?' said the Brigadier.

'Not at all,' said the Doctor, though he looked guilty. 'In view of the circumstances, I think it might be wise to assess the current state of the troops.'

The Brigadier regarded him shrewdly for a moment, then gave a concessionary nod. 'Yes, good idea.'

Offering a brief smile, the Doctor got out of the car and went round to the passenger side of the jeep. 'Do you think I might have a private word with you, Sergeant?' he asked.

Benton looked surprised. He regarded the Doctor as a good friend, but it was not often the Time Lord confided in him. 'Yes, of course,' he said and got out of the jeep. 'Is everything all right, Doctor?'

The Doctor led him a few yards away from the jeep and regarded him gravely. 'How are you feeling, Sergeant?'

Benton frowned. 'You mean since eating the fish yesterday? This infection thing?'

'Precisely.'

Benton considered for a moment. 'Not too bad. I've been having one or two odd thoughts, but I think I'm holding things together pretty well.'

'Good man. And the troops? How are they?'

'A bit edgy. I'm having to give them constant pep-talks to stop them losing concentration.' He shrugged. 'Some are worse than others, mind you. Around a dozen or so have had to be confined to sick bay.'

The Doctor patted Benton on the arm. 'Keep fighting it, Sergeant. You're doing a splendid job.' His voice dropped, even though they were out of earshot of both the jeep and the Brigadier's car. 'The Brigadier's not too good, I'm afraid. I'm not sure how much longer he can keep going.'

Benton puffed out his chest. 'I'll try and keep an eye on things for you at this end, Doctor. You just find a way to beat these things.'

They returned to their respective vehicles, and reached the fairground without further incident. UNIT and the local police had done their job well. The place was deserted, the rides silent. As the car approached the gates, where a lone UNIT sentry stood guard with his rifle clutched in his hands, the Doctor said wistfully, 'There's nothing quite so sad as an empty fairground.'

'Or so eerie,' said Tegan from the back.

They stopped beside the sentry. Tegan noticed that the Brigadier, who had been slumped in his seat for the last couple of minutes, was making a concerted effort to pull himself together. She had liked him the first time she had met him, had sensed a kind heart beating beneath his stern exterior, but now she felt a surge of real affection. He was trying so hard to be the leader his men expected him to be.

Winding down his window the Brigadier leaned out. 'What's the situation, Corporal Manning?' he asked, sounding as strong and alert as ever.

Manning blinked groggily at the Brigadier and swayed slightly as if he was about to pass out. 'Corporal Manning!' the Brigadier snapped. 'Pull yourself together, man!'

Immediately Manning jerked to attention. Flustered he said, 'Sorry, sir. The… erm… creature's taken refuge in the Ghost Train, sir. Some of the lads have got the place surrounded. It can't escape.'

'Excellent,' said the Brigadier. His voice softening just a touch, he added, 'Make sure you keep your wits about you, Corporal.'

'Yes, sir,' Manning said. 'I will, sir.'

'Good man. Now where's this Ghost Train?'

'It's all right. I know,' said the Doctor.

The walkways between the rides and stalls were wide enough for the Brigadier's car to lead the UNIT convoy in single file. They passed the Waltzer and the Log Flume, the Klondike Gold Mine and a looping construction of white tubes that bore the legend: THE TOBOGGAN RUN. The Ghost Train was situated between the Wall of Death and the Viking Longship, and was housed in a tall rectangular building made to look like it was covered in dripping green goo. Its fibreglass, bas-relief surface was further enhanced by a giant rotting-fingered mummy, a witch leaning over a bubbling cauldron, a dayglo-yellow skeleton with a single eyeball hanging from its socket, and a spiky-haired werewolf baying at a cheesy sliver of moon.

A trio of UNIT marksmen was standing guard outside the Ghost Train, one training his gun on the entrance, one on the exit and one hovering in between, ready to give assistance wherever needed. The two access points were marked by black double-doors, each painted with the huge, grinning head of a snake-haired woman. Three cars in the shape of giant skulls stood bumper to bumper outside the entrance.

The marksman in the middle turned as the UNIT convoy approached. The Brigadier's car drew up, and in the time it took for Tegan to reach gingerly for the door handle (her ribs still aching from being slammed into the door during their near-crash), the Doctor had leaped out. As the Brigadier, Tegan and Turlough joined him he finished speaking to the UNIT marksman and turned back towards them.

'Do you have any torches, Brigadier?' he asked, breathless with the nervous urgency that always radiated from him at the prospect of action.

The Brigadier seemed momentarily thrown by the question. 'Um... Benton!'

'Yes, sir?' said Benton, hurrying over.

'Do we have any torches?'

'Yes, sir. We should have.'

'Distribute them among the men, would you, Sergeant?' the Doctor said. 'Then organise them into two groups for a two-pronged attack. I suggest that you lead one of the groups and the Brigadier and I will lead the other.'

'Couldn't we just ask someone to turn the lights on in there?' suggested Tegan.

'We could if our Xaranti friend hadn't disabled the power supply,' said the Doctor. 'He seems to prefer the darkness.'

'Terrific,' Tegan muttered.

'Oh, I wouldn't worry about it if I were you,' the Doctor said, 'particularly as you and Turlough will be waiting for us out here.'

'I don't think so,' responded Tegan hotly, ignoring Turlough's expression of relief.

'Tegan, there isn't time to argue,' said the Doctor bluntly. 'There's no point in you and Turlough putting yourselves at risk for no reason.'

'We didn't come all this way just to sit this out!' she protested.

'Tegan, the Doctor's right,' said Turlough placatingly, taking her arm. 'We'd only be in the way.'

Tegan shot him a look of contempt, and was about to respond when the Brigadier said firmly, 'Besides, Miss Jovanka, may I remind you that this is a military operation under my command, and as such I forbid the involvement of civilians.'

'But the Doctor's going in with you!' Tegan said stridently.

'The Doctor still holds the position of UNIT's scientific adviser.'

'No he doesn't!'

The Brigadier closed his eyes briefly. Then he said, 'May I also remind you, Miss Jovanka, that it is within my jurisdiction to remove all civilians from the immediate area for their own safety.'

Tegan glared round at the trio of faces regarding her. 'Oh, you... you... you *men*!' she shouted.

Less than a minute after the two groups had entered the Ghost Train a blue Ford Escort screeched to a halt behind the Brigadier's staff car and Mike Yates jumped out. Tegan, who had been sitting in tense silence with Turlough in the open-topped back of a UNIT jeep, glanced at him in disgust and muttered, 'Boy racer.'

Mike ran up to them. 'Turlough,' he cried. 'What's going on? Is the creature still in there?'

Turlough nodded. 'As far as we know. They're all inside.'

'How long since they went in?'

He shrugged. 'No more than a minute.'

Mike glanced at the entrance and exit. 'Pincer movement. Am I right?'

'Right,' said Tegan before Turlough could answer. She

jumped down and walked towards him, absently scratching at her arm. 'Are you going in?'

Mike reached under the suede jacket he was wearing despite the heat and drew out a handgun, the barrel of which he kept pointed up at the sky. 'Yes I am.'

'Then I'm coming with you.'

Mike looked at her almost with amusement. 'I don't think so, miss.'

'You haven't got time to stand here arguing about it,' said Tegan. 'And the only way you'll stop me following you is to shoot me.'

The amusement on Mike's face turned to exasperation. 'Come on then. But stay close behind me and don't do anything stupid.' Turning to Turlough he said, 'I suppose you want to come too?'

Turlough looked both alarmed at the prospect and a little shame-faced as he shook his head. 'No, thank you,' he said. 'I'm quite happy to wait here.'

'At least one of you's sensible,' Mike said to Tegan, leading the way.

'An abject coward, more like,' Tegan said, not bothering to lower her voice.

Something touched the Doctor's face, and he flinched before realising it was one of several threads of wool hanging from the ceiling. No doubt it was supposed to feel like cobwebs or a ghostly caress. He smiled sheepishly.

The Ghost Train was a man-sized rabbit warren, full of twists and turns, which made progress tortuously slow as they crept onwards. The passageways were narrow and littered with corners around any of which the Xaranti could have been waiting to pounce. The men were already edgy and aggressive, because of the infection rampaging through their systems, and this situation did nothing but compound that.

The creature, it seemed, had chosen this hideout with cunning deliberation. Each time a torch-beam struck the luminous paint of a green zombie or a bright yellow ghost, it induced a scuffle of panic, a raising and aiming of rifles.

Beside the Doctor the Brigadier, handgun drawn, was struggling. He was doing his best to hide it from his men, but up close the Doctor could see the strain on his sweating face. It was deeply worrying. The usually well-drilled UNIT soldiers were falling far short of the kind of discipline needed here. If the Doctor didn't judge this situation exactly right, then things quickly could turn very nasty indeed.

All at once the Brigadier stumbled, the beam of his torch zigzagging wildly. With lightning reflexes the Doctor turned and caught him before he hit the ground.

'Thank you, Doctor,' the Brigadier breathed.

The Doctor glanced back to see what effect the Brigadier's near-fall had had on the men. Each appeared to be fighting his own internal battle. In the reflected torch-light, their eyes looked glassy, their faces shiny with sweat. The Doctor sighed, and turning to his old friend, whispered 'How are you feeling, Brigadier? Truthfully.'

The Brigadier swallowed. 'I feel a sort of... tugging in my mind. As if... as if something is calling to me with a powerful voice. I can't... hear what it's saying, but... but I feel as though I should... go to it.' His eyelids fluttered and then his head snapped back and he muttered furiously, 'No. I am Brigadier Alistair Gordon Lethbridge-Stewart. I am a soldier in Her Majesty's... Her Majesty's... I will not...' His face twisted in anguish. 'There's something in my head, something... scrabbling in my memories. I can't stop it...' All at once his face slackened, his shoulders slumped and he stumbled to a halt.

'Come on, Brigadier,' urged the Doctor, glancing again at the men. 'Best foot forward.' Ahead of them was another twist in the route, a glowing orange skeleton pointing the way.

He placed a hand in the small of the Brigadier's back, and eased him forward a little. Suddenly, urgently the Brigadier rasped again, 'They know you're here. They know who you are.'

'Let's worry about that when we come to it, shall we?' replied the Doctor, alert for any sound or movement from around the corner ahead. He slowed down, signalling the men to do the same, and reached down to take the Brigadier's torch from his limp hand.

In an uncharacteristic blurt of emotion, the Brigadier suddenly said, 'I'm so sorry, Doctor. This is all my fault. Unforgiveable... Absolutely unforgiveable.'

The Doctor patted the Brigadier's arm affectionately. 'There, there, old chap. Don't concern yourself.'

He edged around the corner, the torch beam dancing ahead. A huge spider in a glowing yellow web sprang out and confronted them. Hastily the Doctor raised his hand and whispered, 'Nothing to worry about. Come on.'

They moved slowly forward again. All at once the Brigadier's head slumped forward and he whispered despairingly, 'I can't go on, Doctor...'

'Nine times seven,' the Doctor responded.

'What...?'

'Quickly, Brigadier. Work it out. Nine times seven.'

'Um... er... sixty-three.'

'Fourteen times eleven.'

'Er... er... I can't...'

'You *can*. Fourteen times eleven.'

'One hundred... one hundred and fifty four.'

'Three thousand, seven hundred and eight minus one thousand, six hundred and forty.' Slowly, the Doctor firing maths questions at the Brigadier, they moved on.

Approaching from the other end, Benton too could feel the

mental tugging. In his case, it was still feeble, half-hearted, a sensation he was able to shrug off by barking out orders to his men, urging them to concentrate. Some of them were bearing up well, but others seemed less able to cope with the Xaranti infection, pointing their guns at every glowing phantom and cheesily grinning skeleton.

Benton wondered what would happen if and when they *did* find the Xaranti. Given the state of the men, he doubted that the Doctor would get much of a chance to communicate with it. It was ironic really: the creature was likely to die at the hands of its own infected prey.

'Go steady there!' he hissed as the men jostled for position behind him, growling bad-temperedly at one another. 'Let's stay in line, stop arguing, and keep an eye out for the real enemy, shall we?'

His words continued to have a placatory effect for now, but how long would it last?

All at once the corridor widened a little, and the track gleaming in the dim torchlight ahead of them cornered sharply to the left. Just before the bend stood a troll-like creature with glowing orange eyes, brandishing a luminous placard announcing: TURN BACK – SWAMP AHEAD. No sooner had Benton taken this in than he heard a commotion behind him. He half-turned, opening his mouth to deliver a few choice words – and someone blundered into the back of him, jabbering incoherently.

Benton was so surprised that he was caught off-balance and careered into the wall with such force that it jarred his shoulder and propelled him on to his knees. His torch went flying, landing with a crack, its beam remaining mercifully intact. Shuffling toward him was Corporal Burke, one of the youngest of his platoon, eyes wide and staring, a mumbled, incoherent stream of words trickling from his slack mouth. He was dragging his rifle along the floor behind him. His right hand was scratching his chest and left shoulder so vigorously that he was probably drawing blood.

'Corporal Burke,' Benton grated, rising to his feet and stretching out an arm to steady the young soldier. 'Corporal Burke, back into line this minute.'

Abruptly the young man's face contorted with rage, he released a gurgling, animal-like cry and suddenly he was lunging at Benton's face with his rifle-butt.

Benton swiftly twisted aside and the butt glanced off his already-bruised shoulder, re-igniting a white flash-fire of pain inside him.

Burke dropped his rifle with a clatter and ran past him as if he intended to engage the troll ahead in physical combat. He was almost there when something black and huge, moving with scuttling, breath-taking speed, appeared as if from nowhere and plucked the man off his feet like a spider snatching a fly.

The young corporal looked up into a face full of bristles and black spider-eyes and screamed. The creature's tail whipped up over its back in a great arc and its scorpion-like sting speared through the back of the man's neck, killing him instantly.

Benton gaped at the creature for a moment, unable to say or do anything, then recovering his wits, he shouted, 'Fire!'

Instantly the small, confined space became filled with the shattering din of gunfire and a lethal, horizontal rain of bullets.

The scream was a jagged blade of sound, tearing through the very fabric of the walls. Tegan jumped out of her skin and grabbed the back of Mike Yates's jacket. As the din was abruptly cut off, she said, 'Please tell me that was just a sound effect.'

Before Mike could answer the air was filled with the cacophony of a hundred small explosions. Instinctively the two of them ducked, then almost immediately Mike raised his head. 'Come on!' he shouted and began to run towards the sound.

Until the shooting started, Turlough had begun to feel like the only person left in the world. He sat on the padded bench in the back of the jeep, gazing at the Ghost Train building until the images on its frontage blurred. The only sound to break the silence was the plaintive cries of seagulls. He stretched and wondered idly whether he ought to find some shade.

He yawned and tried to put aside the guilt he felt at sitting out here whilst the rest of his friends were monster-hunting inside. He was only following the Doctor's orders, he told himself, and he *had* accompanied the Doctor into the heart of the Xaranti spaceship, so he was hardly a coward. He just didn't throw himself recklessly into situations like Tegan did, that was all. He was more thoughtful, had a greater sense of self-preservation. That didn't make him selfish, which was what Tegan had called him on several occasions, merely... careful.

The scream from inside the Ghost Train shattered his thoughts. Turlough sat bolt upright in his seat, half-expecting the doors to burst open and disgorge either a fleeing line of terrified soldiers or the Xaranti creature itself. It struck him that if the creature *did* appear ahead of anyone else, he would be its only possible target. With this in mind, he stood up, intending to shift into the driver's seat for a quick getaway if necessary.

As he stood, two things happened simultaneously. He registered slight movement some distance behind him and a sudden eruption of gunfire exploded from within the building, of such duration and ferocity that it sounded like one long, unbroken roar.

Turlough hunched his shoulders and glanced in that

direction. As yet there was nothing to see. He turned and looked behind him. What he saw made his stomach clench, his throat tighten and his legs turn to water.

About twenty Xaranti hybrids, in various stages of transformation, were shuffling towards him. At their head he recognised the UNIT sentry – Corporal Manning – who had been on the gate. He was still in the early stages of transformation, his eyes staring, his expression zombie-like. Behind him was a policeman in uniform, his eyes black and starting to bulge. A young man in a pair of denim shorts displayed a chest and shoulders covered in Xaranti spines; a girl of no more than thirteen had a hump on her back swelling and squirming beneath a pink *Osmonds* T-shirt. They were all moving slowly as if in a trance. It was if they were being summoned, drawn towards the Ghost Train like metal filings towards a magnet. They seemed oblivious to their surroundings, which Turlough hoped meant they would be oblivious of him too.

Part of Turlough wanted to stay still in the hope that the hybrids would not notice him. However, the greater part – the cowardly part, Tegan would have said – wanted to put as much distance between himself and these… these things as possible. He took a deep breath and jumped to the ground, little clouds of dust puffing up around his feet. The instant he moved, the hybrids reacted, as he had feared they might. The girl in the pink T-shirt hissed, her head darting to follow his progress with an almost snake-like swiftness. Her back bulged more intensely, and then, with a ripping of cloth and a wet tearing of flesh, burst open, to release a thrashing, bloody mass of glistening crab-like legs.

Turlough made an involuntary whimpering noise in the back of his throat. He didn't want to see any more. Panic made his movements jerky as he ran to the driver's side of the jeep and wrenched open the door. He threw himself inside, the smell of hot leather mingling with his fear to make him feel sick. For an awful moment it struck him that the driver of this vehicle might have taken the keys with him, but no, there they were, dangling from the ignition. He leaned over, grabbed the handle, slammed the door shut and locked it. He turned the ignition key and the engine revved into life.

Only now did he look up through the windscreen. He had had a vague idea that he could escape down the route dead ahead, but his heart sank as he saw a crowd of hybrids approaching from that direction.

His stomach turned over and his mouth went dry. Desperately he looked to his left, praying that the aisle directly opposite would be clear.

It was not. The leading hybrid approaching from this direction, no more than twenty yards from the back of the truck, had black, thorn-like bristles sprouting from his face, and was already hunched over and propelling himself grotesquely along on his newly-sprouted Xaranti limbs.

Again, Turlough's panic seemed to intensify the hot claustrophobic stink of leather inside the driver's cab, making him feel faint and nauseous. If he didn't want to be either ripped apart or infected with the Xaranti virus, he had no alternative but to drive forward and hope that the hybrids would move out of his way. He couldn't be half-hearted about it either. If he drove too slowly the creatures would merely scramble up on to the back of the jeep; either that or smash his windows and drag him out.

'Get out of the way! I'm coming through!' he shouted, his words emerging as a hysterical, screaming croak. He slammed the truck into first, released the handbrake, then floored the accelerator.

With a squeal of tyres, which kicked up a billowing wake of dust, the truck lurched forward. Turlough gritted his teeth and tried to thread the vehicle between the leading hybrid shuffling towards him up the centre of the aisle and a 'Hook-a-Duck' stall on the right.

The lead hybrid, a bushy-haired, bearded man in a white shirt and jeans so flared they covered his feet, raised his hands not in a self-protective gesture but a threatening one. Before Turlough could take evasive action, the hybrid (whose black, bulging eyes could have been mistaken for large, round shades at a distance) leapt at the truck.

He hit it with a loud thud and immediately rebounded, cartwheeling spectacularly through the air, a red streamer of blood arcing after him. The truck slewed, but Turlough – through a combination of terror and luck – managed to bring it under control, and tore out of the fairground at seventy miles an hour as the hybrids launched themselves after him in vain pursuit.

As soon as the shooting started, the Doctor left the Brigadier and his men without a word and ran towards the commotion. He bypassed witches and warlocks, ghouls and demons, flapped aside limp-winged rubber bats that ambushed him as he skidded round one corner after another.

He did not exhibit any caution until he was almost upon the scene itself. He paused then to listen, trying to work out the position of Benton and his troops, and more importantly the direction in which they were shooting.

One thing he *was* able to deduce from the din was that beyond the next corner was some kind of open area – not exactly cavernous but with room to move around. This must be where the Xaranti had made its lair after squeezing through the narrow corridors of the Ghost Train. The Doctor took a deep breath, then crouching low to make himself as small a target as possible, crept round the corner.

The roar of bullets struck his ears, the careering torch beams and the tiny but myriad white flashes of gunfire reduced the scene to a rapid, confusing interplay of light and shadow. The Doctor tried to look beyond that, tried to adjust his vision to phase out the distractions.

This area must be the heart of the Ghost Train, the *pièce de résistance* of the ride. It had been designed to resemble swampland, complete with a black, drooping tangle of fibreglass trees and vines which arched over the thread of track. To his right, against the far wall, the 'ground' had been built up to form a bank, beyond which lurked a mechanical serpent-like creature that was designed to rear up out of the swamp.

The serpent was probably effective as part of the ride, but compared to the Xaranti crouching behind it, legs drawn in like a spider under threat, it looked pitiful. The knot of UNIT soldiers on the other side of the room were blasting away at the Xaranti – or rather at the fibre-glass 'nest' in which it was huddled. The creature had been hit; as the Doctor's eyes adjusted he saw some dark fluid – blood or ichor – leaking from several wounds in what he could see of its body. But most of the bullets were going astray, some hitting the walls and sending chunks of plaster flying in all directions, others reducing the sculpted trees to a debris of shattered fibre-glass. Shards rained down on the mangled body of the soldier sprawled across the track like a man hit by a train.

The Doctor tried to attune his mind to the Xaranti thought-patterns and received a tumbling confusion of intense, savage emotions: delirium; abandonment; the desire to inflict pain, to kill. He soon realised these feelings came not from the Xaranti, but from the UNIT troops. Their trigger-happy attack on a creature into which they were gradually transforming must have pushed them over the edge. The Doctor wondered whether in fact the Xaranti as a species had planned this little episode from the outset, had been willing to sacrifice one of their number in order to hasten the recruitment of many more.

Recalling how his attempt to communicate with the Xaranti in their own craft had effectively thrown a spanner into their mental works, the Doctor summoned all his willpower. He took a deep breath and stepped boldly out, not exactly into the line of fire, but certainly into full view.

'Stop!' he shouted, raising his hands and instantaneously transmitting an intense telepathic command to the same effect. The result was startling; the firing ceased abruptly. For a few moments the only sound that could be heard was the stertorous breathing of the wounded Xaranti. The Doctor looked at the troops, who gazed back at him, their eyes glittering in the half-light.

He shifted his attention to the Xaranti, turning his head slowly like a man in the midst of dangerous animals who had been instructed not to make any sudden moves. Concentrating hard he adjusted the message to envelop the creature in a soothing balm of comforting, reassuring thought-waves. Several moments later he sensed the creature relaxing slightly and sent a feathery tendril of enquiry probing deeper into its brain. He gained access with such disconcerting ease that he could only conclude the Xaranti mind operated on similar frequencies to his own. At last he touched upon a few vestiges of human thought and emotion, struggling feebly like a fly ensnared in the sticky secretions of a carnivorous plant. He sensed confusion and fear, plucked out a name: Guy Elkins. Even as he accessed this information he could sense it dissolving, melting down into the substance destined for the controlling mind of the Xaranti queen.

The Doctor moved slowly towards the creature, shards of fibre-glass crunching underfoot. Slowly, shakily, the Xaranti unfolded its legs and raised itself up. The Doctor sensed that the gesture was not a threatening one, but was a display almost of trust, of wary greeting. He continued to sluice the creature in a steady, soothing telepathic tide, speaking gently to it as he did so, like a vet trying to calm an injured dog.

'Hello, Guy. It is Guy, isn't it? Now don't be afraid. I'm here to help you if I can...'

Vaguely he became aware of some kind of kerfuffle behind him in the ranks, but tried not to let it distract him. He would have to rely on Sergeant Benton to sort it out – if he still had enough presence of mind to do so, that was.

Next moment, however, he heard rapid footsteps behind him, accompanied by a warning shout: 'Get down, Doctor!'

His concentration all but broken, the Doctor half-turned and saw Mike Yates skidding to a halt a few feet behind him, levelling his gun at the Xaranti.

'No!' shouted the Doctor, but it was too late.

Two shots rang out. The first hit the Xaranti in the abdomen, fluid spurting out of the wound to spatter on the floor. The second glanced off one of its legs and ricocheted away into the darkness.

The Doctor felt the delicate telepathic link he had established with the Xaranti snap like frayed elastic. The creature opened a flap-like mouth and bellowed like a bull elephant in rage and pain. It reared up into a fighting stance, its legs rigid, back arched. Then, so fast it was almost a blur, it whipped its tail over its head in a huge arc and buried its sting deep into the soft flesh above the Doctor's collar-bone.

Part Four
Changing Times

The thickening fog in the Brigadier's mind was closing in on all sides, obliterating the landscape of his thoughts. The barrage of mathematical questions which the Doctor had been bombarding him with, and his responses to them, had been like a torch beam lighting his way, preventing him from straying off the path.

Even with the Doctor's help, however, the torch batteries had been steadily failing, the light growing weaker the closer they came to the heart of darkness. The Brigadier might well have succumbed completely if it hadn't been for the gunfire.

Although not as swiftly as the Doctor, the Brigadier had been able to do nothing but react to it. To him the sound denoted action and danger, but most especially *duty*. Duty to his men, to his country, to his world.

The fog receded a little. Now that the Doctor was gone, duty was the Brigadier's torch, lighting his way. Hoping that the light would stay with him for as long as he needed it, he set off at a shambling lurch, ignoring limbs that felt stiff and awkward. His heart was heavy as a rock in his chest, and within seconds he was drenched in sweat, gasping for breath. However, he forced himself ion through sheer, bloody-minded willpower.

And then the shooting stopped.

The sudden silence threw the Brigadier into a momentary state of exhausted confusion that almost caused him to blunder off the path, straight into the fog. He thumped to a halt, heart labouring, head pounding.

Then, faintly and hesitantly at first, he heard a voice in his mind, and he realised that his sense of duty, his driving force, had not deserted him, after all.

There might be men dead or injured, the voice told him; men who needed his help, his guidance. He couldn't abandon his duty; he had to lead by example, had to be seen to be counted.

'Yes,' he muttered, 'yes.' He set off again, duty lighting his way once more. When he was almost at his goal he slowed down, allowed his soldier's instincts to take over. His semi-automatic clutched in his hand, he crept along, his back to the wall, towards the place where the track took an abrupt left turn. He wanted a vantage point where he could recce the situation, but before he could do that two further shots rang out, followed by a vast inhuman bellow of rage and pain.

It provoked a deep, almost primeval response in him. For a moment the fog swirled and eddied around him again, threatening to extinguish the light...

Then the enraged roar faded and another sound replaced it – a further cry of pain, from a smaller pair of lungs, but no less agonized.

'Doctor!' the Brigadier yelled. He ran around the corner, gun raised.

The scene before him had frozen into a kind of tableau, lit by a spotlight of torch-beams. Taking centre-stage was a creature from a nightmare, a hideous, giganticised conglomeration of bull, spider, crab and scorpion. Standing rigid before this creature, skewered by its great, ridged arc of a tail, was the Doctor, blood shockingly red on his cream coat, face twisted in agony. Between the Brigadier and the Doctor stood Mike Yates, frozen with horror, mouth agape, gun forgotten in his hand.

Without hesitation, the Brigadier marched forward, barged Yates out of the way and fired six shots point-blank into the creature's face.

Its head disintegrated, spattering the Brigadier with warm,

brown fluid. The Xaranti's legs gave way beneath it and its body slumped like a deflating hot-air balloon. Its tail drooped aside as it collapsed, dragging the Doctor over with it. The creature's body twitched and jittered for a few seconds with involuntary muscle spasms and then became still. For a moment all was silent.

Then the Brigadier began to sob.

He couldn't help it. He had killed before, many times, but this time, even as he had pulled the trigger to fire his final shot, an overwhelming wave of horror, revulsion, shame and, yes, even grief, had swept through him, sapping his strength, forcing him to his knees. He couldn't remember the last time he had cried, but now he couldn't stop. A few feet away from him the Doctor was lying unconscious, the Xaranti sting still buried in his flesh.

Then someone moved into the Brigadier's line of sight and crouched over the Doctor. Mike Yates. Yates glanced at him, and in a split second, even through his tears, the Brigadier was able to read so much in his captain's face. He saw Yates's shock and confusion at his superior officer's display of emotion. And he saw Yates's own mental anguish at having failed to take action, even though one of his friends and colleagues was in deadly peril. Then Yates looked away and turned his attention to the Doctor once more. He grabbed the base of the dead Xaranti's tail, and, with an angry gesture, he wrenched the sting from the Doctor's shoulder.

For a while after that things became a little blurred. The Brigadier remained kneeling on the floor, head bowed, trying to pull his emotions back on to an even keel while everything happened around him. He was vaguely aware of Yates taking charge, organising the men. At one point he saw the Doctor being carried out on a makeshift stretcher, his face waxy and composed, some kind of padding – a jacket perhaps – bound tightly against his shoulder to stem the bleeding. He heard

Yates barking orders at Benton; heard the voice of the Australian girl too, but rather than words he heard only her emotions – the brashness of her anger, the strain of her shock, the muted tones of her concern.

It was she who finally came to him, crouching beside him, putting one hand on his arm as if feeling his biceps, the other on his back. The Brigadier had never been much of a one for physical contact, but now he felt absurdly grateful for the consideration she was showing him.

'Are you all right, Brigadier?' she asked gently, warily.

The tears had mostly run their course, but the Brigadier felt entirely drained of energy. It was as if he was viewing the world through thick gauze; he felt as if great areas of his mind were no longer his, but merely empty chambers waiting to be filled by whatever had cleared out his thoughts.

He nodded, however, and murmured, 'There's life in the old dog yet.'

She smiled and patted him on the back. 'Come on then, old dog,' she said. 'Let's get you out of here. Can you walk?'

The Brigadier would have found it too much of an indignity to say no, so he nodded again and forced himself to his feet. He tried to convince himself that he was escorting her as much as she was supporting him as they shuffled out of the building. The fog was closing in again and he had to channel all his efforts, all his concentration, into remembering who and where he was, into putting one foot in front of the other. After a while he felt his chest and shoulders itching again, but this time it was a pleasant itch; it seemed to send ripples of sensation, like pure energy, coursing through his body.

'Xaranti,' he murmured, lovingly.

'What?' asked Tegan.

The Brigadier felt a flash of irritation. 'We are Xaranti,' he told her.

The girl looked at him anxiously, and suddenly in his eyes

she seemed so puny, hateful, pathetic. 'No. You're Brigadier Lethbridge-Stewart. You work for UNIT, remember?'

For a brief moment he was confused, felt as if his mind was struggling with itself, then the delicious itch flowed through him again, imbuing him with strength and confidence. 'We are Xaranti,' he repeated, snatching his arm from her grip. 'And you...' He stepped closer as if to strike her, then stopped. He sensed... sensed... *yes*. 'You are Xaranti too.

The girl looked shocked. 'No!' she said, backing away from him.

He laughed. 'Soon we will all be Xaranti.'

'*No!*' the girl said again, more venomously this time.

He was about to reply when he felt something in his mind: a tickle, a voice, an instinct, an idea, a compulsion. It was all of these and more, but wherever it had come from – and the Brigadier felt as though it had come as much from inside him, from his memories and knowledge, as from outside – the message was clear.

'The Doctor,' he murmured.

'What?'

'We must –' He stopped abruptly; he was telling her too much. The human influence in her was still too strong. He pressed his teeth together in a tight grin. 'Nothing,' he said.

She stared at him for a moment, her eyes wide, searching. 'Oh no,' she said. 'You're not going to have the Doctor. He's the only one who can help you.'

She turned and ran into the darkness. The Brigadier hissed his displeasure and followed. But his new-found energy burned off quickly, and after a minute or so he was panting again, sweat pouring off him. He struggled along, hands slapping the wall to maintain his balance, but the girl drew so far ahead that soon he could not even hear her footsteps.

It didn't matter. She couldn't get away. He was linked to the group mind now and he knew that there were Xaranti waiting on the outside for her too.

Sooner than he had expected, he burst through a set of double doors and into the light. He stood swaying for a moment, blinking and disorientated. He could hear people shouting, hear his own kind hissing at those who were still transforming. As his eyes adapted he took in the scene before him at a glance.

The UNIT soldiers, many of whom were clinging to their humanity only by the thinnest of threads, were fighting a rearguard action against those of his kind whose transformations were more advanced than his own. If it hadn't been for the man, Yates (backed up by Benton) marshalling them, shouting out orders, pulling them back from the brink, the Brigadier felt sure that most of them would have succumbed by now. At Yates's behest, the soldiers had encircled an army truck, in the back of which lay the Doctor, still unconscious. Crouched beside the Doctor and facing the conflict wild-eyed with fear was the Australian girl. The hybrids were prowling the perimeter of the human circle, looking for a way in. Those who ventured too close were driven back by blows from rifle-butts. The Brigadier knew that they had not yet attacked in force, overwhelming the humans by sheer numbers, because they needed the Doctor in one piece.

The Doctor was important to them. His mind would make an invaluable contribution to their cause. Indeed, it was not an exaggeration to say that the sum of his knowledge could turn the Xaranti into the most powerful race in the universe. It was imperative, then, that the humans were not pushed to firing their weapons. Consumed by blood-lust they would be unable to differentiate between friend and enemy. Under such circumstances the Doctor might be damaged beyond repair.

More subtle methods had to be employed, therefore. The current stand-off needed to be brought to a swift and bloodless conclusion. The one major unpredictable element in this situation was the Doctor himself. Who knew what kind of influence he might be able to exert if, or when, he regained consciousness?

Suddenly, as if the idea had come fully-formed into his mind, the Brigadier knew what he had to do. He drew his gun and stepped towards the small pay-booth at the front of the Ghost Train. From there, keeping low and hiding behind the screen of hybrids, he crept around the perimeter of the circle until he was opposite Mike Yates. Yates was standing in line with his men, gun drawn, still shouting out orders and encouragement, occasionally checking with Sergeant Benton on the far side of the truck to keep the circle tight.

The Brigadier suddenly stood up behind the hybrids and proceeded to barge through them, brandishing his gun, pointing it into the faces of those that made a show of lunging at him, hissing. He even clubbed a couple for good measure to make it look convincing.

'Sir!' Yates shouted, seeing the commotion, and despatched two of his men from the circle as a rescue party.

They were back within seconds, the Brigadier staggering between them, the hybrids making a show of surging forward then falling back as the soldiers swung their rifles this way and that.

'Sir,' Yates said again, 'are you OK?'

'Fine, Captain Yates,' said the Brigadier heartily. 'I see our little problem has increased somewhat.'

'Yes, sir,' said Yates. 'As you can see, we're in a bit of a spot. This lot are hanging back for the moment, but they've got us surrounded. Thing is, I don't want to give the order to fire if I can help it, because... well, because whatever they look like, they're still people, sir. To be honest, I'm damned if I know what to do next. I keep hoping the Doctor'll wake up and come up with something.'

A cry came from behind them, raucous and vehement. 'Don't trust him!'

It was the Australian girl, standing up in the back of the truck, pointing a rigid finger at the Brigadier.

'Miss Jovanka –' he began, speaking her name before he was even aware he'd remembered it.

'He's changing into one of those things,' Tegan shouted. 'He might not look like it yet, but he is.'

'As are we all, Miss Jovanka,' replied the Brigadier, then turned to Yates with a cold smile. 'Except for you, Captain, of course.'

Suddenly he pressed his gun barrel against Mike Yates's temple. 'I suggest the best thing would be to hand the Doctor over to us,' he hissed.

For a moment Yates looked almost comically incredulous. Then an expression of sad resignation appeared on his face and he said, 'You know I can't do that, sir.'

'You have no choice, Captain Yates,' the Brigadier said briskly. 'You can't fight us. You are the only true human left here. We are all Xaranti.'

At that moment something slammed into the Brigadier's back, expelling the air from his lungs and knocking him to the ground with such force that he cracked his forehead on the concrete. A weight landed on his back and a voice muttered, 'Not yet we're not.'

The Brigadier didn't realise he was still holding his gun until it was twisted from his grip. The voice, which the Brigadier quickly recognised as belonging to Sergeant Benton, said, 'Sorry about this, sir, but it's for your own good. We can't let them take the Doctor.' Pinning the Brigadier's arms and legs to the floor, Benton lifted his head and spoke to Yates. 'Get in the truck and go, sir. Take the Doctor with you. Take him somewhere safe.'

Yates's voice: 'I can't just leave you all.'

'Yes you can, sir. The Brigadier's right. Soon we'll all be changing into these bloody things. And then it'll be too late. Just go, sir. Go now.'

A pause, then Yates said, 'We'll never get through.'

'Yes you will, sir.' Benton raised his voice. 'Listen to me, men. Captain Yates is our last chance. If he doesn't get out of here with the Doctor, we're finished. Do you get me? We'll all end up like these poor sods, and eventually like that... that thing in there. So if anyone or anything tries to stop the Captain from getting through, I want you to shoot them. You hear me? If you don't we'll all be dead anyway.'

There was a rumble of assent from the men, the Xaranti aggression within them lending the sound an eagerness, an excitement at the prospect of killing. But as the Brigadier, still pinned face-down on the ground, heard the truck's engine start up, he knew that the Xaranti would not attack. The Doctor might be escaping now, but already Xaranti energy from the sting was surging through his body, attacking his cells. Soon the Doctor would succumb, and the meagre threat that he posed would be at an end. There was no escape for any of them.

It was evident that the Xaranti felt their influence was now well -established enough for them to have no further need for secrecy. In the half-hour or so since the Brigadier had picked up the Doctor, Tegan and Turlough in his car, Tayborough Sands had dissolved into chaos. The seafront streets may have been cleared in the wake of the Xaranti attack on the beach, but there had still been a great many infected, transforming humans holed up in hotel rooms, boarding-houses and B&Bs. As if responding to some internal signal, these hybrids had now emerged and were roaming the streets in groups of anything from three to thirty, hunting down, infecting or killing the minority of unaffected humans who had been foolish enough to venture back out into the open.

Turlough's hope that his nightmare had ended with his escape from the fun-fair was short-lived. As he drove back to the hotel, unable to think of anywhere else to go, the delayed shock of his narrow escape from the fairground was further intensified by the sights around him. There were bodies lying in pools of blood, crashed cars, and even makeshift roadblocks, constructed of anything that the hybrids had been able to get their hands on – furniture, chunks of timber, electrical equipment. Though there was barely any traffic on the roads, discouraged by the diversions presumably set up by the army or the police to prevent people heading into town, several vehicles had still come to grief at these obstructions, including a police car and an ambulance which had been pushed over on to its side.

It was like driving through a war-zone where the indigenous population was hostile and savage but thankfully unarmed. Several times hybrids had run at the jeep; some even throwing themselves at it, their fledgling Xaranti legs scraping the paintwork as they scrabbled for purchase.

Spurred by terror and desperation, Turlough had driven round them, or through them, or slewed from side to side to shake them off. Eventually, after smashing through a roadblock and taking a circuitous route through a number of quiet back-streets to avoid two more, Turlough drew up in front of the hotel. Thankfully there were hybrids in sight and he sat for a moment trying to regain at least a modicum of composure, his hands aching from gripping the steering wheel so hard, his breathing rapid and ragged.

For a moment he honestly didn't think he would be able to make himself get out of the jeep. Though vulnerable, the driver's cab seemed like sanctuary. He wished the Doctor had entrusted him with a TARDIS key. If he got ripped to pieces between here and his hotel room, it would be all the Doctor's fault.

Even when he *did* finally gather the resolve to make a move, Turlough looked up and down the road a dozen times first to ensure it was still deserted. Reassured, he opened the driver's door, and winced at the meaty 'chunk' it made, half-expecting a screeching horde of Xaranti to emerge from all sides like the Zulu warriors in that ridiculous film he had watched with Hippo one wet Sunday afternoon. Though he had hated his time at Brendon, he wished he could be there now.

To his surprise, the ratcheting din of the opening door went uninvestigated, and so he slid out of the jeep and on to the pavement. It was only three paces to the bottom of the stone steps, and another eight up into the hotel, but Turlough felt exposed for an appallingly long time as he dashed across and up, stooped over like an old man.

The foyer sucked him into its coolness, eliciting a gasp from him as if he had just emerged from deep water. Relief mingled with apprehension. Though buildings *seemed* safer than the streets outside, there was no reason why they should be. Indeed, as his eyes adjusted to the dim light he saw the bodies. He flinched from the startling redness of blood and its profusion, but he had seen enough to know that the victims, two women and a man, had not died painlessly.

He scurried across to the lifts, hoping that his trembling body and crumbling nerves would survive long enough for him to reach his room. He jabbed at the lift button, then decided he didn't like the idea of standing around, waiting, and turned towards the stairs. The staircase was wide and carpeted. Turlough had ascended no more than half a dozen steps when the lift announced its arrival with a 'ping'.

His foot hovered above the next step as he dithered over whether or not to run back for it. Then he heard something catapult out of the lift and into the foyer. He turned and saw what had once been a tall, balding man wearing a grey suit.

Now, though, the back of the suit had burst open to accommodate a wavering, clicking mass of Xaranti legs.

Turlough neither moved nor made a sound, but the hybrid seemed to sense his presence. It spun round, hands outstretched and fingers arched like claws. Its bulging eyes gleamed like tar, and spines sprouting from its sallow face scraped together like bone as it opened its mouth in a snarling hiss. With terrifying agility it sprang towards the stairs, its obvious intention propelling Turlough up them.

His back felt wide and vulnerable, and though he was leaping three steps at a time, his breath ragged with panic, he felt he was wading through water. On the first landing the red cylinder of a fire extinguisher stood stoutly in the corner. Turlough lunged towards it, almost sprawling headlong, but managing with a pinwheeling of his arms to remain upright. He grabbed the extinguisher and spun round.

The hybrid was only four steps below him. One good leap and it would bring him down. Turlough had been planning to use the fire extinguisher as a weapon, but he was so shocked by the creature's proximity that he actually *threw* the heavy red cylinder at it.

It was a lucky shot. The extinguisher struck the creature full in the face and caught it off balance. The hybrid fell backwards, arms spread out like a high diver. It looked almost graceful until it hit the steps about half way down, and then it became a spinning mass of arms and legs and thrashing Xaranti limbs. Its head met the floor at the bottom of the staircase with a sickening thump and a halo of brown fluid began to form around it. Turlough didn't hang around. He turned and lurched up the rest of the stairs.

He reached the fifth floor without further incident and hurried along the landing to his room. He fumbled the keys out of his pocket and pushed the largest into the lock. It wasn't until he was in his room with the door locked behind him that he began to shake with reaction. Trying to ignore it, he shoved his bed against the door, then piled every item of furniture in the room on top of it. At last, for want of a better weapon, he grabbed a coat hanger from the wardrobe and sat in the corner of the room, facing the barricaded door. Wishing desperately that he could make himself invisible, he pressed himself as far back into the corner as he could and drew his knees up under his chin.

'You see now?' the Brigadier said.

Benton nodded. 'Yes.'

The Brigadier put his hand on Benton's shoulder. Benton winced as the itching beneath his skin intensified. A wave of sensation that was part pleasure, part pain rippled through his body.

Benton could no longer understand why he had allowed the human, Yates, to take the Doctor away. He only wished he had had his eyes opened in time to prevent it. Human motivation seemed so petty, so pointless, so *alien* to him now. He looked around and saw soldiers and hybrids standing shoulder to shoulder, united in a common cause. It felt good. It felt *right*. And although for the moment he was still aware of who he was, still retained his human identity, he understood and embraced the fact that individuality was no longer important, that it was a human characteristic, divisive and inefficient. Soon there would be no need for it, would no longer even be any further need for speech. For the time being, though, it would remain a useful marshalling device.

'Let's move out,' Benton shouted, and moving across to the nearest army vehicle he slid behind the wheel.

Obediently everyone followed suit, clambering up into the vehicles, squeezing themselves in as tightly as they could. When the vehicles were full to bursting point, Benton started the engine of his jeep and they all filed out, a grotesque slow-moving convoy. There was no need to discuss a plan of attack, no need to issue orders; they were all working as one now, all knew exactly what they had to do. Their immediate objective was clear to them all. They would search tirelessly until they had recovered the Doctor.

At that moment the Doctor was several miles away, still unconscious in the back of a UNIT truck. Tegan was crouched beside him, clinging for dear life to truck's metal framework. She felt not unlike a gazelle being driven through a lion enclosure. At least she had the advantage of being armed, she reminded herself, clutching Mike Yates's Colt .45 in her free hand – though in truth the gun made her feel more nervous than secure.

The journey had been perilous to say the least, but, as they had travelled north, the amount of death and devastation they had seen around them had steadily decreased. They had been pursued frequently by hybrids, and had even been ambushed at one point, a trio of the creatures dropping down on to the truck from above as they had negotiated one of the narrow residential streets that climbed away from the seafront and out of the town centre. One of them had landed on the roof of the driver's cab, the legs that had sprouted from its back clacking against the windscreen like long, jointed, sticks; another had hit the side of the truck and bounced off it on to the pavement, where it had lain, mewling, one of its human legs twisted at a grotesque angle; and the third had landed beside Tegan in the back of the truck, stumbling at first because of the truck's movement, but quickly regaining its balance and springing upright into an attack stance.

It was evident that not so very long ago this particular hybrid had been an attractive young woman with long blonde hair and honey-coloured skin. Now these attributes merely emphasised the extent and hideousness of her transformation.

Her arms and long legs, exposed by the sleeveless yellow T-shirt and denim shorts she wore, were as hackled with Xaranti spines as her fine-boned face. Her eyes were black and bulging and her back had split open to produce the usual bristling mass of Xaranti legs. Moreover, she was hunched over as if her spine was arching, and her shoulders were large and knuckly with excess muscle. When she opened her mouth to hiss, Tegan noticed she was still wearing lipstick.

'Hang on!' Mike Yates yelled and slammed on his brakes. The hybrid scrambling for purchase on the roof catapulted off, landing on the road in a tangle of human and alien limbs. The one which was standing above Tegan, swiftly getting its bearings and readying itself to spring, actually fell forwards towards her. Tegan, still crouched beside the oblivious Doctor, still clinging to one of the truck's metal ribs, screamed and closed her eyes as she twisted her head aside, the gun in her hand forgotten. She sensed the hybrid's presence above her, smelled its dark, rotten-fish smell, then something banged painfully into her outstretched leg. Next instant she was aware of the wind of something swooping past her, followed almost simultaneously by the thump of a heavy and relatively soft object impacting with a hard surface.

She opened her eyes. Although the rotten-fish smell still lingered, the Xaranti hybrid was gone. Tegan looked over the side of the truck and saw it sprawled in the road, already struggling to stand. Before it could do so, the truck moved forward again, picking up speed as quickly as it was able, and Tegan looked away, concentrating instead on holding on. Within seconds the hybrids were too far behind them to launch a further assault, leaving Tegan with a lasting impression of the female hybrid's striking blonde hair streaming behind it, flashing white in the sun, as it climbed to its feet.

The hospital was some five miles away from the

concentration of streets which crammed themselves as close as possible to the sea. In these more salubrious surroundings, the presence of Xaranti seemed non-existent. Nevertheless their influence was clearly felt; it was obvious they had been here and moved on, drawn like lemmings, perhaps, to the sea. Every so often Tegan would see a body sprawled on a road or pavement, or perhaps lying on a neatly-clipped front lawn or gravelled driveway. At one point she saw a man lying on the ground, still gripping the lead of his dead Alsatian; both owner and dog had been eviscerated. The eerie silence that accompanied these appalling sights seemed more sinister than the presence of the Xaranti themselves. Tegan clutched Mike Yates's gun nervously, once or twice even found herself using it to scratch absently at the worsening itch across her chest and shoulders.

It had been Mike's idea to take the Doctor to the hospital where Charlotte and her mother were under observation. He had thought it would be a safe haven for the time being, well away from the point of conflict, but the extent of the hybrids' sudden and violent emergence had taken them both by surprise. Now they were sticking to their original plan simply for want of a better one. If when they got there the hospital seemed too dangerous, Tegan supposed they would move yet further afield, to a place where the Doctor's condition could be assessed and perhaps treated, where he might be given time to recover.

As usual, their reliance on the Doctor to sort things out made Tegan nervous. One day – even today, perhaps – he might not be there for them to rely on and then what would they do?

Once again, she found herself scratching the rash that was now inching down her arm. She was all too aware what it signified and its creeping progress both angered and frightened her. More frightening still, was the way the infection was invading her thought-processes. Her mind kept phasing out like an unstable radio signal for a few seconds at a time, and she knew all too well that as the hours wore on, the tighter the Xaranti hold on her would become.

It was after re-emerging from one such period of blankness that Tegan looked wildly around her and realised she recognised the neighbourhood they were travelling through. Gripped by a sense of urgency, she rapped on the back of the driver's cab.

Mike leaned his head part-way out of the side window. 'Hello.'

'Mike,' she said, 'can I ask you a favour?'

'Ask away,' he replied magnanimously.

'I have a friend who lives near here. No more than a couple of streets away. He was taken ill earlier today. Do you think we could check up on him?'

There was a pause, then Mike said doubtfully, 'I'm not sure that's wise, Tegan.'

Tegan felt a flash of anger, the result of the Xaranti infection inside her, which she managed to suppress. 'Please, Mike, I'm really worried about him. He...' She had been about to say, *He means a lot to me*, but was afraid that giving voice to such a level of commitment might make her more vulnerable than she wanted to be. 'He lives on his own,' she said after a pause. 'He doesn't have anyone to look after him.'

She heard Mike sigh, then reluctantly say, 'All right, we'll have a quick look. You'd better tell me where to go.'

Soon they were pulling up in front of Andy Weathers's pleasant suburban house. The leafy street was quiet, the red-brick semis drowsing in the summer sunshine. Mike waited a moment before turning off the engine. Another pause before he got out of the driver's cab and walked round to lean on the side of the truck.

'I'll go in,' he said. 'You sit behind the wheel. If you see anything you don't like the look of, anything at all, drive away, don't worry about me.' He held out his hand. 'I'd better take my gun. What's your friend's name?'

'Andy,' said Tegan, 'Andy Weathers. He's a policeman.' She gave Mike the gun that she'd been clutching for so long that her hand felt cold and strange without it.

'OK,' said Mike, 'I'll be three minutes at the most. Remember, if you see anything at all that makes you suspicious –'

'I know,' Tegan tried not to snap, 'drive away. Don't wait.'

Mike gave her a brief, reassuring smile, then turned and walked up the short driveway. It wasn't until he was reaching out for the doorknob that he realised the door was slightly ajar. Caution tightened his grip on his gun and he listened at the door for a moment.

Before he could open it, Mike heard a shrill scream of terror, abruptly cut off. It came from next door, beyond a low wooden fence. Mike glanced up and noticed out of the corner of his eye that Tegan had opened the door of the truck and extended one foot to the pavement.

'Stay with the Doctor!' he snapped and jumped over the fence.

This front door was closed and locked, but four savage kicks encouraged it to yield with a splintering of wood. The right hand side of the hallway in front of Mike as he entered became a staircase; the left hand wall contained two closed doors. A third door stood open at the end of the corridor to reveal a split level kitchen made ethereal by a white glare of sunlight filling the window above the sink. Levelling his gun at face height, Mike pushed open the first door with his foot and entered swiftly.

There were bookcases full of Reader's Digest publications, a long dining table stacked with knitting patterns, and a piano. Mike's gaze swept the room and he retreated.

He entered the next room just as quickly and found himself in a lounge with a draylon suite and French windows. Just beyond the oblong of light flooding in through the windows was what he was looking for. A Xaranti hybrid, its back bulging and squirming, was pinning a middle-aged woman to the floor by her throat. The hybrid, a man close to his own age, was grinning and drooling, evidently taking great pleasure in choking the life out of its victim. The woman's tongue and eyes were bulging out of her purpling face and she was scrabbling ineffectually at the hand clamped around her windpipe. Her feet drummed on the carpet as her oxygen-starved limbs spasmed.

Without hesitation, Mike aimed his gun and fired. Just as he squeezed the trigger, the hybrid sprang towards him, swooping low as it did so. The bullet passed over its shoulder and smashed a hole through the French windows. The hybrid collided with Mike's legs, sending him staggering back against the wall.

Mike knew how important it was to stay on his feet. As he bounced back from the wall, the hybrid was rolling over. It was too close now for him to use his gun, it would spring to its feet and close the distance between them before he could even get the weapon levelled. Deciding, therefore, that discretion was the better part of valour, Mike turned and fled.

The hybrid came after him, which was what Mike had expected and wanted. If it had got back to finish off the woman, he would have felt honour-bound to turn and confront it again. All the same, being pursued by a ravening psychotic predator was not a pleasant experience. Mike ran as he had never run before, expecting to feel the weight of the creature slam into his back with each pounding step.

'Start the engine!' he screamed at Tegan, seeing her peering out of the truck at him as soon as he burst out of the house. He saw her face change from surprise to shock as she recognised the thing chasing him – or at least who it had once been. *'Do it now!'* he yelled.

She started the engine. 'Drive!' Mike shouted. 'Drive! Drive!'

If she hesitated they would probably all be dead. He was thankful, therefore, to see the truck pull away from the kerb almost immediately. Mike leaped off the kerb and pounded after it. The truck was doing maybe ten miles an hour when he launched himself at the tailgate. He grabbed it with both hands, ignored a splinter that slid into the ball of his thumb, and hauled himself up and over.

He was lying in a sprawl next to the Doctor's feet, gasping and congratulating himself on his timing, when he heard something thump against the tailgate. Looking up, he saw two hands curled over the top of the wooden flap, a face with tar-black eyes and mouth twisted in a bestial snarl rising between them.

With frightening speed and agility, the hybrid slid its upper body over the tailgate and grabbed Mike's ankle. Its grip was brutally strong, and instantly Mike read its intentions from the glee of anticipation on its face. It meant to twist his foot and break his ankle, and Mike had no doubt that it could do it too. Imbued with the savage strength of the Xaranti, Tegan's former friend could snap his bones as easily as he could have snapped the stick of celery pinned to the Doctor's lapel.

Instinctively Mike whipped up his gun and pulled the trigger. This time the bullet didn't miss. It struck the top of the hybrid's head, sheared it off and scattered it across the road in the truck's wake.

For one terrible moment the hybrid still clung to Mike's foot. Then the grip slackened and the creature tumbled back into the road, arms spread like a horizontal crucifixion.

Tegan stopped the vehicle in the middle of the road and Mike heard her sobbing bitterly. He jumped down from the back of the truck and opened the driver's cab door. She was slumped with her face in her hands as if trying to prevent her near-hysteria from seeping out.

'I'm sorry,' said Mike, 'I didn't want to kill him. I wouldn't have if it hadn't been him or me.'

Tegan didn't answer, didn't even acknowledge him. At least not until he touched her arm, whereupon she wrenched her hands away from her face and snarled, 'Don't you dare!'

The sea boiled and churned, waves crashing on to the deserted beach as if heralding a storm. A hundred feet from the shore, a dark patch appeared on the blue skin of the sea, like a shadow beneath the surface. The patch inched closer to the shore, growing larger and darker as it came. When it had halved the distance between the place it had first appeared and the blood-stained sand it broke the surface.

The Morok battle cruiser, its rusty, barnacled hull rearing up from the waves, was an eminently adaptable ship. It was designed to transform itself to suit whatever planetary conditions presented themselves. It was thanks largely to ships like this that the Moroks would eventually extend their seven-hundred year empire across the nine galaxies. This particular vessel, however, would no longer form any part of their battle fleet, its crew having long since transformed to swell the ranks of its Xaranti invaders.

When the battle cruiser had reached shallow enough waters, it retracted its long submarine-like snout, which had streamlined it to allow easier access through the deeps, drew in its powerful propellers, and extended tank-like caterpillar tracks, which gripped the sea bad and hauled it clanking and roaring on to the sand. On dry land it sat for a while, like some vast behemoth acclimatising itself to its new surroundings. Water streamed from its battle-scarred hull; its prow – if such a shapeless, ugly-looking craft as this could be said to have a prow – peeked over the sea-wall at the promenade.

Suddenly there was a tumultuous grating sound, and a number of doors at ground level slid slowly open, extending ramps that clanged down on to the sand. For a moment the openings contained only darkness, and then the black, bristling bodies of fully-grown Xaranti began to emerge into the light, like ants from a nest.

'It looks deserted,' Mike said.

It was the first time either of them had spoken since Tegan had spurned his attempts to console her after the death of Andy Weathers. She had moved across to the passenger seat and turned her back on him, using her hand as a cushion between her face and the window. Her shoulders had heaved as she sobbed silently. It was clear she was no longer in any fit state to drive. Mike had hesitated over suggesting that she sit in the back with the Doctor again, and in the end had decided that the Doctor would be OK. Around here they'd see trouble coming from far enough away for Mike to provide him with any protection he might need. Besides, Tegan with a gun in her hand while in this state of mind was not a good idea, especially now that he'd noticed she was beginning to scratch her shoulders and arms more and more.

Tegan did not respond to his comment, merely stared dully through the windscreen, her eyes pink as if stained by their red rims. The hospital car park was three-quarters full, but there was no sign of life either out here or at any of the building's many windows.

Mike stopped outside the open gates and glanced at Tegan. 'I didn't *want* to kill your friend, you know, Tegan,' he said again, 'but I had to. If I hadn't he would have killed me, and then the Doctor, and then probably you too.'

Tegan said in a low, bitter voice, 'Don't you think I know that?'

'I don't know. Do you?'

She swung round suddenly, glaring at him. 'Of course I do. I'm not stupid!'

'I never suggested you were,' he said gently. 'It's just that… well, if we're going to get through this, we've got to work together. We've got to know we can rely on one another.'

She gave a snort too mirthless to be termed laughter. 'You can't rely on me. I'm changing into one of those things. Haven't you noticed?'

'Yes, I have noticed. But you're still in the early stages. You'll be OK for a while yet, won't you?'

She shrugged. 'I think so. I hope so. I keep having these… these funny thoughts.'

'Funny thoughts?' he prompted.

'Insights, I guess you'd call them. I seem to know things without knowing *how* I know them. It's like… like I'm tapping into their minds… into *its* mind.' She shuddered. 'It's horrible.'

'What kinds of things?' Mike asked.

'Well, for instance… I know that… that multiplying and expanding is all important to them.'

'You make them sound like fat maths teachers,' said Mike, then saw her face. 'Sorry. Just trying to lighten the mood.'

'I know that a mature Xaranti would always infect you rather than kill you – unless you were unusable, of course.'

'Unusable?'

'Old, crippled, infirm,' said Tegan, her face deadpan, hand straying to the itch on her shoulder again.

'A lot of the dead people we've seen today weren't old or crippled or infirm,' Mike pointed out.

'They weren't killed by mature Xaranti.'

'What's the difference?'

'Inferior races in the mid-stage of transformation can't cope with all the Xaranti energy rushing through them, so they need an outlet for their aggression.'

'Inferior?' Mike exclaimed.

Tegan looked glassy-eyed, as if she'd been awake too long or was under the effect of a strong sedative. 'What?'

'You said inferior.'

'Did I?' She looked confused. 'I meant…' Then she seemed to snap out of it. 'Oh God, it's getting worse.'

'Are you all right?' Mike asked diffidently.

Her eyes flashed. 'Of course I'm not bloody all right!' Then, abruptly, her face crumbled, anger sliding into fear. 'I'm so scared.'

Cautiously he reached for her, and this time she leaned into him, allowed him to hold her. She felt hot, as if she had a fever.

'Hey,' Mike said gently, 'come on. Don't give up hope yet. Any minute now the Doctor'll pop awake and come up with some brilliant solution. You'll see.'

The smile he had hoped his words might raise from her failed to appear. Instead, her voice barely a whisper, she said, 'A while ago, there was this… this creature called the Mara. It took over my mind, made me do evil things. It filled my head with rage and hate. It was awful. I don't think I could ever go through anything like that again.'

'You won't have to,' Mike replied.

She said nothing for a moment, then unfolded herself from his embrace and sat up. 'This isn't getting us anywhere, is it?' she said, 'I ought to tell you what else I know while I still can. It might come in useful later.'

He ignored the doubt in her voice and said lightly, 'Forewarned is forearmed. Fire away.'

'The Xaranti affect different people in different ways, like any normal disease. Some show the symptoms quickly, some hold out for a lot longer. Except that in the last few hours, the whole process has been speeded up. It's as if… as if a switch has been thrown.'

'What kind of switch?' asked Mike.

Tegan thought for a moment. 'A telepathic one.'

'You mean… you mean someone is controlling this infection by thought?'

'Not some*one*,' said Tegan.

'Some*thing* then?'

Tegan's face creased with the effort of trying to express in words the half-formed impressions that flashed sporadically into her mind. 'The Xaranti creatures have no name for it. It controls them. It *is* the Xaranti. The creatures are its… its limbs. Its weapons.'

'How long have we got?' asked Mike. 'How long before everyone in this country is either dead or has turned into one of those things?'

Almost casually Tegan said, 'A week.'

'And what about you? And the Brigadier? And the Doctor?'

Again, that glassy-eyed stare, that dead-pan expression. 'A few hours.'

Mike sighed. A few hours. Which meant that every minute that ticked by was another nail banged into the coffin of the planet. And what was he doing about it? Driving around aimlessly, hoping that the unconscious man in the back would suddenly spring to life and come up with something that would get them out of this unholy mess.

He had never felt so useless. For a while now he had been asking tough questions of himself and his life, had been wondering whether in fact he made any difference at all. His whole existence had been centred around weapons and violence for so long that the real, fundamental issues had been lost somewhere along the way. He believed in peace, *had* believed – or at least had managed to convince himself – that UNIT was in essence a peace-keeping force. But how could you possibly maintain peace with guns and tanks and bombs? All right, so Daleks and Autons and the like wouldn't give a hoot about petitions and marches and protest songs, but surely there must be some other way, some other option to consider?

'We – *they* – want the Doctor,' Tegan said suddenly.

'What?'

Her eyes were wide as if she'd been struck by a sudden realisation. 'It's their overriding imperative. They know all about him from looking into the minds of his friends. They know everything he's done from the Brigadier and Sergeant Benton and anyone else from UNIT who's had contact with him.' She looked momentarily afraid to go on. 'Soon they'll find him through me. I'll lead them to him. I won't be able to help it.'

'We'd better move quickly then, hadn't we?' Mike replied decisively. 'Get him into hiding.'

'Maybe you should just leave me behind,' Tegan said.

Mike shook his head. 'No chance. You're coming with us. I'm not leaving you out here to fend for yourself.'

'Promise me one thing then,' she said.

'What?'

'If I get... uncontrollable... promise me you'll shoot me.'

Mike said nothing for a moment, then he smiled stiffly and squeezed her hand. 'I promise I'll do whatever I have to.' He put the truck into gear and rolled down into the car park.

There was an ambulance parked askew by the main doors. It was only when they got closer that they saw the driver's side window had been smashed and that the top half of a fat man in a paramedic's uniform was hanging out of it, arms dangling and hands outstretched as if trying to reclaim the blood that had run down the side of the vehicle in rivulets and pooled on the tarmac below.

'Cancer,' Tegan said bluntly.

'Pardon?'

'He was killed because he was no use. He had cancer of the colon. We can sense it by –' She stopped abruptly, suddenly aware of what she was saying. Looking at Mike fearfully she wailed, 'I don't want to know these things! I don't want them in my head!'

Mike raised his hands to calm her. 'Just keep fighting it, Tegan. It's all you can do.' He gave her a moment to calm down, then continued, 'I'm going to have to go in there. Do you feel able to cope with sitting behind the wheel again?'

She scratched at a point just below her collarbone, then made herself stop. A small shudder passed through her before she nodded. 'Yes, I'll be fine.'

'Are you sure?'

'I'm sure.'

'Ok. I'll only be a few minutes. I just want to see how the land lies before we take the Doctor in.' He paused for a moment. 'You know what to do –'

'I'll drive away if I see anything suspicious.'

'Good. Oh, and honk your horn too if you can. At least it'll let me know there's something going on.'

He got out of the truck and Tegan moved across to take his place behind the wheel. He walked up to the hospital's main double doors, gun poised. The sun was hurling reflections of itself back at him from the glass panels, masking what lay beyond them until he shoved them open and entered Reception. There was a semi-circular desk to his left, rows of chairs back-to-back, as if someone had set them up for a game of Musical Chairs, to his right. There were bodies on the floor – Mike counted seven of them – all of them lying in pools of blood. Despite the terrible violence that had taken place here, the building was silent now. Either the Xaranti had moved on, or they were lying in wait somewhere.

Going by what Tegan had said, could the hybrids really be that cunning, that restrained? Perhaps if they knew he had the Doctor with him they could be. Perhaps they were receiving orders from on high that were overriding their natural tendencies. He stood for a moment, undecided, though in truth his options were simple. Either he could get back in the truck and drive yet further afield, which meant the loss of more precious time and more ground to cover by returning if the Doctor woke up and could somehow set matters straight; or he could risk bringing the Doctor in here and try to find someone who could treat his wounds or have a go at doing so himself.

'No contest,' Mike murmured, and crossed to the body of an elderly man who had been bludgeoned to death with a desk lamp. The man had been sitting in a wheelchair, which had been tipped over as he had been knocked sideways. He was now lying on the floor, the lamp beside his shattered head caked with blood and hair.

Mike holstered his gun and lifted up the wheelchair, grimacing at the *schlupp* sound it made as it disengaged itself from the pool of partly congealed blood in which it had been lying. He took a handkerchief from his pocket and used it to wipe off as much of the blood as he could.

Tegan was peering out through the windscreen when he wheeled the chair outside. As he passed her window he noticed that she was gripping the steering wheel so tightly that her knuckles were white as bone. Her gaze followed his progress and she licked her lips, but her face was otherwise expressionless. Smiling to compensate for the fact that she wasn't, Mike said, 'Tegan, would you mind giving me a hand with the Doctor?'

She blinked and nodded. Her voice sounded strained as she said, 'Of course.'

The Doctor didn't stir as Tegan lifted up his legs and Mike sat him up then grabbed him beneath the armpits. Mike kept a look out as they transferred him into the chair, acutely aware that for the few minutes his hands were full the three of them were extremely vulnerable. Finally, the Doctor was installed, his head lolling, blond fringe flopping over his face. Mike drew out his gun with relief as Tegan wheeled the Doctor towards the main doors.

'It's not very pretty in there,' he warned her as he pushed the doors open. 'There are bodies.'

She shrugged. 'I've seen bodies before.'

He hesitated a moment longer. 'Are you quite sure you want to go through with this?'

The indifference on her face worried him, but at least there was still a residue of bitterness in her voice. 'Do we have a choice?'

Neither of them said anything as they wheeled the Doctor through the slaughterhouse that had been the hospital's reception area. They proceeded slowly, cautiously, listening hard for the slightest indication of habitation. Everywhere was the same: bodies lay in the corridors in grotesquely twisted positions, most of them exhibiting appalling injuries. There was blood on the floor and up the walls – but thankfully there was no sign of the perpetrators of this violence.

The wards were the worst. Many of the patients had been slaughtered in their beds, the juxtaposition of bright red blood and pristine white sheets like a blow to the system. Mike had seen many people die in his time with UNIT, and to some extent had become inured to the physical shock of it, but the way in which the old and the frail and the sick had been systematically massacred here disgusted and enraged him.

He glanced at Tegan to see how she was taking it all, and was both relieved and disturbed to see the expression, or lack of it, on her face. It was as if a shutter had clanged down behind her eyes. Mike couldn't be sure whether this was because the shock had been too much for her and her mind had decided to draw a veil over itself for a while, or whether the Xaranti infection galloping through her system was deadening her emotions.

'Are you OK?' he asked her, and for a moment thought she hadn't heard him.

Then her eyes flickered in his direction and she said, 'These subjects were unsuitable for Xaranti impregnation. Others have been taken, but these were… unsuitable.'

Her voice trailed off. Mike looked at her for a moment. 'Yes, I gathered that.' He allowed his gaze to roam once more around the ward. If all the beds had been occupied, around half of the patients were missing. He pictured those patients rising from their beds, Xaranti spines and legs erupting from their bodies even as they murdered their fellow patients. He thought of Charlotte up on the fifth floor, and of the foetus which had been clinging to life inside her. A sharp, unyielding block of ice seemed to have taken up residence in his stomach. Instinct made him want to rush out to the lift and jab the fifth floor button to find out the truth as quickly as possible, but he knew he had to do this thing properly, methodically, systematically.

The second and third floors were the same as the first, but the fourth floor delivered a surprise. The wards here were empty, and had been abandoned in a hurry, judging by the way books, meals and personal belongings had been discarded. Perhaps more tellingly, leads had been left dangling from various machines that had evidently been disconnected from patients' bodies.

'What's happened here?' he said, more to himself than to Tegan. But she answered, her voice a mumble, her eyes gazing into the middle distance.

'We took them by surprise. There was so much anger in us. We needed to kill. It was good. Made us feel so good. But we didn't kill them all. We… we wouldn't let ourselves kill them all. We took some. They became us. But the killing. It stopped us hurting. For a little while.'

The block of ice in his stomach extended tendrils along his

limbs and up his back. His instinct was to shake Tegan out of her fugue, but his rationale urged him to use the situation to his advantage, to glean as much information as he could.

'Who are *we*?' he asked gently.

'We are Xaranti,' she replied.

'What happened to the other people in the hospital? The ones who escaped. Where did they go?'

Her eyes widened a little. 'They went up. They got away from us. We couldn't catch them.'

'Up?' Mike said. 'Up where?'

'To the top.'

'The top of the building?'

'Yes.'

'What's up there?'

Her face remained deadpan and he thought she'd switched off. Then she said, 'We couldn't get through. There were barriers.'

Mike pondered for a moment. It seemed his initial theory that half the patients had been killed by the others had been wrong. Perhaps part of the Xaranti plan had been to keep those infected out of hospital – and indeed away from other environments and situations where their affliction may have been discovered – until a stranglehold had been established on the town. Which meant that the missing patients had been infected during, not before, the Xaranti attack.

'Tegan,' he said now, his voice quiet but intense, 'Tegan, can you hear me?'

She stared at him, a tiny frown appearing, her eyes swirling with confusion.

'You are Tegan Jovanka,' Mike said firmly. 'You are Tegan Jovanka and an alien force is trying to take over your mind. But you're strong, Tegan. You can fight it. Fight it, Tegan.'

The frown became a wince of pain. Tegan snatched her hands from the wheelchair grips as if they had become hot and rubbed at her forehead as though trying to erase a stain from her skin – or from beneath it.

'I am... we are... no, *I* am Tegan,' she gasped. Her eyes crinkled into slits and her mouth stretched wide to reveal her clenched teeth. She gave a little scream and fell forward. Mike caught her smartly. She opened her eyes and looked at him, her face etched with fear and dismay.

'Are you all right?' he asked softly.

Her face crumpled and she began to sob, clutching at him. 'So scared,' she whimpered. 'I don't want... this to... happen to me again.'

'I know,' Mike said, 'I know.' He held her until her sobs had subsided. At last he said, 'Are you ready to go on?'

'Where?'

'To the top of the building. That's where everyone is.'

'How do you know?'

'You told me. When you were... when you had your funny turn. It's like you'd clicked in to their thinking again for a minute.'

She was silent, finding the information unpalatable. Finally she said, 'I'm still useful for something then, at least.'

He wasn't sure how to reply, so he gave her a squeeze instead. They wheeled the Doctor out of the ward and across to the lifts. The topmost button was 12, which Mike pressed. As the lift approached their destination he raised his gun, pointing it at the opening doors.

The corridor ahead was as featureless as the rest they had seen. It was silent and deserted, too. Mike stepped out first, checking around, then motioned for Tegan to follow with the Doctor. To their left, at the end of the corridor, were the stairs that led down to each of the lower floors. To their right, the corridor was foreshortened by a huge pair of vault-like doors. In large red stencilled letters on the doors were the words:

208

RESEARCH AND DEVELOPMENT UNIT
STRICTLY LIMITED ACCESS
AUTHORISED PERSONNEL ONLY

Beside the door was a touch-button panel, with numbers from 0 to 9.

'Pretty snazzy for the seventies,' Tegan said, back to her old self for the time being, although she sounded tired.

Mike moved forward and banged on the metal doors with the butt of his gun. 'Hey!' he shouted. 'Hey, is anyone in there?'

There was no reply. Mike continued to thump the door and shout for the next half-minute. Tegan watched him anxiously and scratched at her arms. The Doctor slept on despite the noise.

At last a voice on the other side, sounding no more than the thickness of the doors away, said, 'Who are you?'

Mike raised his eyebrows at Tegan with an expression not quite of triumph and shouted, 'My name is Captain Michael Yates. I'm an army officer who has been called in to deal with the current crisis. I'm accompanied by two civilians, one of whom is severely injured and in need of medical attention.'

There was a pause, then the voice said fearfully, 'How did you know we were here?'

'We worked it out,' Mike replied slickly. 'After seeing the carnage on the first three floors we realised that the only way you could have gone to escape was up. It didn't need a genius to see that this was the only viable option.'

There was an even longer pause this time, then the voice said, 'Stand back. I want to see you on the cameras.'

Mike glanced up and saw two cameras affixed to the ceiling above his head. He stepped back so he was looking directly into their lenses and smiled.

'You don't look like a soldier,' the voice said suspiciously.

'I was employed as an advance guard, to check out the

terrain. That's why I'm in civvies,' Mike explained.

'Have you got any proof?' the voice asked.

Mike reached into the back pocket of his cords and located his UNIT pass, which he held up to the right-hand camera.

'UNIT? What's that?'

'United Nations Intelligence Taskforce. Special peace-keeping force. Affiliated to the British Army. All the information's there if you want to read it.'

The pause was so long this time that Mike thought his credentials had been rejected. Then the voice was back, and saying reluctantly, 'All right, you can come in.'

Turlough was not sure how long he had been sitting against the bedroom wall when he heard the sound outside in the corridor. He stiffened, clutching his coathanger to him, drawing his knees up tighter under his chin.

The sound had been like the scuff of movement that someone who was trying to be stealthy might make. Turlough tilted his head a little as if that might enable him to hear better – and almost leaped out of his skin when someone rapped loudly on his door.

He cringed, praying that whoever was out there was banging on doors at random and would move on if he failed to respond. There was silence for a moment, then a voice he recognised said, 'We know you're in there, son.'

It was the voice of the big, burly soldier, the Doctor's friend: Sergeant Benton. Still Turlough said nothing, but looked around panic-stricken, wondering where he could hide, how he could possibly escape.

A second voice replaced the first, this one more clipped, authoritative; the voice of the Brigadier.

'Be reasonable, lad,' he said, sounding nothing but reasonable himself. 'It's not you we want, it's the Doctor. We just want you to take us to his TARDIS.'

They must have missed it at the fun-fair, Turlough realised. If his plight hadn't been so desperate he would have found that funny. He wondered fleetingly whether he might be able to speak to the Brigadier, reason with him. The man might be infected, but he didn't sound too far gone – though it might well have been the Xaranti themselves who were *allowing* the Brigadier to sound reasonable.

Yes, perhaps that was it. Perhaps the present approach was simply a ploy to lull him into a false sense of security. Or even to get him to give himself away, because, after all, they couldn't know for certain he was in here. They could only be guessing that he was. They had probably been looking for him all over the place. If he stayed quiet they would probably go away.

Then the Brigadier said, 'All right, young man, be it on your own head.'

There was a loud bang, and before Turlough realised what was happening a chunk of wall exploded, not two feet from his left ear. He stared at it for a moment, dumbfounded, then glanced back through the barricade of furniture piled atop his bed and spotted a ragged hole in the door, beside the lock.

They were shooting their way in – and they weren't too worried who was on the other side. Discarding the coat hanger, Turlough scrambled to his feet and ran to the window. He looked out and to his horror saw two fully-grown Xaranti patrolling the streets below.

He ducked instinctively as a second shot blasted through the door and reduced part of the barricade to flying matchwood. Frantically he loosened the catch on the window, flung it open and stuck his head out. There was no way down, but if he could climb up on to the roof he might be able to make his way across it to the building next door.

As a third gun-blast turned more of his barricade to splinters, Turlough grasped the sides of the window frame and stepped up on to the sill.

* * *

Walking through the vault-like doors, Mike and Tegan found themselves in a small vestibule furnished with a semi-circular desk like the one in Reception. On brackets on either side of the doors were a pair of small black- and-white TV screens depicting the now-empty corridor outside.

Waiting for them just inside was a large black man dressed in the blue-grey uniform of a hospital orderly. His face was shiny with sweat and his eyes were wide and wary. As soon as they were inside, he heaved the doors shut again and locked them with bolts and a metal locking-bar as thick as a man's wrist.

'Thanks for this,' Mike said, holstering his gun. 'It's pretty hairy out there.'

'Don't I know it?' said the man and squinted at them suspiciously. 'How did you manage to get through all them... all them *things*?'

'There are none out there now,' said Mike. 'I think they must have all headed down to the sea. We've got a truck, and I've got a gun. We had a few bad moments, but we managed to make it through OK.'

'What's wrong with your friend?' the black man asked, looking at the Doctor slumped in the wheelchair.

'That was one of our bad moments,' said Mike. 'We were attacked. He was wounded. I'm Mike Yates by the way, this is Tegan Jovanka, and the chap having a snooze there is the Doctor.'

He thrust out a hand, which the man cautiously shook.

'Doctors are something we're not short of here,' the man said. 'I'm Max Butler.'

'So what happened here, Max?' asked Mike. 'You were attacked, I take it?'

'From all sides. I've never seen anything like it. Those freaks had taken out two floors before we even knew what was happening. A bunch of us managed to round up the patients

212

from the fourth floor and bring them here.' He shook his head, sending droplets of sweat flying in all directions. 'We're safe enough. Not even a tank could get through those doors. But it's a bad situation. A lot of the patients need special care – medication and stuff. We've got mothers with new-born babies here. The babies that were in the incubation unit we had to leave. One of the nurses stayed with 'em. The doors there aren't as strong as they are here, but at least they can be locked. I just hope to God those freaks didn't break in there and find 'em all.'

'We saw no evidence of it,' said Mike. 'And as I said, it's quiet out there now. You'd be safe going down to check on things and to get what you need. I'll go with you if you like.'

Max nodded. 'Thanks. But let's sort your friend out first.' He flipped a thumb at the doors. 'Any idea where those things out there came from?'

Mike glanced meaningfully at Tegan, hoping she would still have enough of her wits about her to realise that they would have to be careful what they said here. 'They're just people,' he said casually. 'They're carrying an infection which alters them physically and mentally.'

Max looked dubious. 'It's not like any infection I've ever seen before.'

'It's a new strain,' Mike said vaguely. 'We've got experts working on a cure for it right now.'

Max looked at him for a moment longer, then shrugged. 'If you say so. Come on, let's see to your friend.'

He led them out of the vestibule and into a corridor whose widely-spaced doors were linked by viewing windows. The windows looked into medical research laboratories, most of which contained equipment and apparatus whose purpose Mike could only guess at.

'How many people have you got up here?' Mike asked.

Max raised his eyebrows as he thought about it. 'I'd say

around two hundred.'

Mike whistled as Max turned right at the end of the corridor and pointed ahead. 'There's a kitchen and dormitory along here. A real home from home. It's where the doctors sleep when they haven't got time to go home, when they've got experiments and stuff they need to keep an eye on. That's where everybody is.'

A murmur of conversation drifted to meet them as they drew closer. They passed several more labs, these ones full of people. Most of them were patients in dressing-gowns, who were standing or sitting around – talking, reading books and newspapers, playing cards, drinking tea. There was a kind of Blitz spirit in evidence, a sense of pulling together, of cheerfulness in adversity. If Mike had been wearing his uniform rather than his civvies, he had little doubt that many of the older men would have been saluting him as he passed by.

Max led them into the dormitory area, containing around a dozen beds, all of which were occupied by the more serious cases. Most of these patients were asleep, though several were groaning in pain. Some patients were lying on the floor between the beds, draped with spare blankets, heads propped by 'pillows' of bundled-up dressing-gowns and other articles of clothing. Others were sitting with their backs to the walls and their knees drawn up, looking dazed or shell-shocked.

Doctors, nurses and some of the more able patients were moving between the beds, offering care and comfort where they could. Mike spotted Charlotte sitting beside a cadaverous old man who was lying on the floor like a bundle of sticks wrapped in blue and white pyjamas. With one hand she was supporting his head as he raised it, and with the other she was holding a transparent plastic cup, from which he was taking small sips of water.

Mike wanted to call to her, but thought it inappropriate.

Instead he turned to Max and Tegan and held up a finger. 'One moment. I've just seen a friend of mine.'

He crossed to her and waited until the old man had finished drinking and Charlotte had lowered his head carefully back down to the floor. Then he said, 'Hello, Charlotte.'

She looked up, startled, and her face broke into a grin. 'Mike!' she exclaimed. 'What are you doing here?'

He gestured across to the Doctor slumped in the wheelchair, behind which stood Tegan looking tense. 'I've brought an injured friend here for treatment. The whole town is under attack.'

The grin slipped from her face. 'I know. What's happening to everyone, Mike? What's making them change like this? Like my dad did?'

'It's a long story,' Mike said, and quickly changed the subject to avoid having to tell it. 'How's the baby?'

Charlotte touched her stomach and glanced quickly around, evidently not wishing her pregnancy to become public knowledge. 'Fine, as far as I know.'

'And your mum? How's she?'

'Well, she's alive at least. She's over there.'

Mike looked across to where she was pointing and saw a woman sitting against the wall with her face in her hands, so still that he was not sure whether she was awake or asleep.

'Is she –' he began, but was interrupted by a blurted word from Max:

'Jesus!'

Mike turned and saw that whilst he had been talking to Charlotte a little group had gathered around the Doctor. As well as Tegan and Max, there was a doctor who looked young enough to be fresh out of med school and a nurse who looked old enough to be the young doctor's mother. It was immediately evident what had caused Max to react so vehemently. The young doctor had begun to remove the

215

makeshift dressing around the Doctor's wound in order to take a look at the damage, when the Doctor had abruptly woken up. His eyelids had parted to reveal eyes that were completely black.

Mike caught only a glimpse of them before the Doctor closed them again in a slow blink. When he re-opened them a moment later they had returned to normal. The damage had been done, however. Stumbling back a few paces, Max pointed a fat, rigid finger at the Doctor. Fresh sweat bursting from his cheeks, making them shine like mahogany, he cried, 'He's one of *them*!'

Before Max could say anything else, Mike strode forward and grabbed his arm, screening the Doctor from the others in the room.

'Keep your voice down. Do you want to upset *everyone*?' he hissed.

Max turned on him, furiously. 'You knew he was turning into one of them things! You knew it and you still brought him in here. You've put us all in danger.'

'This is probably the only man in the entire world who can help us get out of this mess,' Mike said calmly.

'But he's not a man any more. He's one of those freaks!'

'No, he isn't.'

'*Don't pull my cord, man!*' Max said. 'I saw his eyes. We all did.'

'Look at his eyes now,' Mike replied reasonably. 'They're fine. *He's* fine. There's nothing wrong with him.'

'Oh, I'm afraid there is,' the Doctor muttered.

Max and Mike stopped and stared at the Doctor as if he was a chimpanzee who had just displayed an astounding aptitude for human speech.

It was Mike who found his voice first. 'Are you... all right, Doctor?' he asked.

'Not entirely,' said the Doctor, and raised a hand in Max's

direction. 'The gentleman here is right. I'm metamorphosing.'

'See!' Max said, thrusting his chin aggressively at Mike. 'The guy admits it. We should never have let you in.'

Before Mike could respond, the Doctor said almost heartily 'Quite right. In fact, I suggest you let me out of here before I lose control and kill you all.'

Tegan, who had not spoken a word since they had entered the R and D unit, suddenly said in an anguished voice, 'You can't go, Doctor. We need you. You're our last hope.'

The Doctor flashed her a reassuring smile. 'Believe me, I'll serve you better on the outside.'

'They'll find you,' Mike said. 'There's too many of them. They'll use what's in your head and turn you into one of them.'

'That'll happen anyway if I stay here,' the Doctor said, and suddenly, to Mike's astonishment, he was holding Mike's gun in his hand, pointing it at his own head. 'Now,' he said almost cheerfully, 'are you going to let me out or do I have to kill myself so that I don't kill you all later?'

For every second of the three minutes it took Turlough to climb up on to the hotel roof, he was petrified. Petrified of being shot at; petrified of the hotel's old but stout metal drainpipe giving way; petrified that one of the fully grown Xaranti patrolling the streets below would spot him and scuttle up the wall after him like a spider.

The ledge below his window, along which he had shuffled to the drainpipe, had been just about wide enough, but old and a little crumbly. He side-stepped along it with his back to the sun-baked wall of the hotel, trying not to look down, trying not to rush, trying not to panic, and in the event probably doing all three.

When he reached the drainpipe, he swivelled at the hips, taking care to keep his feet firmly planted on the ledge, and grasped it gratefully with both hands. He would have liked to have rested there for a few moments, but he was afraid that if he stopped he might never start again. He was grateful that the drainpipe was sturdy and not one of the flimsy plastic variety that humans seemed to favour on their buildings in this time period. It was attached to the wall by stolid, chunky brackets which would serve as precarious foot- and hand-holds.

Turlough manoeuvred himself carefully round, his heart pumping fast as his left leg swung out over empty space before clanging against the pipe. He looked up to see how far he had to go, and immediately felt dizzy. The wisps of white cloud slipping beneath the horizon of the hotel roof gave him the impression that the building was toppling over. Turlough gripped the pipe even harder and squeezed his eyes tight shut for a moment, though he had seen enough to know that he had a distance of around twenty feet to climb.

It took him no more than half a minute, but it seemed like an eternity. When he finally reached the overhanging lip of the flat roof, his arms and legs were trembling and his body was drenched in sweat. This time he *did* have to rest in order to summon up the energy to haul himself over the ledge. Finally, first with one hand and then the other, he reached up, grasped the edge of the roof and pulled himself up.

There was an awful moment when he didn't think he was going to have the strength to do it, when his feet pedalled at empty air and his arms began to tremble with the effort. Somehow, though, simply through fear of what would happen if his strength *did* give way, he managed to scramble up and over.

For long seconds he lay there like a beached fish, gasping for air, relief washing through him. Sooner than he would have liked he scrambled to his feet and staggered across to the ledge that ran along the top of the side wall of the hotel.

The building next door was a Chinese restaurant called King

Prawn. The narrow alleyway ran between the two buildings, whose roofs were separated by a gap of no more than five feet. Ordinarily, this would have been a simple leap, but at this height, and given Turlough's current state, the task seemed altogether more daunting. All kinds of possible scenarios ran through his mind as he backed up in preparation for his run-up. He imagined himself slipping as he was about to leap and plunging head-first to the ground below; imagined himself falling short on the far side, scrabbling desperately for a handhold and clutching only empty air. Vertigo swept over him in a dizzying wave, and he had to squat down for a moment, squeeze his eyes shut and make himself take slow, deep breaths to calm his pounding heart. At length he opened his eyes again and slowly stood up. The day seemed piercingly bright and almost preternaturally quiet, with not even a gull's cry to puncture it. By contrast, the gap between the buildings looked as black as the deepest abyss.

Turlough knew that the longer he thought about it the less likely he was to make the jump, so he did the only thing possible: he began to run. The air slid past him, warm and somehow slick; he moved so swiftly that his feet seemed to skim across the roof's surface like a stone over water. He gritted his teeth as he neared the edge, his stomach coiling in on itself. Every instinct screamed at him to slow down, to stop, but he simply made himself run faster, knowing that if he gave in to his fear he was lost.

As he launched himself through the air, the gap between the buildings yawned like a vast black mouth. For an instant he felt like a piece of plankton caught in the downdraft of a fish's maw – then he was sprawling on the roof of the restaurant, having cleared the gap by a good three feet. His palms slid across the roof's gritty surface, but Turlough's relief far outweighed the sting of his skinned hands. He scrambled to his feet and ran towards what he had spotted from the roof of the Lombard – a raised skylight, the glass cloudy with grime.

The skylight had been locked with bolts from the inside, but the wooden frame was rotten with age. It took Turlough no more than fifteen seconds and three good kicks to break in. Lifting the skylight he saw a short drop on to a small, landing and a set of stairs leading down. A minute later he was at street level and hesitating about which way to go.

Straight ahead would take him through the main part of the restaurant and out the front door on to the main street. The opposite way would take him through what he assumed must be the kitchen, where he would hope to find a back door into somewhere narrower and quieter.

It was no contest. He headed towards the back of the building, and opened the door into the kitchen he expected to find. It was large, its stainless steel surfaces gleaming, though no amount of scrubbing could have masked the smell of rice and fish and cooking oil. The back door was green, heavily bolted and padlocked. Beside it and above a large sink was a window covered inside and out with wire mesh.

Turlough selected a large two-pronged implement normally used for skewering meat and set to work on the mesh. Constantly expecting to hear the thump of booted feet on the floors above, he worked feverishly. Several minutes of hacking and twisting later he tugged the mesh away from the frame. That done, he picked up a three-legged stool and smashed the glass of the window, wincing at the noise it made as it rebounded from the outer mesh and shattered into the sink below.

Using the skewer on the outer mesh was tricky as he had to push rather than pull it away from the frame. In the end he climbed into the sink, glass crunching beneath his feet, and kicked the mesh into submission. When he had created a large enough gap, he squeezed through, wincing at the jagged shards of glass still jutting from the window frame that scraped against his skin. He all but fell into the narrow street that the building backed on to, almost landing on the two-pronged skewer that he had decided to bring with him.

He climbed groggily to his feet, bleeding from a dozen stinging scratches, and looked around. There was no sign of either UNIT soldiers or Xaranti, which, only made him think that they were probably lying in wait somewhere. He had to find a place to hide until it was safe to emerge – if it ever would be.

Left would take him back down towards the promenade, so he decided to go right, despite the fact that it was the street in that direction, that bisected this one, that his hotel room overlooked. He only hoped that the two fully-grown Xaranti he had spotted prowling this street had moved on now; certainly they had been moving purposefully enough to have done so.

He moved forward cautiously, keeping close to the wall, shrinking back from the golden thread of sunlight that lay on the road and lapped over the edge of the pavement on his side. When he reached the intersection he poked his head round the corner and looked right and left, ready to turn tail and flee at the slightest movement. However the street, wider and more prominent than this one, was empty. As a right turn on this occasion would again have taken him down to the promenade, Turlough crossed the road, wincing as he stepped through the band of sunlight, and moved to the left.

He crept along from shop doorway to shop doorway, wondering whether he ought to duck into one of them and keep low or try to get as far away from Xaranti Central as he could. But how far away was that? How far did the aliens' influence extend? Was the ship that arrived in Tayborough Sands an isolated one or part of an invasion fleet?

He was still trying to decide what to do when he heard a scuttle of movement from the end of the street ahead of him.

He glimpsed two fully-grown Xaranti turning the corner and heading in his direction a split-second before throwing himself out of sight behind a parked car. Praying that they hadn't seen him and that the scraping, scuttling, clicking of their own bodies would mask his movements, Turlough dropped onto his stomach and crawled beneath the car. Gripping the meat skewer like a talisman, he drew in his legs and lay there in the shade, willing the Xaranti to pass by. If he got out of this one, he told himself, he would take no more risks, would duck into the next shop he could find that contained food and remain there until it was safe to come out.

He could see the Xaranti's spiny crablike legs rising and falling as they stalked closer to his hiding place. When they were almost parallel with the car, they separated, moving to flank the vehicle. Turlough prayed desperately that there was nothing sinister in the manoeuvre – and then the sweat on his body turned cold.

In unison, positioned one either side of the car, the Xaranti came to a halt.

At the entrance to the R and D unit the Doctor had exchanged the gun for the keys to the truck. He knew Mike could have tried to stop him them, or insisted on coming with him despite his protestations, but he didn't. He simply looked the Doctor in the eye, wished him luck and shook his hand.

The Doctor was grateful for Mike's intelligence, glad that it was not the Brigadier he was dealing with. Not that the Brigadier was stupid – on the contrary, he possessed a sharp mind and a quick, dry wit. However his old friend was ingrained with the gung-ho single-mindedness of many of the top military men the Doctor had encountered in his lives. Often the subtle approach advocated by the Doctor baffled and infuriated him, seemed to him to undermine everything he stood for.

Mike was different. He was a good soldier – brave and loyal, dependable and efficient and cool under pressure – but also sensitive and sensible, far-thinking but impressionable too.

The Doctor focused on the matter in hand: he needed to find a way of halting the Xaranti infection before it laid waste to the entire population of the planet.

As he stood in the lift which carried him down through the hospital, the Doctor wondered whether he had done the right thing in leaving Tegan behind. She was infected too, of course – though it would be some time yet before she actually became a danger to those in the R and D unit. The Doctor was hoping to have solved the Xaranti problem long before that moment arrived, though if he failed in his mission he would at least be consoled by the thought that Mike had his gun with which to both safeguard the uninfected and provide Tegan with a merciful release. Despite his guilt, the Doctor knew that taking Tegan with him would have been a bad idea. She – or anyone else for that matter – would have been more of a hindrance than a help.

He took out the square, grey object which was his remote link with the diagnostic programmes he had left running in the TARDIS and flipped open the lid. He pressed a button, then perused the columns of numbers and figures and formulaic symbols scrolling down the tiny screen.

He raised his eyebrows. 'Interesting,' he murmured, then snapped the lid shut and tucked it into his trouser pocket as the lift arrived at its destination.

He rocked backwards and forwards on his heels, hands clasped behind his back, as the doors opened. Despite appearances he was alert for the slightest sound or movement. However, the only sound was the buzzing of flies which had found their way into the hospital, attracted by the sprawled corpses in Reception. The Doctor set his face grimly as he strode through them to the main doors.

He could feel the infection inside him, tingling across his shoulders and chest and back, trying to gain a foothold in his mind. His shoulder wound ached intolerably, but at least it had been treated and properly dressed. That was one thing Mike Yates *had* insisted upon, and quite a crowd had gathered to watch the man who was pointing a gun at his own head being patched up by a young and nervous doctor. After selecting a few items from his coat pockets and transferring them into his trousers, the Doctor had left his ruined coat and sweater behind in the R and D unit (remarking to Tegan that if he didn't have spares in the TARDIS he would be writing a strongly-worded letter of complaint to the Xaranti government) and had strode to the exit, wearing his torn and blood-stained shirt, still holding Mike's gun to his head.

Outside he climbed into the UNIT truck and drove away from the hospital. As he passed through deserted streets he switched to automatic pilot, allowing the Xaranti part of him to lead him to where it wanted to go. Up until now his mind had withstood the siege that the infection had been conducting against it, but suddenly the Doctor lowered the drawbridge, withdrew his defences. The infection swept in, aggressive and triumphant, filling his mind with Xaranti thoughts.

The first phase of the Xaranti recruitment drive was complete, creating a wave of new Xaranti that had broken through and asserted their dominance. Now the infection was speeding up and the second wave would not be long in coming. The Doctor knew that the first wave had taken the unaffected population by surprise, that the new Xaranti had swept through them, killing and infecting, slaking their blood-lust whilst leaving no stone unturned in their search for new recruits. People had been taken in their homes, in their gardens, on the streets. High population centres – hospitals, supermarkets, factories – had been targeted and attacked *en masse.* In other areas of the country the attacks had been swift and invidious, creating ever-expanding clusters of new Xaranti. There was now a lull before the next storm, the streets (around here, at least) quiet because the newly infected, driven by their strange, new alien instincts, had retreated into darkness and solitude to gestate, metamorphosise.

Half a mile from the promenade the Doctor stopped the truck and got out. The new Xaranti, their work done for the time being, had congregated in this area, having felt an instinctive urge to be close to the force controlling their minds. To their queen. To Xaranti Prime. To the brains of the operation. There was no Xaranti word for it, only inadequate human equivalents. Understanding their instinct, the Doctor slipped through the streets, keeping close to the walls, hugging whatever shadows he could. He ducked from one shop doorway to the next, crouching behind parked cars and litter bins, listening and watching not only with his eyes and ears, but also with his mind.

His internal radar – ironically a gift from the Xaranti themselves – allowed him to remain undetected for some considerable time, but at last his luck ran out. The problem was that he was able to detect the presence of other Xaranti only at close-quarters – half a street away at most – which gave him little time to find a hiding place. On this occasion he sensed several Xaranti in the street to his right, heading his way, and so turned to run back the way he had come. As he ran, he realised – too late – that there were more Xaranti approaching from the other end of the street. He skidded to a halt just as this second group came around the corner and saw him.

There were four of them, three males and a female, all relatively young. They were in the mid-stage of transformation, their eyes black, their faces changing shape and bristling with spines, their Xaranti legs and altering musculature causing them to hunch over. Despite this, they moved swiftly, their leader – a shaggy-haired man in a now-ragged denim shirt – actually dropping on all fours to approach the Doctor. The Doctor took a step back, then thought better of it and drew himself up to his full height.

'Good afternoon,' he said.

The denim-shirted hybrid hissed at him, which prompted the others to do the same. All four moved in threateningly. The Doctor stood his ground, looked at them as imperiously as he could, and said, 'Don't you know who I am?'

As he asked the question, he mentally gathered up a sample of the Xaranti thought-patterns that were still roaming through his mind, mixed them with his own, and telepathically threw the whole bundle towards them. The leader flinched and blinked and the Doctor knew that the message had stuck.

The hybrid's mouth opened and in a slurred, guttural voice it said, 'Doctor.'

'That's right,' said the Doctor gently as if speaking to a nervous but potentially dangerous animal. 'I'm the Doctor and I'm one of you now. We are all Xaranti.'

Though he could feel the infection making inroads into his system, for the moment the Doctor was able to control it, to use it. He made his eyes go black simply by letting go, giving in to it for a moment. 'We are all Xaranti,' he repeated softly, 'and I'm on a very important mission. I'm going to see the queen.'

The four hybrids looked mesmerised for a moment, then the denim-shirted one shook his head like a dog with a flea in its ear.

'No,' he growled, the effort of talking apparently difficult for him. 'You... come... with... us...'

'I can't do that,' said the Doctor firmly. 'I'm going to see the queen. I've been *told* to see the queen. If you try to stop me, it will be bad for you.'

The Doctor could sense the hybrids' confusion. They understood that he was indeed Xaranti, and that the Xaranti were all one. However they were unaware of the orders he claimed to be following, knew only that *their* instructions were to find and capture him. The Doctor knew he was fortunate that he had run into this group and not into one which was more fully integrated into the Xaranti communal mind. Not only would those in a more advanced metamorphic state have been aware that he was lying, but they would also have been able to send a telepathic message to every other hybrid and fully-fledged Xaranti in the vicinity, detailing his whereabouts.

'You're confused,' the Doctor said gently, allowing a soothing telepathic pulse to accompany his words. 'Your minds are still clouded. You are not yet fully Xaranti. You still speak in a human voice.'

The Doctor was taking a gamble that the scintilla of human reason that remained in the hybrid's mind was still active enough to enable the creatures to understand his words, but no longer analytical enough to think them through. If it was, it would show the hybrids the loopholes in his argument – the fact that he himself was still in the very early stages of infection, for example, and thus presumably even more prone to confusion and misinterpretation than they were. He needn't have worried. Almost immediately he sensed the hybrids struggling with his arguments. He stepped forward and spread his arms, pressing home his advantage. 'The queen wants to see me. I'm going to her now. The only way you'll stop me is to kill me. So if you're not sure, kill me now, and face the consequences later.'

The female drew herself in and glanced nervously at her companions, her pink – still very human – tongue darting out

227

to lick her lips. The other hybrids hung back, their minds a stew of conflicting thoughts and emotions. The Doctor looked at the leader, keeping his face impassive, trying to project an air of authority not only with his demeanour and his unblinking stare, but also with the steady, uncluttered thought-waves he projected towards them.

The leader groaned and rose from all fours to his feet; it no longer seemed his natural state. He stretched out an arm, the hand blackening, gnarling, and he pointed towards the sea.

'You... go...' he said.

Hybrids, both military and civilian, spread out into the streets around the Lombard Hotel, looking for Turlough. The Brigadier, scratching his chest, feeling the Xaranti spines rasp against his clothing, walked beside Benton. Benton had taken a long time to succumb, but now that the infection had taken hold it was rampaging through his system. His face was red and mottled where the spines were lurking beneath the surface of his skin, preparing to break through, and even his back was a little more hunched than the Brigadier's, who himself had begun to feel a pleasurable tingling between his shoulder blades.

The Brigadier could not now understand why he had resisted the call of the Xaranti for so long. Trying to hang on to the disparate mess of his human thoughts had led only to fatigue and confusion. Finally allowing the Xaranti access had been like seeing the light, admitting a new and astonishing clarity into his life. He was born anew, felt a fresh and glorious future rising from the ashes of his past. He was Xaranti. They were all Xaranti. They were all one.

Despite their failure to apprehend the boy, and the fact that the Doctor was still at large, the Brigadier felt that their plans were moving inexorably forward, coming to fruition. The boy would be apprehended soon enough and he would lead them to the Doctor, or at least to the Doctor's TARDIS. With that in their possession it would only be a matter of time before the Doctor succumbed. And when that happened the Xaranti would be invincible. They would spread out across the stars, engulfing planets and populations. They would assimilate the Zygons into their number and any other species that dared to oppose them. And those races impervious to assimilation – the Daleks, the Cybermen, the Movellans – would be wiped out by the awesome, devastating forces at their disposal, forces that the Doctor would give them knowledge of and access to.

Without so much as a qualm, the Brigadier and Benton walked past the smashed remains of the soldier who had fallen from the ledge above. When they had entered the boy's room and discovered his escape across the roof, the man had gone after him, but the human detritus that still cluttered his mind had resulted in a lack of concentration and he had plunged to his death. It didn't matter. Individuals were of little importance; the man was simply a tiny part of the Xaranti, the equivalent of a human cell, thousands of which died and were constantly renewed. The Brigadier, who at this juncture was still exercising the human convention of individual heirarchy, decided that their efforts would be best served searching for the boy at ground level, that if he hadn't already made his way down on to the streets, he would have to do so eventually.

Suddenly the Brigadier and his fellow hybrids within the immediate vicinity stopped dead, their faces blanking over. As one they turned slowly to face an adjacent street before blinking and swaying as though roused from a trance. There was no need for speech, no need for confirmation; the message each of them had received was clear and unequivocal. Without hesitation, the Brigadier, Benton and their motley crew of infected soldiers and civilian hybrids converged to swarm towards their target.

* * *

Sweat rolled down Turlough's face and dripped on the tarmac beneath the car. He was shaking as if with fever. The two Xaranti were motionless, their spiny legs so close that Turlough could have reached out from his hiding place and jabbed the meat skewer in to one of them. Surely the creatures knew he was here. Why else would they have stopped?

But if they *did* know, why hadn't they attempted to root him out? In some ways he wished they would just get it over with. Maybe they wanted him to make a break for it so they could pursue him, hunt him down. He heard movement at the end of the street and twisted his head to look.

Dozens of feet, many of them wearing black boots into which were tucked green army fatigues, were approaching his hiding place. They did not hurry, had no need to do so. Turlough knew that all was lost, but still he couldn't bring himself to crawl out from under the car and give himself up. He wished he could sink into the ground. His stomach cramped with dread. A pair of boots broke off from the rest and approached the car. They stopped in front of the vehicle.

The owner of the boots dropped down on to one knee and peered under the car. Turlough found himself face to face with the Doctor's friend, Sergeant Benton. Benton's face looked red and blotchy as if he had been out in the sun too long. There was a cloudy darkness, like the reflection of storm clouds, swimming in his eyes.

Benton grinned and saliva gleamed on his blocky white teeth.

'Boo,' he said in a rasping voice.

Since entering the R and D unit Tegan had barely said a word. Mike, keeping a surreptitious eye on her, had noticed her clenched, troubled expression. He had noticed the way she moved too, slowly and tentatively, like someone in pain who was determined not to show it. Several times he had asked her if she was OK, and had received a brief nod and a preoccupied, 'Fine.' Now she was sitting against the wall in the dormitory area, staring into space and taking deep breaths as though resting after an exhausting journey.

'Is your friend all right?' Charlotte asked, glancing across the room. 'She looks very pale.'

Mike had been helping the medical staff tend to those patients most in need of care and attention. He started to nod, then glanced around and drew Charlotte aside. Speaking quietly, he said, 'Well, actually, no she's not. She's been infected by this... this virus or whatever it is.'

Charlotte looked alarmed. 'You mean she's changing into one of those things? Like my Dad did?'

Mike pulled a face. 'Keep your voice down. We don't want to start a panic.'

'Sorry,' whispered Charlotte. 'But what's going to happen when she becomes... uncontrollable?'

'We'll cross that bridge when we come to it,' said Mike. 'For the moment she's harmless enough.'

Tegan chose that precise moment to give a loud groan and slump sideways in a dead faint. Mike rushed to her, Charlotte close behind him. Placing his hand gently beneath Tegan's head he lifted her back up into a sitting position. 'Tegan,' he said, quietly but urgently, 'Tegan, can you hear me?'

Her lips moved soundlessly for a moment, then in a thick, clotted voice, she said, 'We are Xaranti.' Her eyelids fluttered, then parted. The eyes beneath were completely black.

Mike didn't realise they had drawn an audience until he heard the collective gasp from behind him. He turned to see the doctor and nurse who had tended the Doctor's wounds, plus several curious patients, stepping back, shocked expressions on their faces. Next moment Max Butler barged through the crowd, looking harassed. 'What's going on here?' he demanded – then he caught a glimpse of Tegan's eyes a split-second before she closed them again.

'Oh my God,' he breathed.

'She's fine,' Mike said hastily. 'She just needs to rest.'

'*Rest?*' Max said, eyes wide with incredulity. 'She's got the plague, man! You've got to get her out of here!'

'There *is* no plague,' scoffed Mike. 'This is a water-borne infection. It can't be passed from person to person.'

'How the hell do you know that?' Max demanded.

'I just do, that's all.'

Max shook his head. 'No. You've got to get her out of here. We can't take the risk.'

There was another collective gasp as Mike unholstered his gun and pointed it at the ceiling. 'We can and we will. Tegan is my personal responsibility. And I assure you, Max, that if she tries to harm anyone here, I'll shoot her. Is that good enough for you?'

Turlough sat on the sand with his back against the TARDIS door, the faint tingling vibration from the time machine like an echo of the trembling dread in his stomach. He had had no choice but to lead the Brigadier, Benton and four UNIT troops back to the fun-fair, where the TARDIS stood like a curio between two stalls. The hybrids had loaded the TARDIS on to the back of an army truck and driven it down to the beach, where it now stood, dwarfed on the outside at least, beside the vast dripping hulk of the usurped Morok craft. Turlough and the TARDIS were bait for the Doctor – or at least insurance against his departure.

Once again Turlough glanced fearfully at the guns that the quartet of soldiers were pointing at his head. The soldiers' metamorphosis was continuing apace; their eyes now contained a swirling blackness that came and went, like storm clouds scudding across the moon. Turlough tried to avoid eye contact with any of his captors for fear of antagonising them.

He knew how violent and unpredictable those infected by the Xaranti virus could become and didn't want to give them any kind of an excuse to blow his head off.

They had been waiting for twenty minutes and now Turlough was growing increasingly jittery. He wondered how long the Brigadier was prepared to hang around, what would happen if the Doctor didn't show up at all.

At first, when the tingling in his back increased, Turlough thought it was due to the fact that he had been sitting in the same position for too long. Then the tingling became a shuddering, and an instant later was accompanied by the trumpeting bellow of the TARDIS's engines. Irrespective of the guns that were being levelled at him, Turlough scrambled away from the TARDIS and twisted round just in time to see it fade and disappear, dragging the cacophonous din of its dematerialisation with it.

'Doctor!' Turlough called in indignance and despair, but it was too late.

The TARDIS was gone.

For a few moments Turlough stared at the place where the TARDIS had stood, unable to believe his eyes. He realised that the Doctor must have reached it before they had, must have been inside it all the time it was being transported down to the beach. His disbelief, however, was more due to the fact that his friend had left him at the mercy of this bunch of gun-toting lunatics. Surely it wouldn't have taken much for the Doctor to have snatched the door open and dragged him inside? He could have done it before the soldiers were even aware of what was going on.

He turned his attention once more to his captors, whose expressions of shock were almost comical. Then blackness swarmed into the Brigadier's eyes as he turned them on Turlough and the surprise was replaced with cold, hard fury. Like a chain reaction, the same expression spread through the soldiers and, as if responding to some unspoken command, they each tilted their heads to regard him. Turlough, on his knees in the sand, cried out in terror as they threw down their weapons and rushed towards him.

The TARDIS had barely travelled any distance at all. The Doctor had merely allowed the pull of the Xaranti queen to guide his movements and had set the co-ordinates accordingly. As the TARDIS re-materialised, he patted the pockets of the spare jacket he had procured from the TARDIS wardrobe then pulled a lever on the console. When the doors opened with a faint hum, he drew himself to his full height and stepped determinedly out into Hell.

He was surrounded by Xaranti, by the stink of them, their bodies pressed together so tightly that it was like standing on a tiny island in a sea of dark, spiny flesh. Xaranti scuttled over one another, their legs pistoning the air; they clung to the walls like scorpions; hung from the metal roof-supports high above his head.

As he took a step forward, they regarded him balefully with their black, unblinking eyes, but they did not attack. Indeed, they edged backwards on either side as he slowly advanced, creating a narrow channel through which he could walk, increasing the crush of their already tightly packed bodies. Perhaps they had orders from their queen to let the Doctor through, or perhaps they simply recognised him as one of their own. Certainly, his physical transformation was advancing rapidly. His eyes were swimming with blackness, the buds of spines were visible on the backs of his hands and on his neck, and the space between his shoulder blades was already starting to bulge.

The room in which the TARDIS had materialised was large and functional, evidently some sort of security clearance chamber ahead of the energy core that was the ship's heart.

Several hundred yards away, at the end of the channel that the Xaranti had created for him, the Doctor could see a door of dull metal, emblazoned with Morok symbols. Beside it was what had evidently once been some sort of security access panel, now a cannibalised jumble of wildly contrasting technologies. On the metal wall above the door was a large embossed symbol that resembled a flaming star, depicted in vivid purple.

The Doctor did not recognise the literal significance of the symbol, but he did recognise a danger sign when he saw one. Nevertheless he strode forward calmly, confidently, almost regally, head held high, back as straight as the hump between his shoulder blades would allow, hands clasped loosely behind him. When he reached the door he examined the access panel and traced its meanderings to a bulbous metallic nodule that he guessed might have been Kraal in origin. He twisted it and the door slid open.

The corridor beyond was little more than a metal tube with a grilled walkway along its centre. At the far end was another door and another cannibalised control panel. Ignoring yet another star symbol – this one larger and situated right in the centre of the door – the Doctor again operated the access panel. This door, too, slid open and the Doctor stepped through.

The energy core that powered the ship's engines was enclosed in a heavily shielded metal tube, like a vast central pillar, which ascended through a circular shaft in the floor and stretched up to the high ceiling. The grumbling throb of the engines themselves, ticking over somewhere below, made the floor vibrate beneath his feet. Dominating the wall-space of this huge room was a densely packed mass of control panels, again stretching from floor to ceiling, which were accessible via a series of ladders and gantries set at regular intervals.

Intertwined with all this technology, smothering it,

communing with it, *becoming* it, was what the Doctor had come to think of as the Xaranti queen.

It was not a quantifiable life-form as such, but a vast formless entity, an accumulation of the thoughts and emotions and memories of myriad races made flesh. The stuff it was made from was not solid, but free-flowing like liquid glass, iridescent patterns constantly swirling within it. It oozed and curled above and in front of the Doctor, aspects of the many different races whose minds it had absorbed over the years forming briefly within the malleable stuff of its being, as if attempting to break free, before sinking back into the flux. The Doctor saw eyes and claws and mouths; the suggestion of a fur-covered limb; a patch of warty flesh. The impressions were too swift and too vague for him to recognise any of the species depicted, but each and every one of them looked briefly familiar.

'Good afternoon,' he said as the 'queen' coiled and rippled. 'Any chance of a chat?'

The stuff quivered and then bulged in front of him, a vast bubble forming on its surface. The Doctor imagined it bursting and spattering him with goo, but he stood his ground.

The bubble elongated, formed into a gluey tentacle which probed almost hesitantly towards his face. It halted a few feet away from him and almost immediately the tip began to thicken and swell, as if the tentacle were a hollow tube and more of the stuff was being pumped through it.

Slowly, at the end of the tentacle, a shape began to form. The effect was like an impressive display of glass-blowing. The shape started as a blob, which eventually extended limbs of its own before beginning to acquire definition. Within minutes a perfect but featureless humanoid form stood in front of the Doctor, though, like a new-born, remained attached to the main body of the 'queen' via a clear gel-like umbilicus.

The figure could have been constructed from clear glass and filled with colourless, constantly moving oil if it wasn't for the facial features which drifted haphazardly within it, incessantly forming and fading and re-forming, as if attempting to settle on the correct location. Eyes of many different shapes and hues, as many as a dozen at a time, blinked lazily from the flux of the creature's being. Several mouths suddenly opened in the figure's limbs and torso, and one even opened in its head, albeit from the area where its left eye would normally be.

The mouths spoke in unison, though each used a different voice. There was a gruff male voice; a lilting female one; another that was sexless and sibilant. 'I trust that this form meets with your approval, Doctor?' the figure said.

The Doctor shrugged. 'I never judge by appearances.'

The mouths smiled. 'Then that is something we have in common. To we Xaranti, all forms, all species, have something to offer us. We celebrate the great variety of life forms in the Universe.'

The Doctor's face hardened. 'That's not the same thing at all. You don't appreciate variety for its own sake. You celebrate it only because of what it adds to yourselves. By recreating other species in your own image, you're making mockery of life, denigrating the essence that makes each race unique.'

'We *liberate* other species, Doctor,' the figure said. 'We do not destroy them. They grow stronger through us.'

'No,' the Doctor snapped, his face flushing with anger. 'You don't liberate, you enslave. You absorb their individuality into this great repository of yours and turn them into mindless drones, creatures driven by nothing more than negative rudimentary emotions and a basic hive mentality. Conquest through absorption. It's what the Cybermen do, and the Wirrrn. It's the most heinous crime in the universe.'

'Soon you will become part of us, Doctor,' the figure said, its voices imbued with smugness. 'Soon you will celebrate the fact that all life exists within us just as we celebrate it.'

'I don't think so,' the Doctor replied quietly.

'You have no choice, Doctor. You are becoming us.'

'I'm afraid that's where you're wrong,' the Doctor countered. 'I'll never become you. I'll never join you. I'll never see life through your eyes. In fact, I'm here to offer you the chance to withdraw the infection you've set in motion on this planet and leave before I get cross. Rather sporting of me, I think you'll agree.'

'Withdraw the infection?' The voices chuckled. 'It is already too late, Doctor.'

'There's an old Earth saying – it's never too late. But then you probably already know that.' Steel entered the Doctor's voice. 'You know as well as I do how you can withdraw the contagion.'

'Do we?' the voices said innocently.

'Yes. You can think it back.'

The Xaranti queen did not respond immediately and the Doctor smiled and nodded. 'I'm right, aren't I? There are no toxins, no germs, no bacteria involved in this infection of yours. It's psychological warfare, a thought-plague. You simply release this gloop of yours into the water where it's ingested or absorbed, firstly by marine and then by animal life. The gloop contains telepathic suggestions encoded at a molecular level, which then persuade the host body that it is metamorphosising. It's an impressive feat, I'll give you that, making people change physically simply by planting the belief that they're going to do so inside their heads, but it's ultimately flawed. Because when it comes down to it, it's simply a question of mind over matter. All it takes is a stronger mind than your own to expose the whole process for the sham it is.'

The Xaranti queen spoke, and just for an instant its many voices seemed to coalesce into something deep and melodious, before splitting once again into its constituent parts. 'You are a clever man, Doctor. How did you come by your discovery?'

'Oh, process of elimination,' said the Doctor airily. 'There was nothing very clever about it really. I ran some of the infected material through an exhaustive programme of analysis in the TARDIS, but could find no physical reason why the infection was taking place. In desperation I dug out an old lash-up of mine which reproduces thoughts as images, and decided that if I couldn't read the stuff physically I'd try reading it mentally.' He smiled. 'The results were extremely interesting, as I'm sure you can imagine. Improvisation has always been my watchword.'

If the figure had been human it might have shaken its head in dismissal. 'Your discovery is not important,' it said. 'Nothing has changed.'

'Oh, it has,' the Doctor insisted, and, reaching into his jacket pocket, drew out a flask of clear liquid and held it up.

Did the eyes opening and closing lazily within the iridescent flux widen a little in alarm, or was that simply the Doctor's imagination? Certainly its many voices sounded wary. 'What is that?'

'Antidote,' said the Doctor brightly. 'I threw it together in the TARDIS.' He unstoppered the flask and drank the contents in three gulps.

The effects were almost instantaneous. The cloud of Xaranti infection faded from the Doctor's eyes, the spines on his hands and neck withered and shrank until there was no evidence that they had ever been there, and the hump on his back deflated, enabling him to draw himself once more to his full height.

'You see?' he said, holding the flask up. 'Mind over matter.'

'There is no mind that can combat ours, and therefore there *is* no antidote,' the figure said angrily. 'It is a trick.'

'You can't deny the evidence of your own eyes,' the Doctor

retorted. 'I *believed* that this was an antidote and therefore it became one. It destroyed your infection just as I can make you believe it will destroy you.'

The mouths and eyes were forming and fading more rapidly now, the flux quivering as if in agitation. 'Your mind is no match for ours, Time Lord,' the figure said, its voice now sounding like the hiss of its own creatures.

'Isn't it?' said the Doctor mildly, and withdrew a second flask from his other pocket. 'Why don't you take some of your own medicine and find out?'

He hurled the flask at the metal column that contained the ship's energy core. The glass shattered against it, spraying the figure with clear liquid that only the Doctor knew was tap water from the TARDIS. Instantly the strange, shimmering substance of the figure's flesh began to blister and liquefy, to blacken and steam. The Xaranti queen's mouths opened in unison and released a single, fractured, ear-splitting scream. Words formed within the scream, high and undulating. '*Releeeease usssss...*'

'I'll release you when you release this planet!' the Doctor shouted, and his voice became almost pleading. 'Go now before it's too late!'

Without waiting for a reply he turned on his heels and strode from the room.

Tegan opened her eyes and looked around. She saw a sea of faces regarding her with wary alarm. She recognised none of them; nor did she recognise the thin-faced young man who was crouching beside her. She thought his eyes looked kind, and relaxed slightly – then she noticed he was holding a gun.

'Where am I?' she demanded. She glared at the young man. 'Who are you?'

'Tegan,' the young man said, surprising her with her name, 'are you all right?'

'Why shouldn't I be?' Uncertainty was making her angry. Her glance swept across the group of people, many in pyjamas and dressing gowns, still watching her as if she was a wild animal they had cornered in the woods.

'Her eyes look fine now,' one old man said.

A large black man with a sweaty face who was wearing some sort of grey-blue uniform that made Tegan think of hospitals replied, 'It could be a trick. I mean, she's still got those things all over her.'

Tegan looked down at her hands and bare arms and saw black thorns jutting from her flesh. Her voice grew shrill with panic. 'What's going on? What's happening to me?'

'It's OK,' the young man said gently, soothingly. 'How much do you remember?'

Tegan tried to think. 'I remember... I remember leaving Sea Base Four with the Doctor and Turlough. After that, it's all a blur.'

'Look!' a woman said suddenly, pointing at Tegan. 'Look at her arms!'

Tegan looked just as everyone else did, dreading what she might see this time. But the thorns poking through her flesh were beginning to shrivel, to shrink. In less than a minute they had disappeared, the bloodless wounds they had made closing up, leaving not so much as a blemish on her skin.

'She's beaten it,' the woman who had pointed at her arms gasped in awe.

'I still think it's a trick,' the black man muttered.

The young man crouching beside her rounded on him. 'Of course it's not a trick, Max. Don't be so paranoid.' He holstered his gun, turned back to Tegan and took her hands. Smiling, looking into her eyes, he said, 'No, I really think she's cured.'

Turlough's lungs were bursting. If his limbs were not being held in a vice-like grip he would have been thrashing with panic. The urge to breathe was almost overwhelming; he wouldn't be able to fight it for much longer, even though he knew that sucking in a breath would fill him with nothing but sea water. Sergeant Benton's hand on the back of his head was like a massive weight bearing down on his skull. Turlough didn't know whether the soldiers were trying to drown him or infect him, and at that moment he didn't much care. All he wanted was to be allowed to breathe.

As soon as the TARDIS had de-materialised the soldiers had moved in and grabbed him and carried him down to the sea. Turlough had protested, but they had been wordless, robotic. They had waded in almost to their waists before dunking him under. It seemed a long, long time ago now since he had last drawn breath, though it couldn't have been more than a minute or so.

I'm going to die! he thought, and the words were like screams in his head. *I'm going to die on this horrible planet in this horrible century and it's all the Doctor's fault!* He had heard it said that drowning was a not unpleasant death, but this was worse than any nightmare he had ever had. All at once something clenched inside him, some instinctive muscular contraction caused him to inhale, and suddenly sea water was rushing up his nose and down his throat.

This time panic surged through him so powerfully that his body jerked and spasmed in the soldiers' hands. Then he was floating, weightless, and he thought: *This is it. This is death.* It took him a moment to realise that his limbs were free and that there was no longer a hand gripping the back of his skull, holding his head underwater. Turlough thrashed and flapped, kicking down with his legs, trying to find solid ground beneath him. He was disorientated, his lungs were as painful as open wounds, and his heart was a thick, heavy pulse that seemed to be squeezing his thoughts smaller and smaller. The sea felt stronger than he was, the inexorable suck of its tide upending him, dragging him along the sea bed. Just as the crushing weight of unconsciousness threatened to engulf him completely, his head broke the surface of the water.

The sun was a hot, bright slap across his eyes. Turlough desperately wanted to suck in air, but he emerged coughing and retching, seawater rushing back up out of his mouth and nose, tasting like blood. Finally the water stopped coming and Turlough took a deep, gulping breath, then immediately winced; his lungs felt bruised, as if he had been kicked repeatedly in the ribs. He was still floundering in the water, barely holding his head above the surface. Steadying himself, he planted his feet firmly on the ground and stood up.

He was surprised to find that the sea only came up to his thighs. He blinked, swiping water from his face, and saw that he was facing the shore. The Brigadier, Sergeant Benton and the four UNIT soldiers who had been holding him under were behaving very curiously indeed. They were convulsing, their faces twisted in anguish, as if a powerful electrical charge was being passed through them. As Turlough watched, astounded, the six men collapsed one by one, the Brigadier on the beach, the others in the shallows as the froth of dying waves fizzed around them. Up on the promenade, Xaranti hybrids which Turlough had glimpsed patrolling to and fro like border guards, were convulsing and collapsing in a similar manner.

What was happening? Could it be something to do with the Doctor? As if thinking about his friend had willed him to return, Turlough heard the familiar grinding roar of the TARDIS's engines. Next moment, by the sea's edge, a faint blue outline shimmered into view and quickly solidified. The door opened just as an extra large wave surged up the beach and slapped over the rim of the TARDIS, drenching the emerging Doctor's white cricket boots. He looked down at his soaked footwear ruefully. 'Slight miscalculation,' he said. Then, as the wave receded, he leaped out of the TARDIS and ran across the wet sand towards the unconscious Brigadier.

'Help me get these men inside,' he shouted to Turlough, heaving the Brigadier expertly on to his shoulders in a fireman's lift and jogging with him towards the TARDIS.

Turlough, dripping wet, waded towards the shore. He had an entire skeleton of bones to pick with the Doctor. 'You abandoned me!' he exclaimed, hearing the wheedling quality in his voice that Tegan always commented upon, and hating it. 'I could have been drowned.'

'Yes, yes, we'll talk about that later,' the Doctor said briskly. 'Now come on, we haven't got much time.'

'Before what?' Turlough said.

The Doctor nodded up at the vast, drab bulk of the Morok ship towering above them. 'Before that thing takes off and gives us all a tan we'll never recover from.'

He disappeared into the TARDIS with the Brigadier and emerged again almost immediately. Turlough sighed. He could see now why Tegan always got so frustrated. She simply never had time to sit down with the Doctor and properly air her many grievances; there was always something more urgent to do. He splashed through the shallows and lifted Sergeant Benton's legs while the Doctor grabbed him under the armpits. 'Where's Tegan?' Turlough asked as they carried Benton's solid bulk, made even heavier by his wet clothes, into the TARDIS.

'Safe,' the Doctor said, lowering Benton's dripping, unconscious form to the floor of the console room, beside the Brigadier.

As they carried the third soldier into the TARDIS, Turlough exclaimed, 'Doctor!'

'What is it?'

'The Xaranti infection. It's vanished.'

It was true. With everything that had happened in the last few minutes it was only now that Turlough had noticed the spines on the men's skin and the growing humps on each of their backs had disappeared.

'Yes,' said the Doctor, grinning. 'Miraculous, isn't it?' He laid the man next to his colleagues and ran out for the next one, leaving any further explanations still-born.

Less than a minute later, the Doctor and Turlough were hurrying towards the TARDIS with the last soldier. A few steps from the open door, Turlough heard a dry, scuttling sound and looked up. 'Doctor!' he called.

The incoming tide had perhaps another hundred yards of sand to cover before it came up against the sea wall. Swarming over that wall now, and dropping down on to the beach thirty feet below, were dozens, perhaps hundreds of mature Xaranti. They were moving strangely, lop-sidedly, like injured crabs, scuttling and scrambling over one another in their chittering, high-pitched panic. They were moving in one direction only, towards their mother-ship, which meant that in another ten or fifteen seconds they would be swarming over and around the TARDIS.

'Inside, quickly!' the Doctor said. He and Turlough covered the gap to the TARDIS at a run, carrying the soldier between them. They laid the man down, then the Doctor leaped across to the console and yanked back the lever that closed the TARDIS doors. Turlough, meanwhile, switched on the scanner and watched as the bristling mass of Xaranti rushed past them. Their purloined ship had extended ramps like lolling tongues, which lapped up the Xaranti and gulped them into the craft's interior.

'Time to go,' the Doctor said from the console where he had been setting co-ordinates. Turlough was unsure whether he was referring to themselves or the Xaranti. The Doctor pulled the lever that would propel the TARDIS into the Space/Time vortex and then frowned.

'Turlough,' he said sternly, 'you're dripping on my floor.'

* * *

For two minutes after the TARDIS had de-materialised, the Xaranti continued to pour into the Morok ship. At last they were all aboard and the ramps that had extended to admit them were retracted before the doors slid closed. Immediately six portals, evenly-spaced around the body of the ship, opened like eyes, and a cannon-like tube extended smoothly from each one. These tubes extended so far, then bent downwards in the middle at a forty-five degree angle, quickly becoming jointed, telescopic supporting struts. As soon as their tips had embedded themselves in the sand, there was a deep rumbling sound and two large cavities opened at the base of the Morok craft, one on each side. The gigantic caterpillar tracks that had been used to trundle across the sea-bed and up on to the beach lifted up from the sand, tipped slowly sideways with a growling of powerful machinery and folded themselves neatly into the belly of the ship.

Once the cavities had rumbled closed, sealing the caterpillar tracks inside, the Morok ship looked less like the kind of tank that could flatten houses and more like a conventional space craft. There was a pause, then the ship began to growl and shake as if building itself into a rage. Slowly the growling increased in volume and pitch and the shaking grew more intense until suddenly four columns of fire – pink and orange threads twisting like agonised spirits in the blinding whiteness – gouted from the massive thrusters at the base of the ship, accompanied by black, boiling plumes of smoke which sullied the pristine blue of the sky.

The supporting struts snapped back into the ship's interior as the columns of flame struggled to lift the Morok craft from the expanding pool of boiling clinker it was bequeathing the Earth. The ship seemed to groan, its engines screamed – and then it was free, and lumbering skywards. It rose and rose until it was nothing but a black speck trailing fire, and then finally less than that – the merest glint of flame.

The tide rushed over the glowing pool of molten rock that the ship's departure had created, turning instantly to a furiously hissing cloud of steam.

Mike and Charlotte had just finished filling Tegan in on the events of the past two days when the materialising TARDIS swept panic through the R and D unit. Charlotte scrambled clear of the howling roar of the engines and ducked behind the nearest bed. Max Butler took several steps backwards before tripping over his own feet and plumping unceremoniously on to his backside.

'What the hell is *that*?' Max cried, clearly at the end of his tether.

'The TARDIS, of course,' Tegan said as if it was obvious.

Mike jumped up, raising his hands placatingly, as the craft solidified and the roar of its engines faded. 'There's no need to panic,' he shouted, feeling like Corporal Jones in *Dad's Army*. 'This is a friend. He's come to help us.'

I hope, he thought, crossing his fingers, remembering that the last time he had seen the Doctor he had been infected by the virus. He tensed, his hand moving instinctively to the butt of his holstered gun, as the TARDIS doors opened.

The Doctor stuck his head out and smiled. His eyes were clear and normal, his skin unblemished. 'Good afternoon,' he said expansively.

'Are you OK, Doctor?' Tegan asked.

He strode out, a dripping Turlough, rubbing his head ruefully with a towel, in tow, and patted her on the shoulder. 'Never better.'

'What's the situation, Doctor?' Mike asked.

The Doctor turned to him. 'The Xaranti have gone. I managed to persuade them that humanity was a bit too gristly for their tastes.'

'And this infection of theirs?' Charlotte asked, rising from behind the bed.

'I asked them if they wouldn't mind taking their litter home with them. They were only too happy to oblige.'

Mike's hand dropped to his side again. 'So everyone's cured?'

Suddenly the Doctor looked sombre. 'Those who weren't too badly affected should recover relatively quickly. But there'll be a great many casualties. A large number of people won't recover from the injuries that the Xaranti persuaded them to inflict on themselves.'

'On themselves?' Mike said. 'I'm not sure I follow.'

'The catalyst for the infection was not viral or bacterial, but mental, which was why it resisted conventional analysis. It was caused by an incredibly powerful telepathic suggestion. Pure thought in physical form.' He looked around at the roomful of blank faces and said hastily, 'Yes, well, best not to get caught up in idle chit-chat. I've got a console room full of battle-weary soldiers in need of urgent medical attention. Mike, if you would be so kind…?'

Several minutes later, the Brigadier, Sergeant Benton and the four soldiers were laid out on the dormitory floor between the two rows of beds, being attended to by the medical staff.

'Will they be all right, Doctor?' Mike asked, trying not to sound anxious.

'Good as new,' the Doctor said encouragingly. 'Their systems have had a bit of a shake-up, that's all.'

Max sidled up, regarding the Doctor a little suspiciously. 'Is it safe to leave this place yet?' he asked.

'Perfectly,' said the Doctor, but stopped him as he turned away, with a hand on the arm. 'But there are some nasty sights out there. Many of the people here will find them distressing.'

Max met the Doctor's eyes for a moment, then gave a brief nod. 'I'll get on to it.'

'Good man,' said the Doctor. As Max left, he turned back to Mike and thrust out his hand. 'Well, we'd better be off.

Goodbye, Mike.'

Mike looked taken aback by the Doctor's abruptness. 'Aren't you going to wait until the Brigadier wakes up?'

'Best not, eh? That way we can avoid unnecessary explanations.'

'If his memory's anything like mine,' said Tegan, who had risen to her feet and was now standing at the Doctor's shoulder, 'he's not going to know who we are. We're going to have to introduce ourselves all over again.'

'Just so,' said the Doctor.

'All the same –' Mike began to protest.

Turlough sneezed loudly.

The Doctor turned and patted his companion on the shoulder, his hand splatting on sodden material. 'Into the TARDIS,' he said. 'Have a hot shower and put some dry clothes on. I'll make us all some cocoa.'

Tegan and Turlough entered the TARDIS. The Doctor stepped after them. Just as he was about to disappear into the strange eye-defying darkness beyond the doors, Mike stepped forward and took hold of his arm. 'Doctor?'

The Doctor looked back, blond hair swishing. 'Yes?'

Mike suddenly realised he wasn't sure what to say. 'I just… thanks for your help, Doctor.'

'Thanks for yours,' the Doctor said. An odd, unreadable expression flitted across his eyes, and just for a moment Mike had the impression that he was about to say something momentous or significant. Then abruptly the Doctor said, 'Goodbye,' and, before Mike could respond, stepped smartly in to the TARDIS, slamming the door behind him.

BBC DOCTOR WHO BOOKS

THE EIGHT DOCTORS *by Terrance Dicks* ISBN 0 563 40563 5
VAMPIRE SCIENCE *by Jonathan Blum and Kate Orman* ISBN 0 563 40566 X
THE BODYSNATCHERS *by Mark Morris* ISBN 0 563 40568 6
GENOCIDE *by Paul Leonard* ISBN 0 563 40572 4
WAR OF THE DALEKS *by John Peel* ISBN 0 563 40573 2
ALIEN BODIES *by Lawrence Miles* ISBN 0 563 40577 5
KURSAAL *by Peter Anghelides* ISBN 0 563 40578 3
OPTION LOCK *by Justin Richards* ISBN 0 563 40583 X
LONGEST DAY *by Michael Collier* ISBN 0 563 40581 3
LEGACY OF THE DALEKS *by John Peel* ISBN 0 563 40574 0
DREAMSTONE MOON *by Paul Leonard* ISBN 0 563 40585 6
SEEING I *by Jonathan Blum and Kate Orman* ISBN 0 563 40586 4
PLACEBO EFFECT *by Gary Russell* ISBN 0 563 40587 2
VANDERDEKEN'S CHILDREN *by Christopher Bulis* ISBN 0 563 40590 2
THE SCARLET EMPRESS *by Paul Magrs* ISBN 0 563 40595 3
THE JANUS CONJUNCTION *by Trevor Baxendale* ISBN 0 563 40599 6
BELTEMPEST *by Jim Mortimore* ISBN 0 563 40593 7
THE FACE EATER *by Simon Messingham* ISBN 0 563 55569 6
THE TAINT *by Michael Collier* ISBN 0 563 55568 8
DEMONTAGE *by Justin Richards* ISBN 0 563 55572 6

THE DEVIL GOBLINS FROM NEPTUNE *by Keith Topping and Martin Day*
ISBN 0 563 40564 3
THE MURDER GAME *by Steve Lyons* ISBN 0 563 40565 1
THE ULTIMATE TREASURE *by Christopher Bulis* ISBN 0 563 40571 6
BUSINESS UNUSUAL *by Gary Russell* ISBN 0 563 40575 9
ILLEGAL ALIEN *by Mike Tucker and Robert Perry* ISBN 0 563 40570 8
THE ROUNDHEADS *by Mark Gatiss* ISBN 0 563 40576 7
THE FACE OF THE ENEMY *by David A. McIntee* ISBN 0 563 40580 5
EYE OF HEAVEN *by Jim Mortimore* ISBN 0 563 40567 8
THE WITCH HUNTERS *by Steve Lyons* ISBN 0 563 40579 1
THE HOLLOW MEN *by Keith Topping and Martin Day* ISBN 0 563 40582 1
CATASTROPHEA *by Terrance Dicks* ISBN 0 563 40584 8
MISSION IMPRACTICAL *by David A. McIntee* ISBN 0 563 40592 9
ZETA MAJOR *by Simon Messingham* ISBN 0 563 40597 X
DREAMS OF EMPIRE *by Justin Richards* ISBN 0 563 40598 8
LAST MAN RUNNING *by Chris Boucher* ISBN 0 563 40594 5
MATRIX *by Mike Tucker and Robert Perry* ISBN 0 563 40596 1
THE INFINITY DOCTORS *by Lance Parkin* ISBN 0 563 40591 0
SALVATION *by Steve Lyons* ISBN 0 563 55566 1
THE WAGES OF SIN *by David A. McIntee* ISBN 0 563 55567 X

SHORT TRIPS *ed. Stephen Cole* ISBN 0 563 40560 0
MORE SHORT TRIPS *ed. Stephen Cole* ISBN 0 563 55565 3

THE NOVEL OF THE FILM *by Gary Russell* ISBN 0 563 38000 4

THE BOOK OF LISTS *by Justin Richards and Andrew Martin* ISBN 0 563 40569 4
A BOOK OF MONSTERS *by David J. Howe* ISBN 0 563 40562 7
THE TELEVISION COMPANION *by David J. Howe and Stephen James Walker*
ISBN 0 563 40588 0
FROM A TO Z *by Gary Gillatt* ISBN 0 563 40589 9